DEATH AT THE FESTIVAL

A TWISTY AMATEUR SLEUTH MURDER MYSTERY

THE BREAKFAST CLUB DETECTIVES
BOOK FOUR

HILARY PUGH

Housemouse Press

Copyright © 2024 by hilary pugh

All rights reserved.

No part of this book may be reproduced in any form or by any electronic or mechanical means, including information storage and retrieval systems, without written permission from the author, except for the use of brief quotations in a book review.

❦ Created with Vellum

CHAPTER ONE

Clarissa Mayberry opened her eyes. Had she really nodded off for a moment? That was most unlike her, but it was hot and stuffy in the tent, so she could have done. It was the sudden applause that had awakened her. Not rapturous applause; this was no standing ovation. Just a half-hearted acknowledgment that the introduction had ended. Clarissa pulled herself together and glanced at the festival committee member assigned to say a few words about her before she delivered her paper. With a great deal of effort, since her head was buzzing and things were swimming in front of her eyes, she managed to focus her gaze on his name badge. Rupert was the man's name, and he was looking at her with an expectant smile on his face and a hand extended in her direction. It was her turn to speak. She pulled herself unsteadily to her feet, spread her notes on the lectern in front of her and took a long draught from a carafe of water that had thoughtfully been placed on a small table between the speakers' chairs.

What the hell was she doing here, at this Reimagine the Light Festival? No one had told her it was going to be full of woolly liberal vegetarians pushing their trendy, unworkable and no doubt costly ideas. Clarissa was more in the *reduce taxes* camp. Keep things simple and encourage the strivers. Get rid of the shirkers, not to mention illegal economic migrants, and all would be well. Hard-working families would get what they deserved and prosper. And the rest? Not her problem, although while here she was probably surrounded by socialist do-gooders who would insist that in her role as a government adviser it was very much her problem, and what was she going to do about it?

She blamed her agent for her presence today. Patsy Kline had assured her that her opinions would be heard, needed to be heard by a different kind of audience. No use in preaching to the converted, was it? The festival committee wanted a range of views, she told Clarissa. They were worried that there was a danger of the whole thing becoming too left wing. *Something of an understatement,* Clarissa had thought, casting her eyes over the programme of events and noting talks on achieving net zero, progressive taxation, cutting charity concessions to private schools and the re-democratisation of the electoral system. And those were just the main venue events; the discussions that merited the use of two large marquees and a futuristic-looking construction of brown canvas sails called the Flagship, where people could drink beer brewed locally using organic ingredients and discuss innovative ideas; lefty woke ones, in all probability.

Clarissa's lecture, or as Patsy had put it, her opportunity to push sales of her latest book *The Austerity Myth: poverty is all in the mind,* which had not sold in the numbers hoped for, was a chance to make herself known to a new readership. Intelligent people who read actual books and were open to new ideas. Wasn't that what one employed people like Patsy for? But the days when publishers had bottomless publicity budgets were long gone. Clarissa had been shocked to discover she was expected to sell her book more or less on her own. What did she know about advertising and book promotions? She was far too busy with her political causes for any of that, but Patsy had persuaded her that speaking at a festival of ideas would go down well with the publisher, demonstrate that she was willing to do her bit and sell a few of her own books. Signed copies, Patsy had suggested, providing Clarissa with a cardboard box full of author copies for her to arrange on a table at the front of the auditorium. She could hand them over to members of her audience with a smile and a personalised message. So she even had to do her own stage management now? Cart around heavy boxes, set up tables and construct tempting arrays of books. Books that would take her hours to sign. Setting aside half an hour to deliver a short reading, maybe accepting a cup of tea and a biscuit while chatting to a select few of her adoring fans didn't seem to be what Patsy had in mind at all. Instead, she would have to sit at the table while she signed books for an ever-lengthening queue of people who would expect her to write a pithy, individual message before they deigned to pay. Was she also expected to take the money from them?

But Patsy had persuaded her. Threatened her, in fact, because Clarissa had a secret and it would do her carefully constructed family values image no good at all if it got out. Not that it was any more than a bit of trivial fun. She needed to relax somehow, didn't she? All the same, any adverse publicity would do her a lot of harm. So she had agreed to Patsy's demands and now Clarissa was in the auditorium, about to deliver her reading but with an unpleasant feeling that she might pass out before she reached the end of her first sentence.

Auditorium was pushing it. Clarissa's event had been scheduled for one of the smaller tents, known as *Hideaways*, that were erected some distance from the main events. There was an apology for a stage, where there were two chairs, a lectern and a vase of anemones – artificial ones, Clarissa noticed with a curl of her lip. A sign propped against the vase told her they were made from recycled paper by children at a nearby primary school who were doing their bit for the environment – no use of plastic, and no carbon footprint from transporting cut flowers from Africa. In Clarissa's opinion, it would be better if the school involved had them chanting their times tables and taught them to read and write properly rather than letting them play with coloured paper and glue. But at least she wouldn't have to contend with the heady scent of real flowers. And while her mind was on the topic of odours, at least the tent she was in now was free of the smell from the catering marquee that dominated the main area close to the larger venues, and which had turned her stomach earlier in the day. In fact, she still felt distinctly queasy even now, several hours later.

She looked out at her audience, a small one of about thirty people seated on folding chairs, most of whom, she suspected, had not joined the queues early enough for tickets to one of the main events. The faces in front of her became blurred as another wave of nausea hit her and she grabbed the lectern for support. She looked down at her notes, a mass of confused, unfocussed letters swirling around on the sheets of paper in front of her. No matter. She knew her speech well enough. She took another gulp of water and delivered it in what she hoped was a reasonably coherent way, sitting down suddenly as she reached the end. Her head was now aching, but she felt a little better at the thought that she'd soon be able to gather up her notes and escape into the fresh air.

'Thank you,' said the man who had introduced her. She should get better at remembering names, and he was now standing at an angle which made it difficult to see his name badge. Rupert, she thought he was called. 'An interesting take on the state of our current economy,' he said, smiling benignly at the audience; the few that were still awake or who had not already escaped. 'Do we have any questions?'

To Clarissa's relief, no one spoke and no hands were raised. She had just pulled herself to her feet, hoping to make a quick getaway, when a man stood up. He was wearing horn-rimmed spectacles and a T-shirt, the slogan on which, even with her currently blurred vision, she was able to read. It announced in large letters that the wearer was a *Proud tofu-eating member of the wokerati*. He put his hand up.

'Ah,' said Rupert, gesturing to the man. 'We have a question to my left. Your name, sir?'

'Murray Dickinson.'

Clarissa glared at Murray Dickinson in a way that she hoped would intimidate the man. 'Your question?' she snapped.

Murray picked up a copy of her book from the pile on a table at the edge of the stage and waved it at her. 'This book,' he said. 'A book for which you expect people to pay £15.99 a copy, suggests that you can produce a meal for thirty pence. Would you care to explain how?'

Had she written that? Her brain was foggy, her ideas slipping from her grasp. Then a glimmer of a memory. 'I was quoting,' she said, her voice little more than a croak. 'Bulk buying and batch cooking.'

'So,' said Murray Dickinson, 'you're saying if you buy in bulk and eat the same meal every day it can be done?'

Someone at the back of the tent stood up and jeered. 'What are you supposed to do for cash to bulk buy?'

Other members of the audience started to join in. 'What about the cost of power for cooking?'

'And somewhere to keep all these batch cooked meals if you can't afford a fridge, never mind a freezer.'

Murray hadn't finished. 'What if you work three jobs? When do you do all this shopping and cooking?' He turned to face the audience, ignoring Clarissa as small groups started chipping in with their own arguments, which had widened into ever rising rents, cost of school uniforms and mortgage payments.

Clarissa heard none of it. She was wracked with nausea, dizziness and a splitting headache. Breaking into a sweat, she clawed at the collar of her blouse and tore it open, scattering buttons like pebbles into the front row of the audience before grabbing fruitlessly at the lectern and pitching off the stage, collapsing in agony as she fell, gasping for breath, onto the ground.

She'd not fallen silently. She'd taken the table, lectern and carafe of water with her, knocked over chairs and crashed into the stand that held her books. All conversation stopped abruptly as people stared in horror at the crumpled figure writhing and groaning on the ground.

Rupert, who had hoped that volunteering for this event would mean he had an easy, quiet afternoon, stared at her in horror. It took a member of the audience, one who had sat at the side and quietly observed the whole event: the boring presentation; the hostility of the audience and the sudden dramatic conclusion, to take control. He sent someone to find the on-site first aiders, instructed Rupert to clear the tent and then laid the patient on her side in the recovery position.

CHAPTER TWO

To say Jonny Cardew had been surprised at his wife Belinda's suggestion that they spend a few days at the Reimagine the Light Festival would be an understatement. Belinda had recently been kicked off the local council after serving more years than Jonny cared to count, dutifully and conscientiously attending to the needs of her constituents. In a climate of ever-increasing financial belt-tightening, Belinda had fought tirelessly to keep libraries open, and set up drop-in help sessions for the digitally challenged to pay their council tax or complain about the non-emptying of their bins. She battled with the housing department on behalf of tenants with leaking roofs and black mould growing on their walls, and lobbied for funding for schools unable to afford building repairs. And after all of that, she'd lost her seat at the council elections. And it pitched her into an identity crisis, which Jonny could understand but which made him feel helpless. So when Belinda had suggested a few days listening to people who were still optimistic enough to come up with ideas for improving things, Jonny put aside a dislike of sleeping in cramped tents and sharing toilet facilities, and threw himself into the event with an enthusiasm that surprised him. It had been a difficult year and the late summer didn't look set to get any easier, with threatened strikes and weather that was forecast to be anywhere from blisteringly hot to raging tornados. Belinda's idea of some intellectually stimulating glamping, without the need to be stuck in airport delays or fried by forest fires, seemed like an excellent one. And it wasn't as spartan as it might have been. She'd booked them into one of the festival's luxury glamping tents for a few days of enlightening talks, lively music, stand-up comedy, book readings and good food, all within a few miles of home. They had an upmarket tent with comfortable beds, electric lighting and even a carpeted floor. Food was served throughout the day and most of the night by a team of local organic caterers. The beer was excellent and the company good. And unlike the camping experiences of Jonny's youth, he wasn't bitten to death by midges.

It was Jonny's second session in this particular tent. It was one of five small venues known on the festival map as *Hideaways*, situated away from the main events in an area where the talks were likely to appeal to the more eclectic tastes of the attendees, and which offered topics such as Peruvian women's carpet weaving and how to play the Polynesian nose flute. He and Belinda had been in this same tent the previous afternoon, delivering their own presentation. It had been a surprise to both of them when they were asked at the last minute to fill in for a speaker who had cried off within a few days of the festival starting.

Jonny and Belinda had only intended to be part of the audience at the festival; a relaxing few days listening to intelligent discussion, live music and edgy stand-up comedy. But someone on the organising committee had spotted their names on the guest list. After the cancellation of one of the speakers, a woman who had run blogs and written books on ways to cook nourishing meals in times of austerity, and having been made aware of the breakfast club that Jonny and a friend had recently set up, the committee invited him and Belinda to run a session in her place. The idea had terrified Jonny, who had no experience of speaking in public, but Belinda leapt at it. She was a seasoned public speaker after her years as a councillor and was about to supervise the running of breakfast club number two. She would do all the talking, she said. Jonny could be in charge of the slideshow. 'Slideshow?' he'd enquired, only to discover that Belinda had an album on her phone that contained a number of photos of *Jasmine's* – home of the breakfast club – and a video of Belinda herself unveiling a plaque at its opening last autumn. A little reorganising and they could hook it up to one of the projectors thoughtfully provided by the festival organisers. All Jonny had to do was press a button on the phone when Belinda nodded in his direction, and they'd have a fully illustrated presentation.

That afternoon, Belinda was going to a session on women film directors, which Jonny, while he had nothing against either films or women directing them, thought was too intense for a warm September day. The discussion in the main marquee on electoral reform had looked interesting, with speakers Jonny had heard of, but it was fully booked. So it was either a talk given by a woman called Clarissa Mayberry, who had written a book on austerity, or an afternoon snoozing in their tent. He was leaning towards the privacy of their tent with no one to criticise the possibility of him closing his eyes for a while, until Belinda told him it would be a missed opportunity. He could sleep any time, she told him. How often did they have such an exciting array of stimulating entertainments to choose from?

Jonny had never heard of Clarissa Mayberry and had attended the talk with little enthusiasm. Some right wing family values – of the heterosexual kind – bring back the death penalty and flogging type, Belinda had told him. Jonny asked Belinda what the hell she was doing at this festival, which unashamedly reeked of vegan food, ethically sourced clothing and woolly liberal values. Balance, Belinda had told him. She was heartily against any kind of censorship. Contentious views need to be challenged, she told him. Not hidden away to fester on social media.

So Clarissa Mayberry it was. Jonny almost felt sorry for the woman. A lone voice, as it were. And snoozing still wasn't out of the question if he chose his seat carefully. It wasn't unheard of for people to drop off during lectures, and as long as they didn't snore loudly no one minded. Jonny was sure he didn't snore. Belinda would have told him if he did. He chose a seat near the side of the tent, away, he hoped, from the line of vision of the speaker. He had almost nodded off as Ms Mayberry droned on about how people could manage perfectly well if only school curricula included budgeting. She was almost robotic in her delivery. A robot on speed, perhaps, as she rattled through her ideas extremely fast while gazing into the audience with a barely conscious expression. Either way, it compared unfavourably with their own presentation, which had been a lot more interesting than this one. Was the speaker drunk, perhaps? Or just in a hurry to get out into the fresh air? *It's stuffy in here,* Jonny thought, as he felt his head sinking onto his chest and his eyelids drooping. But then things started to get exciting, and he was wide awake. The session had warmed up suddenly and taken a new direction; a direction of which the speaker appeared oblivious. First, one of the audience, a man who introduced himself as Murray Dickinson, asked an entirely pertinent question. One that Jonny himself might have asked if he'd been awake enough to put it into words. He recognised Murray. He'd asked Jonny a question at the session the day before, and he and Belinda had been happy to answer it. Clearly Murray was a regular participant at occasions like this. Today he had a good question about some politician, quoted apparently in Mayberry's book, who had maintained that it was quite possible to feed a family for thirty pence a day. Clarissa Mayberry seemed not to understand the question and stuttered out a vague answer about bulk buying, after which a number of heated discussions broke out, the audience having formed themselves into small factions, ignoring the main speaker entirely while airing their own views to each other. It was definitely more exciting than the lecture and was becoming quite heated. A short step from throwing things at each other and even coming to blows. The member of the festival committee,

Rupert, who had introduced the event, waved his arms around as if swatting a wasp in an unsuccessful effort to keep control.

Jonny sat back in his seat, watching the chaos around him and feeling decidedly smug. Compared to today's debacle, their session the previous day had gone well. Their audience had been polite and interested, the session ran to time and was under the control of a compère who knew what he was doing and wound things up with enthusiastic thanks and on time, allowing everyone to file out and into the beer tent in time for a pre-dinner drink. Today's finale was very different, bringing the session to an end in a moment of drama that no one could possibly have anticipated. Clarissa Mayberry clutching at her throat in a truly melodramatic fashion, her face turning an interesting shade of green before she collapsed, falling off the stage into a pile of her books and writhing in a spectacular way on the coconut matting that lined the floor of the tent.

There was a sudden silence as people stopped talking mid-sentence and stared open-mouthed at the woman gasping for breath on the floor. Rupert was ineffectually trying to herd the audience out of the tent. Did they not get training in what to do in the case of an emergency? Obviously not. Jonny felt a need to step up and take control. He had some memories of his Red Cross training – mandatory for all CPS employees – and knelt on the ground at Clarissa's side, gently turning her into the recovery position. But that was about his limit, first aid wise. He needed more than that. There was a St John Ambulance post near the catering tent, but someone needed to stay with Ms Mayberry. He grabbed the leg of the nearest person to him – Murray Dickinson, who was leaning over Jonny, fanning Clarissa with a copy of *The Austerity Myth: poverty is all in the mind*. Of the two of them, Murray was younger and looked fitter. 'Go and get the first aid people,' Jonny said. Murray scampered off and Jonny turned to Rupert. 'Get these people out of here,' he shouted. 'Give the poor woman some privacy.'

People were reluctantly leaving the tent by the time the first aiders arrived, a woman in her thirties and a man a little older,

Murray following in their wake, apparently keen to be part of the action. The man knelt down and did a few cursory checks while Jonny explained what had happened. 'She looked ill,' said Jonny. 'Then she just clutched at her throat and staggered forwards, falling off the stage.'

He and Murray had both seen Clarissa fall. 'It's very hot in here,' said Murray. 'She's probably dehydrated.' He pushed a glass of water in her direction.

'She drank a lot of water during the presentation,' said Jonny, not wanting to argue, but sure that wasn't why she was ill.

The first aider seemed to agree, pulling a phone from his pocket and calling for an ambulance. 'She's unresponsive. It's more than heatstroke. Are you her husband?' he asked Jonny.

Heaven forbid. He shook his head. 'I'd never met her before.'

'We need to know if there's anyone here with her, a husband or friend perhaps.'

Rupert, who had now successfully emptied the tent of audience and had pulled himself together, said, 'I'll get the public address people to make an announcement.' He stood up and left them, looking relieved to have a reason to escape the drama.

It was an uncomfortable fifteen minutes before the ambulance arrived. No one had responded to the announcement asking for anyone who knew Clarissa Mayberry to contact the festival office urgently. 'We should look in her handbag,' Murray suggested. 'Or her phone. See if there's a number we can contact.'

'Better leave it to the festival office,' said Jonny, not wanting to risk accusations of breaching her privacy.

'They're on it,' said Rupert, returning to the tent. 'I've been asked to liaise with the paramedics and go to the hospital with the patient until they are able to contact someone. You two can leave now,' he said, turning to Jonny and Murray.

Murray looked ready to argue as the ambulance drew up at a gate at the back of the field, fortuitously close to the side entrance of the tent. Jonny was sorry for Clarissa but had no wish to intrude. He patted Murray on the shoulder and suggested a beer. The two first aiders, Rupert and the paramedics nodded appreciatively at Jonny. 'Best thing,' said Rupert. 'You've both had a shock.'

In Jonny's opinion, he and Murray had coped rather better than Rupert, but he didn't argue. A cold beer right now would be more than welcome.

'Do you think I killed her?' Murray asked as he took a slug of the beer Jonny had just placed in front of him.

What an odd question, Jonny thought, looking around the beer tent, which was pleasantly empty as most of the events were still running. 'She's not dead,' he said.

'Yet,' said Murray ominously.

'How do you think you might have killed her?' He hadn't been that close to her, and he was definitely free of any weapons. Unless, of course, he had an air-filled syringe in his pocket and had sneaked up to her without anyone noticing. Jonny couldn't think of anything else that could have done the job without being spotted.

'She might have had a heart attack after the grilling I gave her about her book.'

'Doubt it,' said Jonny, thinking Murray looked disappointed. 'Did you want her dead?'

'She's an epic pain in the arse.'

'Maybe she is. A lot of people are, but we can't go around wishing everyone we disagree with would drop dead.'

'S'pose not. Wouldn't have anyone to heckle then, would I?' Murray grinned at him and finished his beer. 'Love you and leave you. I'm heading off to the Flagship for the jazz.'

CHAPTER

THREE

The following morning, Jonny and Belinda found a picnic table and sat down to enjoy a breakfast of organic oat muesli served with coconut yogurt and fresh raspberries. It was the final day of the festival and they were having trouble deciding what to do.

'There's too much,' said Jonny, spreading the programme out in front of him. It was divided into the different kinds of event: exhibitions – a virtual reality light show that he'd not yet seen; a travel talk; water colour painting or organic gardening. There was a cookery demonstration on how to do away with food wastage by, for example, making pesto out of carrot tops. They'd had a good carrot crop this year so that might be interesting. Politically things were winding down and the only offer this morning was something about arts funding, the discussion led by someone Jonny had never heard of. The afternoon offered a poetry reading, and a how to write your own obituary session. Or they might go to a wine tasting, which would set them up nicely for a gentle jazz concert before everyone packed up and left. He yawned, thinking that, enjoyable as it had been, he'd be glad to get home to his own bed.

'I'd be sorry to miss any of what's left, but we can't do all of it, can we?'

'We don't have to do all of it,' said Belinda. 'Just pick your favourites. I'm going for how to grow organic vegetables in a small garden.'

'We don't have a small garden.' If the amount of mowing and weeding he did was anything to go by, they had a very large garden. 'And aren't you organic already?'

'Not one hundred percent. I need to know how to make my own fertiliser out of nettles and seaweed.'

They were eighty miles from the nearest coast. Was he going to have to go seaweed harvesting and drive it home in his car? Was it even legal to help oneself to seaweed from a beach?

'Don't look so worried. We've plenty of nettles and you can buy dried seaweed online.'

'You wouldn't rather learn how to make carrot top pesto?'

'Why? Are you going to that?'

Jonny shook his head. For him, it was still a toss-up between a talk by a man who had completed a round the world trip without flying, and a session on watercolour painting using natural dyes made from plants. He was leaning towards the painting session, which he hoped would be hands on, when he felt a hand on his shoulder. He looked up into the face of Lugs Lomax, a detective inspector from his local police station.

'Didn't expect to see you here,' said Jonny. He'd not seen Lugs since the end of their murder at the circus case. A narrow escape for Katya Roscoff, founder member and unofficial boss of the Breakfast Club Detectives. He and Belinda had not mentioned the detectives during their presentation, although if it hadn't been for the breakfast club itself, and Katya's love of food, the detectives would never have got started. For Jonny it fulfilled a lifelong ambition to solve murders, and while solving crime was unarguably a *good thing to do*, making sure people had enough to eat was probably a better one and it didn't need sensationalising with a side order of murder.

Jonny wondered if it was a murder that had brought Lugs there that morning. 'Has someone found a body?' he quipped.

Lugs drummed his fingers on the table. 'Not exactly. I'm here with the environmental health people who've been called in by the medical examiner to check on the kitchens. You know about the woman who died yesterday?'

So there was a body. His joke had misfired very badly. 'Clarissa Mayberry's dead?' Jonny said, pushing his muesli to one side. He'd seen Clarissa's dramatic collapse but assumed it was a simple case of heatstroke or possibly mild food poisoning. 'I was with her just before the ambulance came,' he said, feeling the colour drain from his face with shock. 'No one told us she'd died. We didn't think it was anything serious.' But why was Lugs there? Inspecting kitchens was a bit below his pay grade. 'You can't think she was murdered, can you? There was no one near her when she fell off the stage.'

'It's too early to say. There's no evidence yet that it was anything other than a tragic accident and the medical examiner will have to decide if it goes to inquest or not. Initial tests suggest she was poisoned.'

'You think she was poisoned here?'

Lugs shook his head. 'The inspection was just a precaution. No one else on site has had any symptoms, but we had to check it out. And the catering here is in the clear. Mrs Mayberry's last meal was toast and marmalade, presumably breakfast, and a small amount of prawn mayo sandwich believed to have been consumed before her lecture. But everything provided by the caterers here is vegan, so she must have brought the sandwich with her. We'll be looking into that once we've discovered where she bought it or where she purchased the prawns if she made the sandwich herself. But again, there have been no reports of poisoning anywhere else.'

'That's a relief,' said Belinda, finishing the last of her muesli. 'But they don't usually send in a detective inspector to check on kitchen hygiene, do they?'

'The examiner asked for a police presence in case of any trouble. People tend to panic after a sudden death.'

Jonny supposed the sight of the kitchens being inspected after someone had been poisoned could lead to alarming rumours.

'I was having a quiet day,' said Lugs. 'I thought I'd come along myself. A discreet police presence is better than sending in a load of uniforms and creating a panic. And it sounded like a nice place. I remembered Katya telling me you two were taking your holiday here.'

'It's a lovely site,' said Belinda. 'We've really enjoyed it, haven't we, Jonny?'

Jonny nodded vaguely, his head still spinning with the news of Clarissa's death. 'Did she poison herself by accident?' he asked.

Belinda nudged his arm. 'Not everything's a case for the detectives,' she said. 'I'm sure the poor woman didn't mean to poison herself. The prawns were probably well past their sell by date and she hadn't noticed.'

'Looks like it was accidental,' said Lugs. 'But it might not have been the prawns. Traces of α-amanitin were found in her bloodstream. The examiner is leaning towards the idea that she'd been foraging for mushrooms and didn't know enough about them. There's a variety called *amanita phalloides*, better known as the death cap. It's found in birch and oak woods. Easy to mistake a death cap for a field mushroom, apparently.'

Possibly, but Clarissa Mayberry hadn't struck Jonny as a green wellie-wearing forager type. He couldn't imagine her eating anything that hadn't come washed and sealed in plastic from Waitrose or M&S. But he didn't know her well. She could have been doing some research for her next *anyone can eat decently* type book.

'Have you got time for a coffee?' Jonny asked. 'We can order a fresh pot.'

'That would be lovely,' said Lugs, looking at his watch. 'But I'd better get back to the office. I can't sit around sunning myself all day and it looks like you two have plenty to pack in before you head for home.' He stood up and shook hands with the two of them. 'Enjoy the rest of your day.'

They watched him make his way to the car park.

Belinda folded up the festival programme and put it in her bag. Jonny sat and gazed into the distance. 'I'm not sure I'll be able to concentrate on anything,' he said. 'It's tragic, isn't it? Dying so suddenly like that.'

'What do you know about Clarissa Mayberry?' Belinda asked, sitting down again and taking his hand in hers. 'Is there a husband? Family?'

'No idea. Like I told Lugs, I'd never met her before. And I only went to her lecture because it looked like a nice quiet place to sit. I feel as if I should be doing something, but I've no idea what.'

Belinda thought for a moment and then glanced across at the admin tent. 'We should find out what the festival committee are doing. They can't have their speakers dying and not at least express some sympathy for the family. Even if it wasn't their caterers who poisoned her. You could talk to them. I'm sure they will understand when they know you were with her when she collapsed. They might have some ideas about how you could help.'

Jonny supposed there must be a process in place for when things like that happened. The festival might be continuing normally, and someone somewhere would have made the decision about that. But they would be very unlikely to ignore the fact that a tragic incident had happened. 'They'll probably make a statement, send flowers or whatever.' That idea cheered him up a little and made him feel less useless. 'Tell you what. We can send flowers of our own. I was probably one of the last people to see her alive. I'll find out where Clarissa Mayberry lived and if she had any family.'

'Sounds like a mustering of breakfast club detectives again.'

'Lugs is more than likely right about it being an accident so there's no reason for us to be involved. But it has been rather quiet since the circus case.' Could there perhaps be a role for the detectives? Sorry as he was that Clarissa had died, it would be nice to be busy detecting again. He'd call Katya and Ivo as well later and tell them what had happened. They might as well be prepared for the possibility of a new case.

CHAPTER
FOUR

The next morning Jonny was awake early. It had been a warm night and they slept with the bedroom windows open. He was awakened shortly after five a.m. by the dawn chorus. Did they make a racket like that every morning? He supposed they must, and that on cooler nights he and Belinda slept through it. The result of the exorbitantly costly double glazing they'd had fitted some years ago.

Jonny dragged a pillow over his head and tried to get back to sleep. Forty-five minutes later he was still wide awake and decided to get up and make the most of what promised to be a beautiful day. He made Belinda a cup of tea, tried to nudge her awake and left it by the bedside. She'd either wake up properly and drink it or she'd go back to sleep and pour it down the sink later. Whatever she did was her decision and he'd hardly wake her up just to drink a cup of tea. He'd shower quietly and then walk to *Jasmine's* – an early breakfast, a leisurely read of the papers, a few minutes up in the office checking the breakfast club accounts, then a stroll to the florist in town. The festival secretary had given him details of Clarissa Mayberry's next of kin, her husband Anthony, and their home address. He would ask about the most suitable flowers to send a recently bereaved husband and arrange to have them delivered.

Arriving at *Jasmine's,* Jonny was surprised to see a man wearing a red bobble hat sitting at his usual table by the window, nibbling a piece of toast.

'Good morning,' he said, grasping Jonny's hand and shaking it vigorously as if meeting a long-lost relation returning from forty years in Australia. 'Just the man,' he said, slapping Jonny on the back and waving a slip of paper at him, a piece cut from the local paper about the body in the Long Walk. 'I've read all about you.'

Jonny sat down next to him. 'Have we met?' he asked, trying not to be distracted by the bobble on the man's hat, which appeared to have a life of its own, bobbing up and down as he spoke.

'I'm Derek Weatherby, chairman of the East Berks Fungus Conservation Society.'

'Pleased to meet you,' said Jonny.

Derek reached across the table and shook his hand again, and Jonny wondered if fungi had been a lifelong passion. There was something gnome-like about Derek. It was the hat – a pixie hat, and all he needed was a toadstool and a fishing rod to complete the picture.

Jasmine arrived with a tray; three fry-ups and a pot of coffee. 'I've got half an hour,' she said. 'Breakfasts are under control, and I don't need to start on lunches yet. I've asked Ivo and Katya to join us as well.'

'A detective meeting?' Jonny asked.

Jasmine nodded as Katya came through the door followed by Ivo and his dog, Harold.

Katya tucked into a plate of food and grinned at Derek. 'You've a case for us?' she asked.

'Not a case as such,' said Derek. 'Some enquiries. We'll pay for your time.' He finished his slice of toast and poured himself a cup of tea. 'Members of the Fungus Conservation Society are concerned about the recent death in the area,' he said, sounding as if he were addressing a public meeting rather than a group of amateur sleuths. 'We understand that it was not believed to be a suspicious death. However, we find that the idea of an accidental death by mycological misadventure to be alarming.'

'Death by what?' Ivo hissed at Jasmine.

'Posh word for mushroom poisoning,' she whispered back.

'We would like to draw up a code of practice for the use of foragers – not that we encourage foraging, too detrimental to the environment. But people will still do it and we would prefer to avoid further fatalities. Before we can action this, we need to know how the deceased obtained the *amanita phalloides* that caused her death. The society is prepared to agree a number of hours at your usual rate and we realise that you will incur expenses, for which we will reimburse you.'

Ivo stared at him blankly, Jonny tried to suppress a laugh and Jasmine refilled all the coffee cups. Katya continued eating.

Derek pushed his plate to one side. 'If you are willing to take the case,' he said, 'perhaps you would discuss it among yourselves and inform me of your action plan.'

'We'll definitely take it,' said Katya with a glance at the others, who all nodded.

'In that case,' said Weatherby, 'perhaps you would furnish me with your terms and conditions.'

'We'll discuss it and get back to you,' she said, smiling at Weatherby.

Derek nodded enthusiastically, the bobble on his hat joining in.

'Excellent,' said Katya, shaking his hand. 'I shall email you this afternoon.'

They watched as Derek straightened his hat and scurried towards the door.

'Shouldn't we have discussed terms now?' Ivo asked. 'We might get to work and find he doesn't agree with them.'

'He will,' said Katya. 'Once we've drawn up our plan. Meeting in the office this afternoon? Four-thirty?'

'I'd better have a clean-up,' said Jasmine. 'We've barely used it for weeks.'

~

Jasmine and her dad were due to go on holiday in a couple of weeks. Hopefully they'd have the new case sorted by then. How difficult could it be, finding out how Clarissa Mayberry had come by the mushrooms that killed her? The office wasn't used much unless they had a case on the go, but it wasn't right to neglect it. It had been so generous of her dad to let them use the room. The least they could do was look after it. She gathered up dusters, polish and a vacuum cleaner and dragged them up the stairs.

Once the room was the way she wanted – the floor polished, table cleared of heaps of papers and cobwebs successfully removed – she returned to the kitchen, where her dad was showing Jonny how to oversee *Jasmine's* while they were away on holiday. He'd have help, of course; the café could probably run itself for a week. The kitchen staff they employed were thoroughly reliable and any one of them could take over at a moment's notice. Jonny already did a good job running the breakfast club and pitching in with some washing-up when they were stretched. But if Belinda was going to do as good a job with a breakfast club of her own, she'd need to know what a well-run café looked like.

It would be strange leaving it for a week. It was the first time Karim had been on holiday for years. And Jasmine herself had barely spent a night away from home apart from occasional sleepovers with friends when she was a teenager.

'It'll do us good,' said Karim, not looking completely convinced about it.

'It'll do you both the world of good,' said Jonny. 'And don't worry about a thing. You've got an excellent team here.'

Karim shrugged. 'I'm not worried,' he said, not sounding too sure. 'But it's only for a week and Norfolk isn't so far away. We can be back in a couple of hours if necessary.'

'Right,' said Jonny, slapping him on the back. 'You'll find the time passes in a flash and you won't want to come back.'

'What about this new case? Will you be done with it in two weeks?'

Jonny laughed. 'Probably. It's not going to stop Jasmine going on holiday. We'd better head up to the office and get things going. The sooner we start, the sooner it will all be solved.'

'It won't be a long meeting,' Jasmine promised her father. 'Stevie's coming in to help with the teatime rush and I'll be done before we close.'

It was a couple of months since they'd last sat round the table like this and they were all looking good. Ivo still had the remains of a suntan from his Greek holiday, even after a couple of weeks of being back home.

'You're looking well, Ivo,' said Jasmine. 'Still topping up the suntan?'

'I've been spending a lot of time in the open since we got back. The weather's been lovely, and I've had to cut the grass and check on the residents' cabin roofs and windows, making sure everything's watertight before the autumn.'

'Harold must have missed you. Did he go wild when you got back?'

'Pretty much,' said Ivo.

The dog looked the same as ever. He'd stayed with Jonny and Belinda while Ivo was away, and Ivo had worried that he might put on weight. But Jonny had walked him twice a day to ensure that he didn't, and in the process he'd dropped a few pounds himself. Jasmine was pleased to see him looking fit as well. Would she and her dad return from their own break looking as well as these two did? Jonny really should think about getting a dog of his own.

Perhaps she'd ask around in case anyone knew of a puppy in need of a home. Belinda would be up for it. Running the new breakfast club wouldn't take up all her time and she was always complaining about how little exercise she got since her council work had stopped. Jasmine knew she enjoyed Harold's stays with them and missed him when he went home.

Jasmine could hear Katya plodding up the stairs. She puffed into the room, her arms full of bags of pastries Karim had given her. Once she'd finished her chores, she'd nodded off and missed her usual lunch. 'Been sleeping better since my holiday,' she said, yawning and putting the bags down on the table. 'And now I'm raring to go with this new case. Karim's keeping some soup for me for when the meeting's finished.'

'We wouldn't want you to fade away,' said Jonny, turning on the coffee machine and picking himself a pastry.

'Not much chance of that,' said Katya, taking her usual seat at the head of the table.

'How was your holiday?' Jonny asked. 'You look well.'

'Excellent. I stayed with a very old friend who has a lovely cottage near Ripon. We went for long walks and ate most of our meals in pubs.'

'Nothing new there, then,' said Ivo.

'The pubs are nicer in Yorkshire. They've not been tarted up like they have round here. You can get proper pub grub, not this gastro stuff.' She took a bite of almond croissant. 'It's good to be home again, though. I've missed Karim's pastries.'

'What about this new case?' said Jasmine, sitting down and booting up the computer. 'We need to get on with it. Dad and I are going away in a couple of weeks.'

'We need to go over what happened,' said Katya. 'Jonny should start. He was there.'

'Where?' Ivo asked. 'And what happened?'

'It was while Belinda and I were on holiday.'

'At the festival? Remind us about that,' said Katya.

'It was a festival called Reimagine the Light. A lot of discussions about creating a better future.'

'It doesn't really sound like a holiday,' said Ivo, stretching out an arm and admiring his suntan. 'We spent most of the time on the beach or in tavernas eating olives.'

'It was a nice break,' said Jonny. 'Belinda booked us in for four days of uplifting presentations, music and comedy. We had a comfortable, very upmarket tent with real beds and a carpet on the floor. It was great. One of the speakers dropped out at the last minute and Belinda and I were asked to give a talk about the breakfast club.'

'The breakfast club itself or the Breakfast Club Detectives?' Ivo asked.

'It was about the breakfast club. Belinda did all the talking but she dropped in the fact that one of our members is a retired police sergeant and that we'd got together and solved a few murder cases.'

'Let me guess,' said Jasmine. 'One of the audience popped up and said he had a murder that needed solving.'

'Not quite,' said Jonny with a laugh. 'One of the other speakers collapsed at the end of her presentation and was taken to hospital, where she later died.'

'Did someone kill her?' asked Ivo. 'Is that what Derek was on about? The phally thingies?'

'Better known as death cap mushrooms,' Jonny explained.

'No post-mortem?' Katya asked.

'The medical examiner was brought in. It's something that happens now in cases of unexpected deaths. It's supposed to catch people like Dr Shipman before they do too much damage. But in this case, he okayed the signing of the death certificate without the need for further investigation.'

'The woman who died was poisoned by mushrooms?' said Ivo.

'She was. There are only a few cases of mushroom poisoning a year, in this country.' said Jonny. 'I checked it out but couldn't find exact figures. In this case, the hospital carried out its own PM to establish the cause of death and found it was food poisoning as a result of eating the death caps. They reported it to the examiner, who decided there was no reason to think it was anything other than an accident. The body was released to the next of kin and the authorities don't expect to hear any more about it.'

'I can see why this fungus man wants to know more,' said Ivo. 'It's not doing much for their image, is it? It might mean people go out destroying all the fungi they can find.'

'Exactly,' said Katya. 'The society want to draw up a leaflet that will reassure people, but first they need to know exactly how it happened. Then they can make a list of what to look out for and avoid. You're all smiling. Can I assume that we want to go ahead with this case?'

'Of course,' said Jasmine, nodding enthusiastically.

'Definitely,' said Ivo.

'Right,' said Katya. 'Jonny, perhaps you could talk us through what happened at the festival. Give us a few names.'

Jonny stood and picked up a pen. 'The woman who died was Clarissa Mayberry. She works for a right-wing political think tank as an adviser on social economics. She's written a book called *The Austerity Myth: poverty is all in the mind*. She was invited to the festival to talk about it.'

'I thought the thing you went to was all lefty vegans,' said Katya.

'Not exclusively. They wanted a range of opinions.'

'So this Clarissa Mayberry gave her talk. Then what happened?'

Jonny opened his notebook. He'd written down everything he remembered as soon as he knew Clarissa had died. He was expecting to be asked for an eyewitness account. No one had asked him at the time, and he was glad now that he'd kept the notes. 'She looked odd from the start,' he read. 'Kind of glassy-eyed and spaced out. She delivered her talk rather robotically and then there was some quite vicious heckling, and it all got a bit out of hand.'

'Violent?' Ivo asked.

'Not really. It just turned into a lot of breakaway heated discussions.'

'Didn't they have someone to keep that under control?' Katya asked.

'They did, a guy called Rupert who was on the festival committee, but he wasn't really up to the job. The audience was quite small. I guess he was expecting it to be rather dull and that everyone would have nodded off after the first ten minutes or so. They probably would have done if there hadn't been a carefully primed heckler. It was a guy called Murray Dickinson, who had read the book, probably done a lot more research into Clarissa Mayberry and was armed with a battery of awkward questions. He was pretty forceful and obviously had a fair number of the audience on his side. I didn't know the guy, but I should think he's a practised disrupter of talks he doesn't agree with.'

'And what was Ms Mayberry's reaction to all of that? Did she have answers for him?'

'She muttered something and then collapsed and fell off the stage. The first aid people came and called an ambulance and as I said, she died later in hospital.'

'And they traced the poisoning to death caps. Not, I assume, part of the festival menu or there would have been a lot more sick people there.'

'That's right. The environmental health people came and examined the festival kitchen. All their food was tested but nothing bad was found. No one else had suffered even mildly. Mushrooms hadn't been on the menu, so they were in the clear.'

'And none of this woman's friends or family were there?'

'There'd been someone there with her in the morning, but the organisers didn't know who it was. I suppose the hospital would have contacted her husband later, once they'd gone through the contents of her handbag.'

'There was nothing on the local news about it,' said Jasmine. 'Is that unusual?'

'The festival committee kept it very quiet for obvious reasons, I suppose. Belinda and I didn't know Clarissa had died until Lugs told us on the last morning we were there.'

Katya looked at him in surprise. 'Lugs was there? Someone called the police because they thought it might not have been an accident?'

'The hygiene people asked for police cover in case anyone turned nasty while they searched the kitchen. It didn't need a DI, but Lugs felt like a morning out of the office and thought it sounded like a nice place to visit.'

Ivo laughed. 'Not everyone's idea of a fun day out.'

'Police work's not all excitement and chasing criminals,' said Katya. 'It can get quite dull doing paperwork in the office. I can absolutely understand Lugs wanting to get out for a bit.'

'Did Lugs think there could be anything suspicious about the death?' Jasmine asked.

'No,' said Jonny. 'I think he went along with the accident theory.'

'He might be wrong,' said Katya. 'I think the first thing we need is to do some research. Find out all we can about Clarissa Mayberry. See if there's anyone who might have wanted to get rid of her.'

'You're assuming it was murder?'

'We need to consider it.'

Jonny wrote Clarissa's name on the board, leaving space for more notes. 'What should we do first?'

'Find out about the family,' said Ivo. 'Family are always the first suspects, aren't they?'

'I've done a bit of research,' said Jonny. 'And made a list of people who knew her.'

'That was quick,' said Ivo. 'We only knew about the case this morning.'

'I was interested before that. Lugs told us it was an accident, but I couldn't help thinking, suppose it wasn't?'

'Well done, Jonny,' said Katya. 'What did you find out?'

'Her husband is Anthony Mayberry.' Jonny wrote his name on the board. 'He and Clarissa were married for twenty-one years and they have two children, eighteen-year-old twins, Tristan and Amelia. Tristan is retaking his A levels at a college in town. Amelia finished school after hers and must have got good results. She's been offered a place at Cambridge. I don't know if she's accepted it yet. After her mother's death she's taking time to consider her options. A euphemism, I think, for loafing around doing nothing.' He added their names to the board.

'How did you discover all that?' Jasmine asked, sounding impressed.

Jonny grinned at her. 'You're not the only one who can nose around social media,' he said. 'There was plenty there about Clarissa. She has upset quite a few people who have been rather vocal about her on Twitter – what used to be Twitter. It doesn't feel right to call it Cross, does it? Anyway, sooner or later, these trolls start on the family and a couple of posh kids are easy game.'

'The son doesn't sound like the kind of offspring someone like Clarissa Mayberry would have expected,' said Katya, tapping her pen on the table. 'Probably nagged him about failing his exams. And even the daughter could have been bullied by her. Perhaps she was one of those tiger mums. Who thinks twice about accepting a place at Cambridge?'

'Someone whose mother pushed them into applying?' said Jasmine. She'd only ever experienced gentle nudging from her dad. All the same, she resented it when he suggested she should be a lawyer rather than run the café with him.

'Precisely,' said Katya. 'Did the twins get on with their mother or were they fed up with her nagging?'

'I don't know,' said Jonny. 'But it's hardly motive for murder, is it? There'd be very few mothers surviving into middle age if it was.'

'Quite right,' said Katya. 'We don't want to start suggesting anything too soon.'

'But we should check them out, shouldn't we?' said Jasmine. 'Even if they loved their mum, they might have noticed something odd about her behaviour.'

'A sudden desire to go foraging?' Ivo suggested.

'You never know. They might have picked some mushrooms for her without knowing what they were,' said Jasmine. 'We should find out more about them.'

'Definitely,' said Katya. 'They were probably in the best position to poison their mother, accidentally or otherwise. But let's get the full picture first. Who else needs to be on our list?'

'There's a family friend and business partner, Carl Archer. He was tagged on Anthony Mayberry's Facebook page. They used to belong to the same sailing club, but he's known Clarissa for longer. They were at university together.'

'Was that on his Facebook page as well?' Ivo asked.

'Clarissa studied at LSE. There was a link to an alumni page. Carl Archer was there at the same time.'

'Could be an interesting history there,' said Katya. 'We'll come back to him and find out a bit more. Who's next?'

'Magda Nowak. Cleans for them.'

'Live in?'

'No. She lives in town.' Jonny studied his notes. 'Little Frampton, where they live, is about six miles from Windsor. They found her through an agency that's based in the town. I got that bit of gossip from one of our contract cleaners at CPS,' he added proudly. He wrote her name on the board. 'We should find out when she was last at the house. She may have seen something.'

'Okay,' said Katya. 'Who's next?'

'Clarissa's agent, Patsy Kline. She was mentioned on Clarissa's own website.'

'Why did she have an agent?' Ivo asked.

'She did a lot of speaking engagements, not all through the people she worked for. But she didn't deal with any of that herself. All her bookings were organised through the agent, who also took care of her publishing contracts. I wondered if there might be a problem with her contract and perhaps this was the woman who was at the festival on Friday morning. She might have been there to discuss it.'

'Pure speculation,' said Katya. 'Don't let it lead us into blind alleys. We should find out more about her, though.'

'She had the opportunity to poison Clarissa,' said Ivo.

'Maybe,' said Katya. 'But I can't see her feeding mushrooms to her during a discussion about a contract.'

'No,' said Jonny, 'but a contract problem could have been a motive.'

'Again, speculation and it would have to have been a seriously bad problem for that,' said Katya. 'But it's worth following up.'

Jonny added Patsy Kline's name to the board and then looked at the list in his hand. 'Those are the people I've identified as having contact with Clarissa in the days immediately before she died. But we should investigate this guy as well.' He wrote Murray Dickinson's name on the board. 'He's the bloke who heckled her at the festival. He had a very low opinion of her and didn't do anything to hide it when he questioned her after her talk.' Jonny sat down and made himself a cup of coffee from the machine.

'Well done, Jonny,' said Katya. 'That's an excellent start.'

'Where do we go from here?' Jasmine asked. 'Are we looking for a killer or just someone who made a mistake?'

'Someone who innocently left a heap of deadly mushrooms lying around?' asked Ivo.

'Who would do that?' Jasmine asked. 'No one leaves poisonous mushrooms in places where someone could mistake them for the ordinary sort. It sounds deliberate to me.'

'Maybe someone who didn't know they were poisonous. One of the kids, perhaps, out for a country walk, thought they'd found some mushrooms and decided to leave them in Clarissa's kitchen.'

It was usually Ivo who had outlandish ideas about murders and Jasmine who tempered them with more practical theories. At that moment, they seemed to have switched roles.

Katya tapped the board thoughtfully. 'That could be the most obvious conclusion. It's clearly what the medical examiner thought.'

'He thought she'd picked them herself,' said Jonny. 'If someone else had, wouldn't they have said so?'

'Not necessarily. Not if it meant admitting to having caused a death,' said Ivo. 'They'd be feeling dreadfully guilty and scared.'

'You're probably right,' said Jasmine. 'It's not as if anyone was accused. They'd probably just keep quiet and let everyone assume it was Clarissa who'd made a mistake.'

'We should consider that first, I think,' said Katya. 'We'll check everyone on Jonny's list and find out what they were doing the day before she died.'

'How are we going to do that?' Jonny asked. 'We can't just call them up and ask if they were out gathering mushrooms. We'd be virtually accusing them of killing Clarissa.'

'No, you're right,' said Katya. 'We need to be way more subtle. Let's go through these people one at a time and work out how to engage with them. We've done it before. It just takes a bit of careful thought.'

'Magda Nowak would be a good person to start with,' said Jasmine. 'I could pose as someone looking for a cleaner. I could contact her and say she's been recommended by a colleague and ask if she's looking for more work.'

'That would also be a good way to learn more about the twins,' said Katya. 'She probably has to clear up their messy bedrooms. She'll know all about what they are interested in and what they get up to.'

'Definitely worth a try,' said Jonny. 'But do teenagers go for long healthy walks to pick mushrooms? Don't they usually skulk in their bedrooms listening to loud music?'

Jasmine laughed. 'That's just a stereotype. You shouldn't assume all teenagers are the same.'

'This agency,' said Katya, as she circled Magda's name on the board. 'Do you suppose it's the same one as that woman who does your house, Jonny?'

'Possibly,' said Jonny. 'I can find out.'

'That could save me a few phone calls,' said Jasmine.

'Jonny, you're probably best placed to find out more about this friend of the family. And more about what Anthony does for a living at the same time.'

Jonny made a note of it. 'I'll call round. See how the funeral arrangements are going.'

'What about me?' Ivo asked.

'Go and poke around the festival ground,' said Katya. 'It only finished a few days ago. With any luck they won't have completely cleared the site yet. We're assuming Clarissa ate her sandwich while she was there, so poke into litter bins and see what you can find.'

'You think the sandwich came with a side order of mushrooms? Wouldn't they have shown up in the PM alongside the prawns?'

'I hadn't thought of that,' said Katya. 'She must have eaten the mushrooms earlier in the day. I don't know how pathology works. Presumably the prawns were still in her stomach while the poison was in her bloodstream.'

Jonny looked at the list of names again. 'That leaves Murray the heckler and Patsy Kline.'

'I might take a look at their social media and see what I can find out,' said Katya.

'On your phone?' Jonny asked, wondering if her eyesight was up to it.

Katya shook her head. 'I can do it here. Or there's a nice little out of town library where they make you a cup of coffee and there's free use of the computers. Let's send an email to mushroom man with a contract and let him know what we're planning at the same time. We can meet back here tomorrow evening. See how we've all got on.'

CHAPTER
FIVE

Jonny picked up the small envelope that had landed on the mat in the hall and carried it into the garden, where Belinda had set out their evening meal. It was nice to be home again. Jonny had enjoyed the festival, but it had been full on, and his brain had been bombarded with ideas, which he needed time to process. He handed the envelope to Belinda, poured them both a glass of wine and sat down in front of a seafood salad – a Belinda special – with prawns, smoked salmon and crab meat from a local fish deli, lying on a bed of home-grown salads and tomatoes. Being vegan for a few days was fine. They'd both come home feeling healthy, not to mention smug, after days of eating nothing that wasn't plant based. They'd done their bit for the planet and their own blood pressure – a tiny drop in a very large ocean – but Jonny was quite pleased that Belinda's dietary views hadn't shifted to full-on veganism. He'd miss cream and eggs, fish and the occasional steak. But they seemed safe enough for now. However, Belinda's political views did seem to have shifted. Not to the left or even to the fringes of woolly liberalism, but they had moved away from those of her party.

She denied it. 'It's the party that's shifted, not me,' she told him.

'So where does that leave you?' he asked. Was she about to shift her allegiances to another party? Or would she stand as an independent? She'd hinted as much a while ago, but she'd had so many changes of heart he was beginning to lose track of them.

'Out of politics,' she said.

That was a surprise. Was she really giving up something that had been her driving force for as long as Jonny had known her?

Apparently she was. 'I won't stand for election again,' she said as she poured herself another glass of wine and downed it in a single gulp.

What was she going to do with all that time? The council had been her whole life. There was the new breakfast club, of course. But the current breakfast club didn't keep Jonny fully occupied and Belinda had way more energy than he had. He wasn't sure what to say, so he speared a prawn, dipped it in the dressing Belinda had made and enjoyed the tangy taste of it on his lips. 'Are you going to open that?' he asked, eyeing the envelope.

'You do it.' She pushed it in his direction. 'It's addressed to both of us. I'm just popping inside for a cardigan.'

She was right. There was a chill in the air as the sun set. There wouldn't be many more meals in the garden this year, apart from bonfire night, which had become a bit of a tradition since they had been grandparents. Marcus and his family would come round, loaded with treacle toffee and cans of beer. Belinda would heat up baked potatoes and roast chestnuts in the embers of the bonfire and they'd watch as neighbours let off fireworks in their gardens.

He picked up the envelope, opened it and read the card that was inside.

'Interesting?' asked Belinda as she returned with a cardigan wrapped around her shoulders. She was also wearing a scarf and carrying two cups of coffee. She handed a mug to Jonny and sat down.

'It's from Anthony Mayberry, Clarissa's husband,' said Jonny, warming his hands on the mug, thinking it was time they went inside. 'To thank us for the flowers.' After a discussion with the florist, he'd arranged for a bouquet of white lilies, roses and chrysanthemums to be delivered to the Mayberry home.

'That's thoughtful,' said Belinda. 'He must have a great deal on his mind at the moment.'

Jonny was sorry now that he'd been so prompt with his flower sending, which he'd done before the meeting with Derek Weatherby. Katya said he needed to talk to Anthony Mayberry and the delivery of flowers would have given him an excuse for calling at the house. Could he just drop in and say he'd come for a chat? He tried to imagine who he'd want to talk to should Belinda die without warning. He didn't think chatting to someone who'd never met her before would be what he needed, but everyone reacted differently. Then he remembered he'd been one of the last people to see Clarissa Mayberry alive, and that perhaps Anthony would welcome the chance to talk to the person who'd been with her in what had turned out to be her final conscious moments. Not that she'd said anything to him, or even realised he was there. He hoped Mayberry wasn't going to want a blow-by-blow account of her talk. He'd find it hard to be complimentary about a presentation that had been rushed and incoherent. And then there was the angry reaction from the audience. Surely Anthony wouldn't want to know about that. Jonny would need to be tactful, while at the same time trying to discover more about the Mayberry family dynamic. Were they the kind of family who went in for affectionate little gestures like picking gifts of mushrooms? If they were, one of them must be feeling mortified right now at the thought that their gift had been deadly. Was it more likely that they hated each other? But enough for murder? On the other hand, could Clarissa have been feeling suicidal? Or was the solution the obvious one? A tragic accident of the kind that could be avoided in the future if the mushroom society, or whatever they called themselves, provided the right information. Jonny wasn't sure what they had in mind. Warning notices in areas where mushrooms grew, perhaps, or leaflets in places that recommended country walks.

He tucked the note into his pocket and drank his coffee before helping Belinda to clear away the remains of their meal. He'd spend the rest of the evening trying to think of nice things to say about Clarissa Mayberry and questions that might help him learn more about the family and what they'd been up to the day she died. He'd call first thing the next morning and ask if he could visit to express his condolences in person.

~

THE MAYBERRY HOME, Limetree Cottage, was in Little Frampton, a village a few miles from the centre of Windsor. It was a mock Tudor building approached by a gravel drive and surrounded by a garden of bowling green standard lawns and colour-coordinated flower beds. From the size of it, Jonny guessed there must be at least six bedrooms, which stretched the term 'cottage' to its limits. A short distance from the house was a double garage, its open doors revealing a lack of cars, the reason for which was a collection of cardboard boxes and wooden tea chests taking up most of the available floor space. Was the family planning to move? Or were they just decluttering? Three cars were parked near the front door: a black Audi A4, a white Evoque and, something of a blot on the landscape, an old-style, bright green Polo with a number of scratches and dents.

Jonny parked behind the Evoque and climbed out of the car. He crunched across the gravel and knocked on the front door, which was opened after a few moments by a girl of about seventeen or eighteen. She was dressed in ripped jeans and a T-shirt decorated with a pink unicorn, and which had been made for someone at least eight years her junior. It revealed more bare midriff than Jonny had seen since a group of belly dancers had turned up for a Christmas party at work.

'What?' she said, scowling at him.

'I've come to see Mr Mayberry,' said Jonny. 'He is expecting me.'

The girl eyed him suspiciously and then stood back, letting him through the door. She led him into a hallway, past an elaborate umbrella stand and a narrow oak table, on which stood an arrangement of dried flowers in a tall white vase with a design of green herons, and a marble model of the Taj Mahal. He followed her past a flight of stairs and along a polished wood floor. 'In there,' she said, pointing to an open door into a study.

A man, Anthony Mayberry, Jonny assumed, looked up from his laptop. 'What is it, Amelia?'

'Some bloke to see you.'

Mayberry leapt to his feet. 'Mr Cardew, of course, come in. I'm sorry. I didn't realise the time. One tends not to, you know, when...' The sentence trailed away. 'Come in and sit down. It's good of you to drop in.' He led Jonny to a couple of armchairs near a window with a view of the garden. Jonny sat down while the girl stood in the doorway and stared at him.

'Amelia,' said Mayberry. 'You couldn't rustle up some coffee for us, could you?'

'Nah,' said Amelia, turning her back on them and heading for the stairs.

'Sorry,' said Mayberry again.

'Please,' said Jonny. 'Don't worry about it. I really don't need coffee.'

'I'm afraid Amelia's taken her mother's death very badly.' Mayberry gazed up at the ceiling. From the room above they could hear heavy footsteps and a sudden burst of loud music.

'I'm sure it's been very distressing for all of you,' said Jonny. 'You have two children, I believe?'

'Amelia has a brother, Tristan. Still asleep, I expect. Teenagers, you know. But they'll be back at college soon,' he added with an expression of relief.

He might find them annoying, Jonny supposed. But that would

probably be nothing compared to the loneliness that would surround him once they left for college.

'I've a colleague coming to visit,' said Mayberry, looking at his watch, apparently having read Jonny's thoughts. 'More of a friend, I suppose. He's been through a tough time. A messy divorce, you know.' He gazed out of the window for a moment as if reflecting on this. 'His wife is a close friend. Puts one in a difficult position, doesn't it?'

'I suppose it would,' said Jonny, never having been in a position of that kind.

'He had to move out of the family home in a hurry,' Mayberry continued. 'Left all his stuff in our garage. Hopefully he'll find somewhere of his own soon.'

'But I expect you'll be glad of his company right now,' said Jonny.

'He should be here any minute,' said Mayberry, not commenting on whether he'd be glad of the company or not. 'There's so much paperwork after a death.'

'Perhaps he'll be able to help with that.'

'Maybe,' said Mayberry, looking less than enthusiastic about the idea. 'Of course, we've known Carl for years. He and Clarissa were at university at the same time and we used to sail together. He may be able to help me plan the funeral. I can't really ask the children to do it.'

Jonny wondered why not. Surely it would help all of them to plan the funeral together. 'Have you settled on a date?'

'Not really. In a couple of weeks, probably. Hard to decide when it was all so unexpected.'

'Have they found out how your wife got hold of the poison?' Jonny asked.

Anthony sighed. 'I had a call from the medical examiner. He told me the post-mortem report just showed Clarissa had died from poisoning. He ordered a search of the kitchen at the festival site and found nothing suspicious. No one else had reported any ill effects that day. In any case, the post-mortem suggested Clarissa's last meal had been a prawn sandwich, which wasn't sold in the festival cafeteria. All vegan, apparently. And anyway, if the prawns had been off they might have made her very sick but wouldn't have killed her. That ruled them out as the source of poisoning. The chemical analysis found traces of alpha-amanitin in her blood. That's a poison that comes from the death cap fungus, but mushrooms hadn't been on the festival menu at all. They had a problem with their supplier apparently.' He stared out of the window into the garden for a moment. 'Can't imagine how it happened,' he muttered. 'Better to put it behind us and move on.'

Jonny couldn't understand why Mayberry wasn't asking more questions. It didn't seem enough to know that she'd died from poisoning. Didn't he want to know if it was an accident or if someone had deliberately fed Clarissa poisonous mushrooms? It was probably all too painful to think about. He remembered reading somewhere that poison was a woman's method of murder, but perhaps that was only in Agatha Christie novels – not the most reliable source. 'Do you know where your wife ate that day?'

'I don't know. I was away for a couple of days. Left on the Thursday morning. She usually made a flask of soup to have at her desk when she was working here at home. She took a salad or a sandwich when she was out all day.'

'Would she have made that herself?'

'I don't think so. She wasn't very domestic like that, not much of a cook. When she was working at home, she filled a flask with soup made from one of those packets and took it up to her study. But on Friday she planned to be at the festival from late morning. She was meeting her agent there for a discussion before her talk. Some problem with her contract, I think.'

'So she could have bought a sandwich on her way there?'

'There's an M&S Local on the way into town. She usually stopped there and bought herself something when she was going to be out all day.'

It was very unlikely that anything from M&S had been spiked

with poison. Half the local population would have been wiped out if it had. 'Did the medical examiner have any idea where the mushrooms might have come from?'

'They're found in the woods around here. He suggested that Clarissa might have been for a walk and picked some. But I think he's wrong about that. Clarissa wasn't keen on country walks, any kind of nature. She was busy with some conference in London earlier in the week and was tied up with the festival on the day she died. The only day she was home was Thursday, and as I said, going for a walk in the woods would have been entirely out of character. If there were mushrooms in the house, it wouldn't have been Clarissa who brought them in. Why the interest?'

'I'm a detective,' said Jonny, deciding to come clean about why he was there. 'The local mushroom society are anxious to prevent any more accidents like this one and have asked us to look into it.'

'Yes, yes, I think I've heard of you. You don't work alone, do you?'

'No, there's a group of us. I wanted to do something useful with my retirement, so I set up a breakfast club with Jasmine Javadi, the co-owner of a café in Windsor. The detectives were a spin-off from that. Jasmine and I joined up with a retired police sergeant and a young man called Ivo Dean, just after the royal funeral when a body was found in the Long Walk. The police weren't particularly interested, assumed it was a natural death and didn't take it any further. But I was intrigued and wanted to know more. Jasmine felt the same and along with DS Roscoff and Ivo, we decided to take a closer look at it.'

'I read something about that,' said Anthony. 'You worked out that it was a murder and even managed to detain the perpetrator. I also read a bit about the talk you and your wife gave at the festival. I suppose that's how these fungus people found you. Worried about their membership, I suppose. Giving mushrooms a bad name and all that when they are trying to promote foraging.'

'Actually, they discourage foraging.'

'Because my wife was poisoned?'

'No, they think it's bad for the environment. They want to know how your wife died in case there is a way they can avoid it happening again without having to ban people from the countryside during mushroom season.'

'The examiner bloke seemed happy to sign the death certificate,' said Anthony impatiently. 'I don't see the need to stir it up any further. Death from poisoning was obvious and he assumed it was an accident. He said it wouldn't be necessary to call in the coroner.'

'You think he was correct?'

'Why wouldn't he be? He's a highly trained professional. I'd trust him over a group of amateur fungus groupies any day.'

'I don't think they are disagreeing,' said Jonny. 'They just want to trace the source of the poison and work out how Clarissa was able to get hold of it.'

'Don't see what good they think that will do. The bloody things grow in the woods. It could have happened to anyone.'

But it hadn't happened to anyone. It had happened to his wife. There were very few similar deaths reported each year, so what made Clarissa Mayberry different? Why would she break the habit of a lifetime and go out into the woods to pick mushrooms?

'You must have known Clarissa better than anyone. What do you think happened?'

He shrugged. 'God knows. A sudden desire for some fresh air and a chance to sample the delicacies of the forest. I really can't imagine why she'd do that.'

Jonny felt he was getting nowhere and irritating Anthony Mayberry in the process. But there was one question that needed to be asked, quite possibly one that Anthony Mayberry wouldn't want to face. Had she eaten them deliberately? There'd been no hint that Clarissa Mayberry had any intention of doing away with herself. All the same, it had to be considered. 'Do you think she poisoned herself deliberately?'

Anthony stared at him with a mystified expression. He hesitated before answering. 'Wouldn't have thought so,' he said, having obviously considered the idea. 'Not impossible though, I suppose.'

Could someone have given her the mushrooms without knowing what they were? An innocent mistake? A horrible, deadly bit of generosity on the part of a person she trusted. A neighbour, perhaps. Jonny wondered, should he ever poison someone inadvertently, whether he would come forward and admit it. He liked to think he would. But of course, he couldn't actually imagine himself in that position. Could she have eaten them deliberately, knowing she'd make herself extremely ill and probably die? Thinking it over, this was highly unlikely. Jonny doubted that Clarissa had poisoned herself, whether deliberately or not. She wasn't the type to gather mushrooms herself and even if she was, wouldn't she be suspicious of anything that wasn't shrink-wrapped and sold by a reputable supplier? There was nothing to suggest she was suffering any kind of mental health issues, and she led a privileged life, free from worry, apart from the hint that there was a problem with her contract. And an apparently anti-social daughter. But no one would kill themselves because of a stroppy teenager, would they? And self-poisoning wasn't a nice or even common way to do away with oneself. In any case, she wasn't a country lover and probably couldn't tell one type of fungus from another. There was one other answer, and he wasn't prepared to bring that up right now. But they couldn't ignore the fact that Clarissa had some strong and unpopular views, and he knew that a search for her on social media revealed a lot of hate messages. Was that enough to suggest murder? He imagined Katya would consider it. There was nothing like the hint of a murder hunt to get her enthusiasm working at full tilt. He jotted down a few notes. Then he put the notebook away in his pocket.

He was pulling on his jacket when the sound of car tyres crunched across the gravel drive. Anthony peered out of the window. 'That's Carl,' he said as Jonny joined him at the window, and they watched a slim figure in a well-cut suit climb out of the car and make his way to the door. 'I'll let him in,' said Anthony. 'Amelia won't have heard him arrive and anyway she's in a foul mood.' He opened the door and led Carl into the living room, where he introduced him to Jonny.

'Cardew?' Carl asked. 'Anything to do with the packing company?'

'Yes,' said Jonny. 'But my son runs CPS now. I've retired.'

'Bet you still have a seat on the board, though.' Carl shook his hand energetically and beamed at him. 'Plenty of time for the golf course and all that.'

'Jonny works as a detective now.'

'Really?' said Carl, not looking particularly impressed.

'He also runs a breakfast club.'

'Very noble of him,' said Carl with a smirk.

Anthony ignored him. 'He's trying to find out how Clarissa was poisoned.'

'What?' said Carl. 'I thought it was all settled. It was an accident, wasn't it? Why do you need a detective?'

'I don't. He's working for some fungus people in case Clarissa's death gives mushrooms a bad name.'

'Huh,' said Carl. 'A load of busybodies.' He frowned at Jonny. 'Wouldn't have thought you'd give them the time of day.'

Jonny was thinking it might be time for him to leave. He was getting nowhere with these two arrogant types. He was even developing some sympathy for Clarissa, and he really wanted to know the truth about what had happened to her. He faced Carl head on.

'You don't think Clarissa killed herself, do you?' He'd already asked Anthony, but a second opinion was always valuable.

'Don't be ridiculous,' said Carl. 'Clarissa was... well, she was always so sure of herself, thought she was right about everything. Killing herself would have been admitting she was wrong. And in any case, she was far too much of a coward to take poison. And she didn't leave a note. Isn't that what suicides usually do?'

'Do you know anyone who wanted to hurt Clarissa?'

'I can't think of anyone who might have wanted to do her in,'

Carl scoffed, blundering into the elephant in the room in a way Jonny found arrogant.

'Let's hope it doesn't come to that. It was a horrible way to die, but hopefully it will turn out to have an explanation. If it was an accident, we may be able to stop it happening to anyone else.'

'Good luck with that,' said Carl, turning to a sideboard and helping himself to a tumbler of whisky.

Anthony stood up and walked with Jonny to his car. They shook hands, grudgingly on Anthony's part, Jonny thought. 'Thank you for seeing me,' he said.

Anthony Mayberry turned his back and headed into the house without answering.

APART FROM DEVELOPING a deep dislike for both Anthony Mayberry and Carl Archer, Jonny hadn't achieved very much with his visit. It was probably too close to home. Neither of them seemed to want to know any more about what had happened. He realised Clarissa could be difficult, but it didn't seem right to bury her without knowing more about the reason for her death. Jonny wondered how he would feel if it had been Belinda who had died from something that clearly wasn't natural. He shuddered at the thought. But Clarissa's death certificate had been signed and the body released, and Anthony Mayberry appeared to accept that. No date had been set for the funeral. Jonny didn't know what processes were in place for altering a cause of death once certified, but there must be ways. Katya would know what they were. Somehow Jonny had the feeling that this was far more than an unfortunate accident, and he meant to get to the bottom of what had really happened and why Clarissa Mayberry had died in such a horrible way.

CHAPTER SIX

It was a busy morning in the café. Jasmine wasn't sure why. The tourist season was coming to an end, children were back at school and there was no train strike so no delayed commuters; no reason at all why there should suddenly be an extra demand for breakfasts. Sometimes that was just how things were. It had happened before and would probably happen again. And she shouldn't complain. Extra people meant extra money in the till. But she was glad that Jonny had somehow got wind of the rush of customers and had come in early to help with the washing-up. But then she realised that Jonny didn't have any kind of second sight. This was just his day for dropping in to update the breakfast club records.

'You're in luck,' Jonny told Jasmine, hanging up a damp tea towel and reaching for a dry one. 'Mrs Gage knows Magda Nowak.'

'They work for the same agency?' It would be great if they did. Jasmine wouldn't have to call all the cleaning companies in Windsor, enquiring about a cleaner she didn't really want to hire. She'd planned to do that after the lunch rush, but thanks to Jonny's Mrs Gage, she was now down to one, or at most two phone calls.

'They both work for Windsor Mops,' said Jonny. 'Mrs Gage was a bit huffy about giving me Magda's details. They're not supposed to take on private work. The agency loses their commission, I suppose, if they do.'

That was fair enough. 'How did you persuade her to pass on secret info?' she asked.

'I used my irresistible charm.'

Jasmine didn't doubt it for a moment. Jonny was good at using his good looks and winning smile to elicit information from women of a certain age. But once Jasmine had thought it over, she had no intention of poaching a cleaner from Windsor Mops. She did, however, need to think of another reason for inviting Magda to chat to her. If she went with her original plan, Magda might take her up on the offer of a job, and Jasmine wasn't sure she could afford anyone else right now. Particularly if it was going to land Jonny in Mrs Gage's bad books. She decided there was no harm in telling Magda she'd been asked to enquire about where Clarissa could have found the mushrooms that killed her. It was the kind of thing anyone with an interest in fungi would want to know, wasn't it? Families as well, and grieving relatives would be unlikely to want to make their own enquiries. The Breakfast Club Detectives were quite well known in town now, so the fact that they were looking into Clarissa Mayberry's death would hardly come as a surprise.

HAVING SERVED THE FINAL LUNCHES, Jasmine went up to the office and called Magda. She tempted her with the promise of a free cup of coffee and a pastry of her choice if she could spare half an hour or so to talk to her. Magda agreed to come round right away. She'd just finished work at an office nearby and had not had time for lunch, so Jasmine's suggestion of pastries was more than welcome. Jasmine went back down to the café and put aside a plate of sandwiches and a couple of her dad's best. Breakfast had been busy, but they still had a few leftovers from lunch. It was the least she could do in exchange for some information.

It was a good decision. Magda, when she arrived, was red-faced and out of breath, having walked, carrying a bag of cleaning equipment, from the other side of the bridge. She dropped her bag onto the floor, sank gratefully into a chair and helped herself to an egg and cress sandwich from the plate Jasmine placed in front of her. She was a well-built woman in her mid-twenties who, having finished the sandwich, chose one of Karim's raisin whirls and asked for coffee with whipped cream. Not a weightwatcher then, Jasmine thought as she poured the coffee, adding a generous swirl of cream. She led Magda up to the office, where they could chat without interruption and without anyone overhearing what they were saying. Jasmine asked her if she enjoyed working for the Mayberry family.

'No,' said Magda, taking a hefty bite of her bun. 'They are horrible people. Mr Mayberry perhaps is not so bad, but he is not usually there when I clean. Mrs Mayberry is mostly working at home in her office, where she must not be interrupted. How can I clean and make no noise?'

Jasmine offered her a sympathetic smile. 'Will you go on working there?'

Magda shook her head. 'They don't want me back.' She looked at Jasmine with a defiant expression. 'I'm not worried. Windsor Mops give me as much work as I want.'

Jasmine sensed some tension and wondered if the Mayberrys had dispensed with her services before Clarissa had died. And if so, why? Good cleaners were hard to come by and Jasmine didn't suppose Windsor Mops moved their staff around for no reason. If there had been some hard feeling and they had asked for Magda to be removed, could she expect an honest account from Magda herself? Well, she didn't have a lot of choice. Magda was here and Jasmine needed to find out what she could. She'd just have to accept that Magda's account might not be an unbiased one. 'How did you get on with the twins?' Jasmine asked. Hopefully Magda's grudge, if she had one, would be with the adults in the family.

'They have very messy bedrooms,' said Magda, with obvious disapproval. 'They should have been made to clean them. In Poland, even small children clean their bedrooms. But Tristan, he leaves dirty plates and cups on the floor, all mixed up with his clothes. I have to tidy it all up. He is a repulsive young man.'

To be fair, Jasmine thought, most teenage boys' bedrooms were probably not squeaky-clean examples of orderliness. 'Did you see much of him?'

'He was supposed to leave for college at eight-thirty, but usually he was still in bed when I arrived. His mother shouted at him to get up so I could clean, and once he was gone, I could get into his room. I put his clothes in the washing machine. I took his crockery and cutlery to the kitchen and put it in the dishwasher. Why does he eat in the bedroom? Is that an English habit?'

Jasmine was not sure how to answer that. It was more a symptom of a dysfunctional family, she thought. Had she ever decamped to her room in a huff when she was a teenager? She didn't remember that she ever had, but she and her dad had always got on. She'd be better keeping off the topic of teenage bedrooms. 'And in between him getting up and going to college, did he talk to you?'

Magda studied her hands. 'Sometimes,' she said slowly.

'What did you talk about?'

'About going out. Once he wanted to buy me a drink, but I told him he was too young.'

'And how did he react to that?'

'He threw more of his stuff on the floor. Like a toddler. After that I tried to avoid him.'

'And his sister?'

'Amelia? She was very rude to me and shouted at me to keep out of her room, so I left it and sometimes her mother shouted at me for not cleaning it. I tell her Amelia will not let me in and she just says, "Amelia lives in a tip, not my problem," and goes back into her office.'

It sounded like the cleaning job from hell. Jasmine was quite tempted to ask Magda if she would like to work at *Jasmine's*. But although she was sure Magda would be great as a kitchen hand, she didn't actually need any extra staff. And anyway, she was supposed to be solving the puzzle of Clarissa Mayberry and the mushrooms, not reorganising her employees. 'Did you often see Mr Mayberry?'

Magda shook her head. 'I did meet him once or twice, but he usually left for work before I got there, so I didn't know him well. He seems nice enough, but Mrs Mayberry complained about him quite often. Said she didn't like it when he hung around the house while she was trying to work.'

'When were you last there?'

'The day before Mrs Mayberry died. They said not to come after that. But I don't care. I am starting a new job next week.'

A bit abrupt, Jasmine thought, wondering again if there had been some kind of trouble. Had Magda resigned or had Clarissa Mayberry sacked her? It wasn't really Jasmine's place to ask that kind of question. Even if she did, she would probably not get an honest answer.

'I went three days a week,' Magda continued. 'Tuesday, Thursday and Saturday. So I wasn't there the day she was at the festival. I should have been there the day after, on the Saturday morning, but Mr Mayberry told me not to come. Windsor Mops said I would be paid for that day so I wasn't worried. I was just glad not to go back there.'

Even if Magda was leaving, why wasn't she working out her notice? Could that be because Mayberry couldn't have anyone in the house so soon after his wife's death, or did he want to get rid of evidence? How much did Magda know about Clarissa's comings and goings? 'Did Mrs Mayberry go out a lot?'

'Quite often she would go for meetings, and she gave lectures.'

'Did anyone visit her at the house?'

'Not much. But on my last day there, when I was leaving, a car pulled into the drive. Amelia was out and Tristan was at college.'

'Did you see who was in the car? Was it just one person?'

Magda nodded. 'A man.'

'What did he look like?'

'Smart suit, good haircut.'

So not someone to fix the washing machine or do the garden. 'What kind of car was it?'

'I don't know cars very well. It was a big one. Black.'

'A people carrier?'

'No, more like the ones that take people to the airport.'

An executive taxi? But driven by a man in a suit, so probably not there to pick Clarissa up and take her to a speaking engagement. But people visited houses all the time, not usually with any sinister intent. Although, when the person being visited was dead two days later, one did wonder if the visitor was someone with an evil plan. Delivering a gift of poisonous mushrooms, perhaps? But how would she find out who the visitor was? Jasmine felt this was probably a bit of a blind alley. She should focus more on Clarissa's actions on the days before she died. 'Did Mrs Mayberry usually take her lunch with her when she went out?' Jasmine asked, changing tack. Was that an odd question?

If it was, Magda was unfazed by it. 'No, she liked to get the free lunch that goes with speaking engagements. But the festival was all vegan. Nothing but nuts and carrots – rabbit food, she said. She kept some meals in the freezer, and she might have taken one of them with her. Or bought a sandwich on her way.'

Clarissa's last meal was a prawn sandwich. Sandwiches, Jasmine knew from experience, froze quite well and were a useful standby. If she'd planned to eat it for lunch, she would probably have taken it out of the freezer in time to thaw out, so perhaps she'd left it on one of the kitchen counters, where she might have added extra mushrooms herself after a walk in the woods to clear her head before her lecture. Prawn and mushroom? Not a sandwich filling Jasmine had ever tried, but not impossible. But mushrooms were not listed alongside prawns as Clarissa's last meal, so she must have eaten them earlier. The black car was there on Thursday and Clarissa had died on Friday evening, so it wasn't impossible that whoever was driving the car was also the bearer of mushrooms. Perhaps Clarissa had eaten them on toast for her breakfast on the Friday morning. Had anyone checked the contents of the fridge? They should, as a matter of urgency. There could be other meals contaminated with death caps. She made a note to ask Jonny and get him to suggest Mr Mayberry throw everything out before there was another nasty death. She also wondered if it would be worth checking out the car. Big and black wasn't a lot to go on, but one of the neighbours might have noticed what make it was, maybe even recognised the driver.

What else could she learn from Magda? Cleaning the kitchen must have been one of her tasks and she might have noticed any food left lying around. 'Did you see any mushrooms in the kitchen the day you were there?' she asked.

Magda shook her head. 'Only dirty crockery and pans and the flask Mrs Mayberry used for her soup. I washed the pans and loaded the dishwasher but left the flask. She'd probably take it to her study later. There was no food left out when I left.'

'Any mushrooms in the fridge?'

'It wasn't the day for fridge cleaning. I only opened it to put away the milk, but I don't think so.'

Was it safe to assume the mushrooms were not in the house during Magda's last visit? That would mean they must have been delivered that afternoon, which didn't rule out black car man, or early the following morning. 'So on the days you worked there, you just drove to the house and away again when you'd finished? You didn't go for a walk after work?' If she had, she might have noticed if the black car was making a quick call or if it was still there.

'Why would I? I just wanted to get home.'

Jasmine couldn't blame her for that. Only a committed rambler would go for a walk after a hard morning's cleaning. 'What about the rest of the family? Did any of them go out while you were there?'

'Tristan went out. To college, I suppose.'

'Did he walk to college?'

'Him, no,' Magda scoffed. 'He always took his car.'

He probably crawled out of bed straight into his car. No time for a mushroom foraging walk. 'And Mrs Mayberry and Amelia were there all the time?'

'Most of the time. I could hear Amelia's music all the morning but then she went out in Mrs Mayberry's car. And Mrs Mayberry was on her phone most of the time.'

'Did Mrs Mayberry have lunch at home that day?'

'She usually had a flask of soup at her desk.'

'I don't suppose you know what kind of soup it was?'

Magda shook her head. 'No idea. Probably just one of those packets. There were some in the store cupboard.'

Jasmine wrote that down in her notebook and tapped it with her pencil. She wasn't sure that she'd discovered anything very useful. She read through the notes she'd made and decided there were no more questions to ask. She thanked Magda for her time.

'No problem,' said Magda. She stood up but seemed reluctant to leave. Did she have more to say?

'Do you need anyone to work for you here? I have waitress experience.'

'I don't need anyone right now, but I'll let you know if I do.'

Magda looked disappointed. Was that the only reason she'd agreed to come? That and the free sandwiches and pastries. Not to mention a coffee with added cream. Not exactly a financial drain, but possibly something she could add to Mr Weatherby's expenses.

CHAPTER
SEVEN

Ivo drove up a bumpy lane and parked his van at the edge of the field that had been the festival site. Harold, sensing a good place to go for a walk, tugged at his harness and sniffed the air as Ivo lowered the window. He stared out at a more or less empty field. Most of the tents had gone and there were patches of dead grass where the marquees had been. At the far side of the site there was still a collection of rubbish skips, some stacks of folding chairs and tables waiting to be hefted onto a fleet of flatbed trucks along with strings of bunting and fairy lights that had been dragged out of trees and now lay trailing along the ground. There were still people clearing up, piling stuff onto the trucks, coiling up electrical wire and spiking up discarded flyers and sandwich wrappings. Ivo put an excited Harold on his lead and strolled across to talk to a man who was emptying bags of litter and sorting it into bins labelled paper, glass, food and other waste. Ivo noted that the bin for other waste was by far the fullest. Was this laziness or had the festival not lived up to its green credentials? Although, to be fair, the only plastic in evidence were the rolls of black bags they were collecting the rubbish in.

As Ivo and Harold stood and watched the clear-up in progress, a man came up to them and patted Harold on the head. 'Can I help you?' he asked.

Ivo very much hoped so or the whole trip out there would be a waste of time. 'Were you at the festival?'

The man pulled off a stout black and yellow glove and shook Ivo's hand. 'Name's Andy, one of the festival committee. I was here throughout. Are you looking for something?'

'I'm after information. Were you here when Clarissa Mayberry gave her presentation?'

'Who? Oh, the woman who collapsed. I saw the ambulance leaving. Hadn't had much to do with her, though.'

'You didn't talk to her at all, or the first aid people?'

'I deal more with the site itself and don't have a lot to do with the speakers, or the public for that matter. None of my business what people get up to. Someone's hurt, I leave it to the first aiders. Best to keep out of their way. They know what they're doing and people like me barging in just make it worse.'

Ivo nodded. 'Probably best if everyone does what they know about.' He wasn't sure he agreed. If someone was in trouble you tried to help them, didn't you? But he supposed there were plenty of people there to do that. Properly trained people, and it didn't sound as if Clarissa would have been any better off with Andy's help.

'I wondered why the food hygiene people were here the next day,' said Andy. 'Blooming cheek. We have professional caterers. They're thoroughly recommended – awards, certificates, five star reviews, you name it. Why would they poison anyone?'

'I suppose they have to check when someone dies,' said Ivo. 'They can't risk it happening again.'

Andy looked surprised, shocked even. 'Didn't know she'd died,' he muttered. 'I'm sorry to hear that. Accounts for the health inspection, though.'

Ivo was surprised he didn't know. He'd have expected the festival to be buzzing with it. Jonny and Belinda hadn't known either until Lugs told them, so he supposed the committee had wanted to keep it quiet and play the incident down. It wouldn't have been good publicity to make too much of it. And Clarissa had died in hospital, not at the festival. As far as Ivo knew, she'd been there on her own. It wasn't as if they'd had to deal with grieving relatives demanding medical attention. 'Did you see her before that? At one of the other events, perhaps?'

Andy scratched his head. 'Not as far as I know. I'm not sure I'd recognise her. But ask Tommy over there. He was stewarding that day. He'd be the one most likely to have seen her.'

Ivo and Harold made their way to where Tommy was piling up folding chairs and lifting them onto a truck. Having loaded the final one and fastened the back of the truck, he rubbed his hands and smiled at Ivo, who asked him the same question he'd asked Andy. Had he seen Clarissa on site on the morning of her talk?

'Dunno, mate. What did she look like?'

Ivo scrolled to a photo on his phone and found the picture Jasmine had downloaded from Clarissa's website. It was a photo that had also been on the back cover of her book, copies of which had been scattered around the festival; in the tent where she was speaking, in a pop-up bookstore on the edge of the site and advertised on the pages of the festival programme. It must have been a face that was well known to anyone who had anything to do with organising the event.

'Oh, yeah,' said Tommy, taking the phone from Ivo and studying the picture. 'I saw her. She was sat outside the bookstore, on the Friday morning, I think. There was a heap of books on a table. Reckon she was expecting to sell signed copies, but no one was interested. Not when I was there, anyhow.'

'Was she eating anything?'

'That's an odd question. Why do you want to know that?'

'Because something she ate that day killed her. We want to know what and where and of course, how she got hold of it.'

'You police?' Tommy asked, with a look of suspicion that made Ivo wonder if he had something to hide.

'No,' said Ivo. 'It's not a police matter.'

'One of them private investigators, then?'

'You could say that.'

'Well,' said Tommy. 'I think she had a cup of coffee. They both did.'

'Both?'

'She was with this other woman.'

'One of the festival organisers or a visitor?'

'Not one of the organisers. I hadn't seen her before, and I didn't see her later that day. I don't think she was one of the speakers, either.'

Could be the agent, Ivo thought. 'What did she look like?'

'Skinny, dressed a bit arty, if you know what I mean. But that would go for a lot of the people here.'

'Did either of them have anything with them? A picnic basket, perhaps?'

'Didn't really notice. Oh, I remember now. There was a green carrier bag on the ground near where they were sitting. Might have had a picnic inside. Harrods,' he added. 'That posh place in London.'

'Thanks,' said Ivo. 'Mind if I take a look at your bins?'

'Be my guest. Takes all sorts,' Ivo could hear him mutter as he and Harold left him and made their way to the bins.

Ivo found a long stick, leant over the side of a skip into which the general rubbish bin had now been emptied, and started poking into the garbage. He could probably ignore the paper and glass bins. Even a hard right recycling refusenik wouldn't ignore a sign that said glass or paper only. At least, Ivo hoped they wouldn't. Rule keepers rather than breakers, weren't they? Law and order types. He poked at the bags of food refuse, which were buzzing with wasps and smelt horrible. Even Harold showed little interest, slinking away and curling up by the paper bin. Ivo was trawling back through five days' worth of litter, and it was slow going. He began by pushing as much as he could to one end of the skip and gradually sifted his way through the rest. His stick was not a lot of help, so he pulled on the latex gloves Katya had given him and did the job by hand. He was about to give up when he spotted it. A dark green plastic carrier bag with *Harrods* printed on it in curly gold lettering. He lifted the bag out, rolled it up and pushed it into an evidence bag. Another bit of kit that Katya had given him. He did a quick check to make sure it was the only bag of its kind in the skip. Then he slipped it into his pocket and headed back to the van with Harold at his side.

He drove back to *Shady Willows,* stopping briefly at *Jasmine's,* where he pinned the evidence bag to the board ready for their next meeting.

CHAPTER
EIGHT

Katya navigated her way to Patsy Kline's flashy website. It must have been built by an over-enthusiastic computer science undergraduate on work experience. It had every web-building gizmo in the book, from irritating gifs that jumped around on the screen, to rapidly scrolling background images, both of which made Katya's eyes hurt. Luckily, the one page that kept still long enough to make notes was the *Contact Us* section. The most high-tech part of that was a link to a map for the street address in Ealing. Katya clicked it and a map opened with a number of options. The website designer must have a side-line as an animator. A small car, a slightly bigger bus and a train bounced up and down at the edge of the map inviting her to choose her means of transport. Katya didn't have a car, so she ignored that. There was a dizzying array of buses that would take her there, but they were all from central London. None from Windsor or even Slough. Which left the train, and that suited Katya well. She could nip up on the train from Slough, a journey of around twenty minutes. She clicked the small image of a train and a little orange man popped onto the screen and trotted along the map from the station to Patsy Kline's office in Ealing Broadway.

There was nothing on the site to suggest that drop-ins were welcome. Katya decided she wasn't going to go all that way only to be told she needed an appointment, so she called and said she would like to speak to Ms Kline as soon as possible. The receptionist Katya spoke to insisted that the first available time was in two weeks, until Katya dropped in the name of Clarissa Mayberry, at which point she discovered a slot that same afternoon.

Katya grabbed her best tote bag; one stamped with a picture of Windsor Castle that someone had left dangling from a chair at *Jasmine's* months ago and never claimed. It was empty when Jasmine found it, so it couldn't have meant very much to its owner and Katya had no qualms about requisitioning it for her own use. She took it from its hook on the back of her kitchen door and shook out the dust and some ancient sandwich crumbs. Then she filled it with an umbrella, an exercise book and pen, a wallet containing her senior travel card and a packet of Murray Mints, a recent BOGOF deal at Tesco. Having packed the bag, she hefted it over her shoulder, tucked her phone into a zipped pocket of her trousers and set off.

The map had told her it was a six-and-a-half-minute walk from the station to Patsy Kline's office. Katya did it in five and felt pleased with herself. She wasn't even out of breath. The map must have allowed for people walking in high-heeled shoes, something Katya had never worn. The image on the website had clearly been doctored to make the office look far grander than it was. Generated by AI, she wouldn't wonder. Rather than the grand Victorian villa she'd been led to expect, she found the office consisted of three rooms on the second floor above a red brick parade of shops in the Broadway. Katya pressed a buzzer on a door at the side of a betting shop, announced her name and was buzzed in. She puffed up two flights of stairs and was greeted by a receptionist, who indicated a purple sofa next to a fern in a brass pot and asked her to wait.

Katya sat there for twenty minutes without so much as the offer of a cup of tea and was then shown into another office, this one overlooking the shopping street below, and where Patsy Kline herself sat behind an oak desk, on top of which and slightly to one side sat a large screen iMac. Patsy, an extremely thin woman dressed in a black trouser suit with a purple silk scarf and the largest earrings Katya had ever seen, was sitting on a yellow swivel chair. She indicated that Katya should sit down on one of a similar colour on the other side of the desk. Katya was a little disappointed to discover that this one was static. Probably just as well; whizzing round on a chair didn't give quite the right impression during a serious interview. And discussing a death by poisonous mushrooms was definitely at the serious end of all the possible interviews that Patsy was likely to take part in.

'You want to talk about poor dear Clarissa?' said Patsy, reaching for a box of perfumed tissues and dabbing her eyes with an audible sniff.

Somehow Katya didn't feel the *poor dear* rang true. She suspected this was not a best buddy type of relationship. 'I believe you were with her the day she gave her talk at the Reimagine the Light Festival.'

'Clarissa didn't have time to come here to discuss her contract, apparently. I knew she'd be at the festival – well, she couldn't get out of meeting me there. I suggested a coffee at the bookstore. Just as well I went,' Patsy sighed crossly. 'When I arrived, she'd done nothing with the box of books I'd sent her. She was supposed to arrange a display and sign them for people. Typical Clarissa. Expects to have everything done for her. Anyway, I helped her get things organised and left before her presentation.'

'Did you have lunch together?'

'I don't eat lunch,' said Patsy.

Katya believed her. She didn't look as if she went in for breakfast or dinner in a big way, either. 'Do you know where Clarissa planned to have lunch?'

'Why would I? All I know is that she didn't plan to eat in the festival cafeteria. She said it smelt of cabbage. And she doesn't approve of vegans.'

'Do you think she brought something with her from home, or would she have bought it on her way to the festival?'

'I haven't the least idea. My clients' refreshment arrangements are nothing to do with me. She did have a bag with her that might have contained food.'

The receptionist arrived with a wooden tea tray, lacquered in gold and with a design of blue lilies. It contained two cups and saucers, a teapot and milk jug, all in white with gold rims. She poured the tea and passed a cup to Katya, who took it with a slightly shaking hand, nervous about spilling it on the pale cream carpet at her feet. She took a sip and perched it on the edge of the desk. 'Are you a nature lover?' she asked Patsy.

'What an extraordinary question. I walk in the park now and then, but I'm not one for the countryside.'

No, she looked as if she spent more time with a personal trainer in a posh gym than yomping around the countryside, which – disappointingly – would probably rule her out as a suspect. 'And Clarissa?'

'Well, she lived out of town, but she was a busy woman. I don't imagine she had much time for country rambles.'

'So neither of you have any interest in plants?'

'Certainly not.' She looked at Katya as if she'd suggested an interest in do-it-yourself brain surgery. Katya glanced at a Monstera that sat in a corner of the room in a navy-blue ceramic pot. It looked glossy and well cared for.

Patsy followed her gaze. 'We were advised to have plants in the office. They improve oxygen levels, apparently, although I can't say I've noticed. A man calls in once a week to care for them. Clarissa has a gardener, and as far as I know she has no plants in her house.'

A gardener? Katya scribbled that in her notebook. 'So if Clarissa had seen what she thought was a mushroom, she'd not be suspicious?'

Patsy laughed. 'Would you?'

Katya supposed not. She'd bought mushrooms from Tesco and eaten them on the top of pizzas, never giving a thought to whether or not they were likely to kill her. One trusted the likes of Tesco more than, for example, a gift from a friend. 'You didn't pick mushrooms on your way to the meeting? As a gift, perhaps?'

'I'm afraid I can't help you with that. If I was going to meet a client with a gift it would probably be a perfumed candle or some chocolates from Fortnum's. Not that I give my clients gifts very often. Just a small token at Christmas or after a particularly successful book launch.'

Katya believed her. She didn't look like the type to shower her clients with generosity. In any case, she would have been unlikely to admit giving Clarissa mushrooms. But the question had to be asked and Patsy didn't look particularly fazed by it. She was either an excellent actor or she had a clear conscience.

Patsy took a small sip of tea, put the cup down and blotted her lipstick with a tissue. 'So did poor Anthony ask you to trace the source of the poison that killed Clarissa?'

Katya shook her head. 'It was the local fungus society. They want to know what happened so they can publish a brochure to warn people.'

'I'm sorry, I can't help with that. We don't do publicity brochures.'

'No, that's not why I'm here. I just needed some background on Clarissa.' Stupid woman. Wasn't it obvious why she'd come? 'Well,' she said, gathering up her bag and standing up to leave. 'Thank you for seeing me.' She extracted a card from her wallet and handed it to Patsy. 'Give me a call if you think of anything I need to know.'

'I can't think what that would be,' Patsy said, pushing the card to one side without reading it and turning back to her computer screen. Katya was obviously expected to see herself out. She made her way back past the receptionist, who barely glanced up as she left. Katya didn't bother saying goodbye to her and it was a relief to be back in the street. No one spoke to her there either, but they seemed a lot friendlier than Patsy and her assistant. One or two of them even smiled at her as she passed them.

The next train to Slough would arrive in twenty minutes, and as she sat on the platform waiting for a it, she remembered that she had a packet of Murray Mints in her bag. Particularly welcome, given the lack of biscuits with her cup of tea. Clarissa clearly hadn't been a favourite client, but perhaps Patsy was like that with all of them. Katya wrote her off as an accidental poisoner. If she had poisoned Clarissa, it would have been deliberate and carefully planned. But try as she might, Katya couldn't see her gathering death caps on her way to see Clarissa. She'd go for something far more sophisticated. A beautiful miniature liqueur laced with arsenic, probably. So as a suspect, Patsy fitted the profile – an obvious dislike of Clarissa. But she was short on means. Even opportunity was dubious. At least it was for mushroom poisoning. Was there, she wondered, any way one could lace a liqueur with liquidised mushroom? The train arrived and Katya climbed aboard, telling herself not to be so silly. Even Ivo wouldn't have come up with that idea.

CHAPTER NINE

Jonny typed Carl Archer's name into Google, hoping that as it was a fairly unusual name there would not be too many entries for him. He was wrong. There were a surprising number of them. He contemplated adding *arrogant prat* to the name but decided it wouldn't help much. However, when clicking on possible hits, Jonny discovered a lot of the Carl Archers were on family history sites and had been dead for many years. It was also a more common name in America than the UK and Jonny decided to rule those out as well. Anthony hadn't mentioned that the Carl Archer he knew was American. He'd been at university with Clarissa and he and Anthony belonged to the same sailing club, so for now Jonny decided to focus on the UK.

The most likely lead he could find was something called Archer Investment Advice. The chairman was Carl Archer and the company operated from offices in West London. There was a flashy website complete with photographs of senior members of staff. He'd struck lucky. This was definitely the Carl Archer he'd met, and he looked about the right age to have been at university with Clarissa. After further research, he discovered a London School of Economics alumni list and he and Clarissa were indeed contemporaries. Digging a bit deeper led to a Facebook page belonging to Carl's wife, Leonora; a nice-looking woman, Jonny thought. It was hard to tell from a Facebook profile head and shoulders, but she didn't seem to have Carl Archer's air of arrogance. She and Carl had a sixteen-year-old daughter and a son two years younger. Both were attending boarding schools on the south coast. The couple were in the process of divorcing and Leonora's page was full of sympathy messages which ranged from *Thinking of you, darling – hugs*, to *He was a rat – you're better off without him*. Leonora sounded upbeat about it all. She'd posted a picture of a village in Provence with a message: *Taking a break in the sun to do some painting*. On later pages she'd uploaded some of her paintings and posted a link to a site that was selling them for her. Jonny clicked on it. Bearing in mind the richness of Provençal colours, he thought them a little dull, but her prices suggested she was sought after. He was unable to find an address for Carl, but then he remembered all the boxes and tea chests in Anthony Mayberry's garage. Carl Archer was in the process of moving.

He decided to check out Clarissa and Anthony's social media. Clarissa's own Twitter and Facebook accounts were obviously operated by someone else, presumably her agent as they mostly contained links to her books and were devoid of anything personal. Jonny still thought of it as Twitter in spite of its recent rebranding to something he assumed was now called X. Jonny had never been much of a Twitter user and was even less inclined to post anything to a site merely named with a cross – was it now a place for people unable to write their own names and who communicated entirely with irritating gifs? But plenty of people did still use it, and many of those were less than complimentary about Clarissa Mayberry and her opinions. There were no doubt those who thought she was the answer to all the country's problems, but he left them alone, partly because they would make him angry but more because they would be less likely to want to kill her. Some of the Clarissa haters had made threats but none of them mentioned poisonous fungi.

Anthony Mayberry's Facebook page, like Carl's, was there solely to promote his business, that of financial adviser. One thing it contained was a link to Archer Investments, but that was no surprise as the two of them were already friends. He remembered Anthony mentioning sailing and checked out a number of sailing clubs within a reasonable distance from Windsor, none of which gave any information about membership. He typed Anthony Mayberry yachting into a Google image search and found a photograph of Anthony standing in front of a small sailing boat, clutching a trophy for a race he'd won in the summer of 2018. Standing next to him was a boy of about twelve. Tristan, presumably, before he hit teenagerhood. He had probably changed a lot over the last five years, but photos were always useful, if only to make the incident board look more colourful, so he bookmarked the picture ready to download and print it next time he was in the office. He then tracked back and saved the pages with Carl Archer's photograph and Leonora's Facebook page.

It was half an hour or so before Jonny needed to head to *Jasmine's* for the meeting, so he decided to check out the Mayberry twins. A search for Tristan Mayberry revealed a school prizegiving from just over two years ago, when he'd won a medal for outstanding achievement in his GCSEs. And yet he'd gone on to fail his A levels. Anthony had told Jonny Tristan was retaking them at a local college. Had he just chosen the wrong subjects or had something happened that led to disastrous results first time around? Not that unusual perhaps – teenagers went through a lot of angst – but to go from record high achiever to failure in two years seemed to suggest something far more catastrophic. He made a note of it and planned to ask the others what they thought.

Amelia ran an Instagram page on which she commented on her favourite bands, uploading and subscribing to a huge number of reels of the kind of music that would likely only appeal to other eighteen-year-olds. Jonny had little experience of that. His own son Marcus had been a rather serious teenager, weighed down by concerns about global warming. Once again, he made a note of Amelia's musical interests, hoping that Ivo or Jasmine would be able to shed some light on them.

CHAPTER
TEN

Jasmine arrived early in the office. It had been a quiet morning in the café – fewer students and schoolchildren now the new term was starting. Karim had made too many muffins, so she'd brought a plate of them with her. They were always popular, particularly with Katya. Harold wouldn't turn one down, either. She shovelled some beans into the coffee machine and turned it on, enjoying the aroma of freshly brewing coffee, which was usually overpowered by the smell of frying bacon downstairs.

She turned on the computer, thinking that while she was waiting she'd find out a bit more about the death cap. A lot of what she found she knew already, but then she came across an article on food foraging that had appeared in a national newspaper a couple of days ago. It was headed *Food for Free. With supermarket prices still on the rise,* she read, *why not get out into the countryside and see what you can find for free.* The article mentioned blackberries, sloes, hawthorns and rosehips. It also had some recipes and Jasmine wondered if Karim fancied trying out blackberry muffins. She'd seen plenty of blackberries along the river path, on the roadside, even creeping over the fence between *Jasmine's* and the shop next door. She read on and discovered that after the damp summer they'd had this year, mushrooms and toadstools would also be plentiful. *But be careful,* the article continued. *Some are poisonous. Buy a good guidebook, or better still join a group with a professional fungus expert.* She scrolled down to a comments page where someone had posted a warning with unpleasantly graphic details regarding the effects of eating death caps. She already knew that, of course, since that was what Clarissa Mayberry had died from. What she didn't know was that they took up to twenty-four hours to kill you. Clarissa would most likely have been suffering stomach pains and vomiting the day before she died. She would then have felt a little better, only to be struck down again as the poison attacked her liver and kidneys. So Clarissa was unlikely to have eaten the death cap mushrooms at the festival. Her presentation began at five in the afternoon, and she died shortly after arriving in hospital later that evening. It was most likely that she'd eaten the mushrooms either for lunch or an early dinner the day before. She would have felt ill that evening, but in all probability woke up the next day feeling better. All of which could change the focus of their enquiry. They needed to find out what Clarissa had eaten on Thursday. The day before she died. Magda had been at the house cleaning that day. She'd said there weren't any mushrooms in the kitchen, but perhaps she hadn't looked carefully enough. Anthony Mayberry had been away on Thursday night, but the twins should know what had been on the menu.

She printed out the article and was just pinning it to the board when she heard Katya stomping up the stairs. Jasmine poured her a cup of coffee and offered her a muffin.

'Thanks, love,' said Katya, sitting down at the head of the table and spreading out the notes she'd made after visiting Patsy Kline.

'What was she like?' Jasmine asked.

'A bit of a cold fish and not very helpful. She's a real townie type. Thinks a walk in the park is the same as a country ramble. Even the office plants are cared for by someone else. I don't think she liked Clarissa much, but I doubt if she wanted her dead – she's too much of a cash cow. She didn't seem the type to shower her clients with gifts, particularly not wild ones she'd gathered herself, although she did admit to giving away the odd scented candle. Never saw the point of those myself. And even if she had wanted to kill Clarissa, she didn't strike me as the type for do-it-yourself poisoning. She'd probably have hired a hit man.'

'A wasted trip, then?'

'She did tell me one thing that could be useful. Clarissa didn't fancy eating in the festival cafeteria. She didn't hold with vegans, apparently.'

Jasmine laughed. 'Why not?'

'Dunno, too woke for her, perhaps. Or too left wing.'

'We do a vegan selection in *Jasmine's*. They're quite popular, but I don't think there's a *type*. I don't think it's a political choice.'

'What's not a political choice?' Jonny asked, catching the end of their conversation as he arrived.

'Being a vegan,' said Jasmine. 'We were just discussing Clarissa Mayberry's choice not to eat at the festival canteen.'

'She probably should have done. She might still be alive if she'd trusted their vegan menu. Do we know where she ate before her talk?'

'She had a bag with her that Patsy Kline, her agent, thought might have contained a packed lunch.'

Ivo and Harold arrived. 'I've got the bag with the remains of her lunch,' he said, holding up the evidence bag.

'Well done, Ivo,' said Jasmine. 'It will be interesting to know what she ate. But it won't be what killed her. Death cap mushrooms take twenty-four hours.' She tapped on the article she'd pinned to the board, and they gathered around to read it.

Ivo sighed. 'You mean I was poking around in all that rubbish for nothing?'

'It will still be interesting to know what was in the bag,' said Jasmine. 'Did you look inside it?'

'No. I just sealed it into the evidence bag like Katya told me to.'

'Good lad,' said Katya. 'As this isn't a police case, I don't think there'd be any harm in looking inside. But let's get organised first. We need to make a note of everything you've discovered so far and see if we can make any sense of it.' She stood up and cleaned a section of the board. Then she drew a line down the middle. On one side she wrote *Accident* and on the other she wrote *Intentional*. 'You start, Jasmine,' she said. 'What did you make of Magda Nowak?'

'She said the Mayberrys were horrible people to work for.'

'That's suspicious,' said Ivo.

'Hmm,' said Katya. 'It's not a reason to kill them. She could have asked the agency to send her somewhere else.'

'Unless it's more personal than that,' said Jonny. 'Not just a general dislike. Do you think one of them had done something specific to make her hate them?'

'It's possible,' said Katya. 'Did she say why they were horrible?'

'Clarissa worked at home quite often. She ticked Magda off for making too much noise and was never satisfied with her work. When she wasn't at her desk, she would follow Magda around and nit-pick about what she'd done.'

'Did Magda see much of the rest of the family?'

'I think the son, Tristan, tried to make a pass at her. She was a bit cagey about it. He'd asked her out for a drink, and she avoided him after that. She said Amelia was rude to her and told her to get out of her room. She went out at lunchtime the last day Magda was there. Magda didn't know where she went, but Clarissa let her take her car.'

'Mushroom gathering, perhaps,' Ivo suggested.

'Possible,' said Katya. 'But from what I've learnt about Amelia so far, unlikely. She was probably off to meet friends. And she borrowed her mother's car so most likely she was headed into town.'

'She could have walked from the house to pick mushrooms,' said

Jonny. 'There's a path at the side of the garden that goes to the woods.'

'If Amelia used her mother's car to go out the last day Magda was there,' said Katya, 'I don't suppose she said where she was going?'

'She didn't, but Magda saw a man arrive in a black car soon after Amelia left. She said he was wearing a suit so probably not a workman.'

'Interesting,' said Katya. 'I wonder how often Clarissa let Amelia drive her car. Do you suppose it was a bribe to get her out of the house when she was expecting a visitor she didn't want anyone to know about?'

'Do you think she had a lover calling on her?' Ivo asked. 'Makes sense, doesn't it? Husband away for the night. Daughter allowed to take the car to get her out of the way.'

'We mustn't jump to conclusions,' said Katya. 'But we do need to know who was driving that black car. We could ask the neighbours, perhaps.'

'Anyone fancy trekking round the village on the off chance someone can identify the driver of a black car?' said Ivo.

Jonny grinned at them. 'I can do better than that.'

'Okay,' said Katya. 'Tell us how.'

'There's this bloke I know who lives in Little Frampton. He makes a real nuisance of himself. He was forever calling Belinda when she was on the council to complain about people speeding in the village. He spends a lot of time sitting at the side of the road with one of those speed checker gadgets. He waits at the bit after the turn off from the main road at a bend where he's hard to spot. It's where drivers tend to speed up after the crossroads. He would send Belinda lists of car numbers of people he thought were driving too fast. I assume he still sends stuff to one of the new councillors. He's been in the local paper a few times demanding speed bumps.'

'Would he talk to you?'

'I think he'd probably be thrilled to. He's not much listened to.'

Katya wrote a *Things to do* heading and added *Jonny to talk to speeding man*. 'Jonny, what have you dug up about the family?'

'Anthony and his friend Carl Archer are both in finance. They use Facebook business pages, which don't reveal very much, but links from their web pages suggest they work together some of the time. Carl and his wife are in the process of divorcing. Having met Carl, I'd imagine it's Leonora, the wife, who is divorcing him rather than the other way around.'

'You met Carl Archer?' said Jasmine. 'It sounds as if you didn't like him much.'

'He was an arrogant prat.'

'A murderer?' Ivo asked hopefully.

'Couldn't say, I'm afraid,' said Jonny. 'And as Katya is always reminding us, we mustn't jump to conclusions. He doesn't seem to have had a motive, and even if he did, he was wearing expensive calf leather shoes so I can't see him out in the woods foraging. He'd have found another way to do it.'

'We're going too fast,' said Katya. 'We don't know if it *was* murder. We should still be working on the possibility of it being an accident.'

'Not so much fun, though,' Ivo muttered.

'What did you find out about Clarissa?' said Katya, ignoring him.

'She didn't use social media a lot herself. Everything that's posted looks as if it has been managed for her. Probably to sift out all the unpleasant posts. She didn't use Twitter, or whatever it's called now. But there's a huge amount of really vitriolic stuff about her.'

'I'm afraid that's probably normal for a woman with strong views,' said Jasmine. 'It will include death threats, I expect.'

'There were some,' said Jonny. 'But none that mentioned death cap mushrooms.'

Katya looked up in surprise. 'Doesn't anyone mediate that kind of stuff? Remove death threats?'

'If she'd had her own feed then she could have had it removed, but this stuff is on other people's.'

'Twitter is a cesspit of insults and threats,' said Jasmine. 'I think they used to try and moderate it, but I don't suppose anyone bothers now. We might keep an eye on it and see if someone claims responsibility for Clarissa's death. I'm not sure how reliable that would be, though. Anyone who hated her views could claim to have killed her without revealing their real identity.'

Katya added *Keep an eye on social media* to her list. 'So, let's take a look at the bag Ivo found.' She fished into her pocket and pulled out a pair of latex gloves. 'It was your find,' she said, handing them to Ivo. 'You do it.'

'Do I need the gloves?' Ivo asked, looking puzzled.

'Just a precaution. We've no reason to suppose she had any mushrooms with her. But she may have been using the bag the day before and I don't know if poisonous mushrooms leave a residue, so we shouldn't risk it. Also, if we do discover that Clarissa was murdered, we don't want to contaminate the evidence.'

'We're coming round to the idea of murder, are we?' Ivo asked. 'I thought you said we should still be treating it as an accident.'

'I'm saying we should keep our options open.'

Jasmine smiled to herself. This was typical Katya. She'd probably hoped all along that this would be a murder. And she'd been correct before, on at least the two occasions that Jasmine knew about. Who knew how many more there had been when she was with the police?

Katya found another evidence bag and spread it out on the table. 'The Harrods bag will already have your fingerprints on it, but be careful not to leave any more on the contents.'

'I won't,' said Ivo. 'I wore gloves when I was going through the rubbish.' He picked up the bag and placed it on the table, carefully opened it and peered inside. The first thing he pulled out was an opened pack of Marks and Spencer prawn mayo sandwiches, partially wrapped in a paper table napkin and well past their sell by date. He pushed the edges of the napkin aside, revealing the sandwich cut into two triangles, one of which had been bitten into. They all stared at it. How much evidence could a pack of sandwiches reveal? Even when one of them had a bite missing? All they had discovered was that someone had started to eat a sandwich and then changed their mind and replaced it in the pack. That could be because the someone was already feeling ill and couldn't stomach more than a single bite. Or it could just mean that whoever it was just didn't like the taste.

'That's odd, isn't it?' said Jonny. 'It's only partly eaten. Not enough to keep her going for the rest of the day.'

'It makes sense though,' said Jasmine. 'You need to read this again.' She unpinned the newspaper article from the board and handed it to him.

'Of course,' said Jonny. 'I'd forgotten that. She died on the evening of her talk at the festival, so if this is correct, she must have eaten the mushrooms the previous day. She'd have started to feel better and fancied some lunch, only to start feeling ill again after the first mouthful.'

'That's right,' said Katya, having re-skimmed the article herself. 'She would have felt nauseous an hour or two after she ate the mushrooms but felt better the next morning and recovered enough to buy herself a sandwich. But then the second wave started to take hold and she was probably feeling ill again, exacerbated by the sight or smell of the prawns.'

'If I don't have to worry about death cap contamination, can I take the gloves off now?'

'Better keep them on. We still need to avoid fingerprints. Is there anything else in the bag?'

Ivo found an unopened plastic box of prepared peaches and put it on the table next to the sandwich. There was also a packet of tissues, a lanyard with a speaker's pass to the festival and a flyer for her talk with *Hideaway Five* scribbled on the back.

'What does that mean?' Ivo asked.

'It's where she gave her presentation,' said Jonny. He clicked into the festival website, found a map and pointed to a section that was labelled *Hideaways*. 'It's the collection of smaller marquees at the back of the site. They were for the less popular, quieter events.'

'What's that?' Jasmine asked, pointing to some numbers and a question mark handwritten at the bottom of the flyer.

'Looks like a phone number,' said Ivo. 'Should I call it?'

'Probably not right now,' said Katya. 'I'll see if I can get Lugs to trace it for us first.'

'It might just be the agent's,' said Jasmine. 'She was there with Clarissa that morning. Perhaps she'd got a new phone.'

'People usually transfer their old numbers, don't they? Particularly someone like an agent who needs to keep in touch with clients.'

'Perhaps it's a burner,' Ivo suggested.

Jasmine sighed. Ivo was always coming up with wild ideas. 'Why would Clarissa need a burner phone?'

'To keep in touch with her lover,' said Ivo. 'The driver of the black car.'

'But she was a strictly hetero family values type,' said Jasmine. 'Wanted to make divorce harder and ban gay marriage. She's hardly likely to have an affair herself.'

'Who knows?' said Katya. 'People don't always practise what they preach.'

'It could have been a motive for killing her,' said Jonny. 'There were plenty of threats on Twitter but mushroom poisoning sounds like someone far closer to home.'

'Are you suggesting her husband?'

'Possibly,' said Jonny.

'Wouldn't he have jumped at Jonny's suicide suggestion? It would have deflected any suspicion from him.'

'He didn't totally dismiss the idea,' said Jonny. 'It was his friend Carl Archer who was set against it. He was pretty insistent that it was an accident.'

'Jonny might have a point,' said Katya. 'It could be a double bluff to throw suspicion from himself.' She started a new column on the board headed *Persons of interest* and wrote *Anthony Mayberry* at the top of the list.

'Any more suspects?' Katya asked.

'One of the twins?' said Ivo. 'Or both of them. They could be working together.'

'To murder their mother?' Jonny asked. 'Not very likely, is it?'

'Not impossible,' said Katya. 'We need to find out more about their motives.' She wrote Amelia and Tristan's names on the list.

'Might as well add Magda,' said Jasmine. 'Although I can't imagine what her motive would have been. She hated working there but Windsor Mops are not short of work. She is about to start working somewhere else.'

'What about the agent?' Jonny asked. 'We know she was with Clarissa the day of her talk. Could she also have been at the house the day before?'

'Having conveniently come across a crop of poisonous mushrooms on the way?' said Katya.

'It's possible, though,' said Ivo. 'We shouldn't rule her out.'

'I wonder if Murray Dickinson knew where she lived,' said Jonny. 'He's said some pretty vicious things about Clarissa.'

Katya added his name. 'Anyone we've missed?'

'This family friend,' said Jasmine. 'Carl Archer.'

'Why him?' Ivo asked. 'One minute we're saying he and Clarissa were lovers, the next he's on a list of suspects.'

'The two aren't mutually exclusive,' Katya pointed out, adding Carl's name to the list then standing back to stare at it. 'Seven suspects,' she said. 'We need to dig deeper into all of them.'

'Who's going to do which?' Ivo asked.

'I suggest you take the twins, Ivo. You're not so different in age. Ask around town, chat up some of the boy's college pals. Try clubs and coffee bars where they might mix with friends.'

'I'll check out the speeding bloke,' said Jonny. 'See if he spotted the black car that Magda saw. And I'll check with Windsor Mops and find out if there's anything we should know about Magda. Belinda knows the woman who runs them.'

'I'll check out Murray Dickinson and Carl Archer,' said Jasmine. 'See if I can get further into their online presence.'

'Which leaves me with Patsy,' said Katya. 'I don't think there's much to gain from meeting her again, but I might be able to pick up some online gossip. And I'll check out this phone number on the flyer. Talk Lugs into finding out whose it is. That's quite a lot to do. Shall we meet back here the day after tomorrow? Four o'clock?'

CHAPTER
ELEVEN

Harold was scratching at the door to be let out. Sun was streaming through the cabin windows and Ivo wondered if he'd overslept. He opened a bleary eye and grabbed his phone to check the time: six o'clock. He hadn't overslept, but he had forgotten to close the blinds last night. The trouble with dogs was that they didn't use clocks or watches, or even as Ivo did, a phone, to check the time. Harold's day was regulated by the hours of daylight. He was set in his ways and liked to stick to his routine: an early morning walk the moment it was light – a habit Ivo found more convenient in the winter than the summer; home for a light breakfast, in Harold's case a handful of dog biscuits; a wander around *Shady Willows* to be petted by residents while Ivo completed his various maintenance jobs and repairs; a snooze in the back of the van and eventually home again for a meal.

Ivo groaned and climbed out of bed, dressed quickly and reached for Harold's lead. Upriver, he decided. There were fewer swans further away from town. Harold was a generally fearless dog. He'd caught a burglar and detained murderers, twice. But there were two things that scared him. One was cats, which was understandable. It was a run-in with a cat that had led to the loss of half of one of his ears. The other was swans and Ivo could think of no reason for that. He was probably suspicious of the way they stood on one leg with their heads tucked under a wing, one eye gazing menacingly at anyone who passed by. But at this time of year Harold's fear was a good thing. The birds were viciously possessive about their offspring. Ivo wasn't sure that the myth that a swan could break a man's arm was true, but he wasn't taking any chances. Harold was battered enough already.

While walking, Ivo planned his day. A quick round of the site – sweeping the paths and putting the bins out, a couple of repairs that residents had asked for. For once there were not very many - a leaky tap and a cracked window frame. He could complete those in double quick time and hopefully, probably to Harold's disappointment, avoid too many cups of tea and offers of cooked breakfasts.

Once he'd finished, he and Harold walked to *Jasmine's,* where he hoped the office would be empty and he would have sole use of the computer to do some uninterrupted searches for the Mayberry twins. He was in luck. Jasmine and Jonny were both busy with the breakfasts and there was no sign of Katya. Tristan first, he decided. Where did posh kids go when they'd failed their A levels? He logged onto the computer, opened Google and searched for *A level courses in Windsor.* He rejected the schools. He doubted that Tristan would have returned to school to retake his exams. It was a toss-up between the further education college and a private establishment that claimed to provide a fast-track experience to acquire the necessary qualifications for university entrance. He checked out the fees and winced. They'd need to get students through the exams at lightning speed to make that amount worthwhile. Or was it just a way for those with means to get their kids through exams without them having to mix with the common herd? But given the choice between a free two-year course and one that was fast but expensive, Ivo assumed the Mayberry parents would opt for the latter in order to pack Tristan off to university at the earliest possible opportunity.

Ivo clicked away from the fee page and looked at details of the college itself. It was housed in a large Victorian villa, not unlike the one Jonny lived in, on the edge of town. There were some photos of happy-looking students clutching certificates, and a list of the college facilities, which were minimal. No sports, social clubs or even catering. But the lack of anything to do in what were probably short breaks between classes could work in Ivo's favour.

He and Harold walked to the college and found it was close to a small park. It was midday and Ivo assumed that even at this nose-to-the-grindstone crammer, the students would be allowed a lunch break. As there was no catering and it was a good fifteen minutes' walk into town, the students would most likely bring a packed lunch, and on a nice mild day like this, the obvious place to eat it would be in the park. He sat down on a bench and threw sticks for Harold. It was a small park and not over-stocked with benches. In fact, the one he was sitting on was the only one and it wasn't long before a couple of students – Ivo assumed that's what they were because they looked young, well off, and had just emerged from the door of the college – asked if they could join him while they ate their sandwiches. Ivo was more than happy for them to do just that and shifted up to make room for them. 'I'm Ivo Dean,' he said. 'This is Harold.' He pointed to Harold, who was sitting at his feet, alert to the whiff of food.

'I'm Sarah and this is Evie.'

Ivo wondered if they were sisters; both had similar glossy hair, faultless make-up, and the confident bearing of the rich and privileged.

'Sisters?' he asked.

Sarah giggled. 'Just good friends.' She opened a padded green carrier bag with the logo *Keep cool and carry on* and took out a plastic box with a lid. She opened it and sniffed. 'Fish salad,' she said with an expression of disgust. 'What've you got, Evie?'

'Ham sandwich,' she said, opening a paper bag.

'Swap?' Sarah offered.

'Not a chance.' She took a bite of the sandwich. Sarah reached into the bag, found a fork and started picking out some small tomatoes.

'Doing your A levels, are you?' Ivo asked as Sarah slipped some scraps of smoked salmon to Harold, who gobbled them up before Ivo could object.

'Yeah,' said Sarah, screwing up her face. 'Parents kind of insisting. Threats of cutting off my allowance.'

'So you go to that college across the road?'

'Yeah, more's the pity. Whatever happened to finishing schools in Switzerland?'

'Brexit, probably,' said Evie, finishing her sandwich and scrunching up the paper bag. 'I fancy drama school, but Daddy won't pay unless I've got A levels. Such a drag.'

All right for some. Ivo had never had the chance of either drama school or Switzerland. He didn't even know what a finishing school was, but Sarah was probably wrong about Brexit. Switzerland wasn't in the EU, was it? But he was allowing himself to be side-tracked by the lives of the rich and privileged. 'Do you know Tristan Mayberry?' he asked, hoping to get back to why he was there.

'I do,' said Sarah. 'He's in my geography class. Not in today though. He's a lazy sod. Bet he gets a top grade though.'

'He's really clever,' said Evie. 'But he misses loads of classes.'

'I don't think he's been in since the field trip,' said Sarah. 'That was so boring. I don't even know why he bothered turning up then.'

Not an ideal student, Ivo guessed, wondering what had happened since his dazzlingly good GCSE results. 'Where did you go for the field trip?' *Probably some posh field centre in the Lake District,* he thought. But he was wrong.

'It was a forestry place quite near where he lives. That's probably why he came. No need to get up early.'

'Part of the geography course?' Ivo asked. 'Never really got into geography when I was at school.'

'Don't blame you, but it's supposed to be an easy option for A level.'

'Can't imagine where that idea came from. It's all about environmental stuff and essays about landscapes. We were supposed to write about sustainable forestry.'

'So that's what the field trip was for?' Ivo asked.

'Supposed to be. But it was just trekking around the woods in wellies looking at trees.'

Evie giggled. 'Don't forget the funny little man in the bobble hat who told us not to pick the mushrooms in case they were poisonous. What was his name?'

'Eric? Something nerdy like that,' said Sarah.

'Could it have been Derek?' Ivo asked. 'Derek Weatherby?'

'Dunno,' said Evie. 'Wasn't really listening. I didn't even know there were mushrooms in the forest. We always get ours from Waitrose. You won't catch me eating wild stuff.'

'It wasn't even a real forest. Just a little wood with, like, really old trees that they are trying to keep alive.'

Sarah pulled out her phone and gasped. 'My God, look at the time. We'll be late for study skills.' She jumped up and pulled Evie up with her. 'Got to dash,' she said. 'Thanks for letting us sit here.'

'You're welcome,' said Ivo. He watched the two girls run back across the road to the college. It had been a useful chat. Tristan Mayberry had a reputation among his peers for being brainy but lazy. Knowing Katya wouldn't take him seriously, he tried, and failed, to avoid constructing theories in his head about why Tristan was like that. Braininess was not something he could do anything about. He could cover it up, but he obviously didn't because Evie and Sarah, and probably all the other students at the college, knew he was clever. Laziness was different. People chose to be lazy, didn't they? Had Tristan Mayberry, having proved himself with dazzling exam results, suddenly decided there was no need to put any more effort into schoolwork? Did he plan to sit around for the rest of his life doing nothing and living off his family's good fortune? Or had something happened, post GCSE, that had changed him? There could be any number of reasons, the most obvious, bearing in mind that Tristan was eighteen and had cash in his pocket, was drugs. That could be why he had fallen out with his mother. But whatever the reason, Ivo couldn't help thinking that Tristan Mayberry had just shot to the top of the list of suspects. He might have unwittingly poisoned his mother as a result of foraging on a geography field trip. Perhaps he'd not listened to the warning they were given. Or he could have hoped only to make his mother feel ill, some kind of revenge perhaps, but not knowing just how poisonous death caps were. Or he could have deliberately picked poisonous mushrooms in order to kill her. An uncomfortable thought, but one that needed to be considered.

Harold was tugging impatiently on his lead. Time to go home. Ivo still needed to talk to Amelia, because she and her brother could have been in it together. But not right now. Amelia wasn't at college with Tristan and she didn't have a job. She didn't seem to do anything other than sit at home playing loud music and drive around in her mother's car. There was no way he was going to call at her house and ask if she'd killed her mother. He decided to go back to *Shady Willows* and mow the verges. Cutting grass was a good time to think things through, so with any luck the hypnotic hum of the mower might give him some ideas.

CHAPTER
TWELVE

Saturday lunchtime and the town centre pubs were crowded with shoppers, or husbands and partners of shoppers who hated the whole process – hanging around outside changing rooms trying not to look shifty, being tactful when confronted with a new dress or jacket – do you say you like it when you don't? Or say you don't like it when you catch a glimpse of the price tag? Then there was the carrying of the shopping: bags with string handles that cut into your hands; bulky packages that caught people on the shins; the trek back to the car park trying to remember where you'd parked. Getting home and the news that it was all having to go back because it looked a different colour in daylight, or there was a previously unnoticed mark or a rip in the seam.

Lugs and Katya were lucky not to be part of any of this. Mrs Lomax had discovered online shopping and now rarely ventured into town. And Katya only shopped at Tesco – choosing its least busy times – or at charity shops, and those were rarely crowded. The two of them had squeezed into the pub and pushed their way to the bar, where they grabbed a couple of high stools. Lugs who was a regular, was known to be a police inspector and rarely needed to do more than lift an arm in greeting to be served instantly. And not only that, but the bar staff also knew what he liked to drink.

The barman put two pints of Theakston's Old Peculier down on the bar in front of them and Katya pulled a wallet out of her bag and paid for them. 'My treat,' she said.

'Thanks very much,' said Lugs. He drained half the glass, put it down on the bar and sighed happily. 'Just what I needed.'

Katya heaved herself up onto the stool and took a long slug of her own beer. It had been a busy week for Lugs, but she needed to know about the phone number they'd found on the festival flyer as soon as possible, and she hoped that tempting him out for a lunchtime beer would speed him up a bit.

'Want anything to eat?' he asked.

'Oh, go on then.' She'd not really been expecting a meal. She shouldn't push their friendship too far, but since he'd offered... She studied the menu that was resting on a metal stand at the end of the bar. 'I'll have a bowl of chips.' Not too extravagant, but hopefully mouth-wateringly crisp and garnished with a sprinkling of grated cheese and some fried onions. She'd had them before in this pub and they were a far cry from the soggy type one now paid an arm and a leg for at the chippy in town.

Lugs ordered for the two of them. 'So how's things?' he asked.

'Good,' said Katya, not wanting to bring up the matter of the unknown phone number too soon.

Lugs pulled a folded slip of paper from his pocket. 'I could have emailed this,' he said, 'but it seemed a shame to pass up the opportunity of a pint with you.'

'I'm flattered.'

'Well, we don't often meet up when you're not working on a case, although asking me to trace a number for you suggests you might be.'

Their bowls of chips arrived impressively quickly. They must have a continuous fry-up going on in the kitchen. Katya picked one up, blew on it to cool it and lingered over its delicious crunchiness.

'Might be,' she said, wiping her fingers before unfolding the paper and reading what was on it. 'Or might not,' she added, feeling disappointed with the result of Lugs' search. The number was registered to Carl Archer. An old family friend who must have just changed his phone. Odd to change his number when these days it was so easy to keep to an old one, but otherwise uninteresting. She'd really hoped it might give them a lead to someone who perhaps didn't have Clarissa's best interests at heart, and an old friend from university didn't fit the bill at all. Assuming her death wasn't an accident was a leap in the dark. She realised that. Everyone accepted that the poor woman had died after an unfortunate, thankfully rare, but accidental case of mushroom poisoning. So why couldn't Katya accept it and get on with what Derek Weatherby wanted, which was to trace how the poison had made its way into Clarissa's food, in order to produce a warning leaflet to prevent it happening to anyone else?

Lugs was looking at her quizzically. 'You're up to something,' he said. 'I recognise the signs. Want to give me a heads up?'

'It's probably nothing.'

'Tell me anyway. I may be able to help.'

Katya sighed. 'It's that woman who died of mushroom poisoning. Looked like an accident and no one questioned it. We've been approached by a local society.'

'Another secret one like the Followers of Herne? They're not regrouping, are they?'

'No, nothing like that. It's a group of people who are interested in preserving mycology in nature.'

'You're losing me, Katya.' He squeezed some ketchup out of a plastic tomato and dipped a chip into it.

'They're a group of fungus experts and they want us to trace the source of this particular incident of poisoning.'

'Why?'

'So they can produce a leaflet. The man we spoke to says he wants to take steps to stop it happening to anyone else.'

'Not sure how he can do that,' said Lugs. 'Except to make sure people are warned about foraging for potentially dangerous food. He could write an article for the paper. Why does he need to know exactly where the mushrooms came from?'

'I don't know, and we'd probably have told him we weren't interested, only there's something not right about Clarissa Mayberry's death. And this Derek Weatherby is paying us to look into it.'

'Everyone was satisfied that it was an accident.'

'You're right of course, but... what if it wasn't an accident? No one asked a lot of questions, did they? Not once they'd given the festival kitchen the all clear.'

'You think she was deliberately poisoned?'

'I dunno. I've no reason to think she was, and the medical examiner was satisfied. It's just a feeling I have.'

'And you hoped that knowing the owner of this phone might lead you to someone who had it in for her?'

'Like I said, it was just a feeling I had. I should probably ignore it. You know how I get carried away.'

Lugs swallowed the last of his chips and mopped up the scraps with his fingers. 'Yes, I know you do. And you see a murder where no one else does. But I'll tell you something else.' He paused for a moment to drain his beer glass. 'Unlikely as it seems, you are usually right – the man in the Long Walk, the body in the river and cases we worked on before you retired. You remember that lad who was accused of stealing from the riding stables? Well, that wasn't a murder but your feeling that he was innocent turned out to be correct, didn't it?'

'You're saying I should treat this case as a murder? Then I'd have to let you take over?'

Lugs laughed. 'I've no evidence to suggest opening a murder case. We can't override the medical examiner's decision unless something else comes to light. I'm just saying you shouldn't ignore your instincts. But if you do find any evidence that suggests foul play, then of course you must come to me with it.'

'We've a long way to go before that happens.'

'Of course, but tell me what you've done so far.'

Katya swallowed her remaining chip. They'd been delicious but the bowl had been far too small. She wondered if the pub did desserts and spotted a blackboard on the wall that promised sticky toffee pudding, apple pie and chocolate fudge cake. Lugs noticed the direction of her gaze and fumbled in his pocket for his wallet. 'Sticky toffee pudding?'

'You're a mind reader. Order a couple of those and I'll tell you everything we've got so far. Although I'm not sure it's enough to earn a pudding.'

'Never mind,' said Lugs, taking out a bank card and waving it over the bar. 'Tell me who's in the picture and I'll give you the benefit of my vast experience of poisonings.'

Katya talked him through their list of everyone who'd had contact with Clarissa at the relevant time.

'Hmm,' said Lugs. 'Statistically, the husband would be the most likely. Have you ruled him out?'

'He was away from home at the critical time.'

'Have you checked that out?'

No, but they should have done. 'That will be next on my list,' said Katya, although she wasn't sure how she would set about it. Ivo was getting to know the kids, so perhaps they'd be able to tell them more. But of course they could be suspects themselves. 'Would you rule out the family? Eighteen-year-old twins?'

'You'd need to be very careful. They are only just adults, but you should probably keep an eye on them.'

'I've already got Ivo on watch. It's not too hard to keep tabs on teenagers. Unless, of course, you happen to be their parents.' She laughed. 'I've not had my own, but I remember being one. Ran circles round my parents. They rarely knew where I was or what I was getting up to. I was a right stroppy mare.'

'No change there, then.'

Katya ignored him. 'Any other ideas?'

'Assuming no one else appears, I say you should look into the heckler. He sounds like a real Clarissa Mayberry hater. You should check out his social media.'

'Jonny's been doing that. There was a mass of vile threats against her but all anonymous.'

Lugs nodded. 'Of course it was, and I wasn't suggesting this guy was openly admitting to planning murder. But you could learn a lot more about him by looking at what he's been posting.'

'That's the sort of thing Jasmine's good at. I'll get her to keep an eye on it.'

'And let me know if you need more from me.' He stood up, put his jacket on and headed for the door, Katya following him.

'Thanks for the meeting,' said Katya. 'Much appreciated.'

'Happy to help. Do you want me to check this lot out on the police database? See if any of them have previous?'

'As murderers? Not very likely, is it?'

'There could be other things – arrested at demos, perhaps.'

'Let me know if you find anything,' said Katya, heading out of the pub and back into the busy shopping street. It was good to talk things through with Lugs. The phone number was probably a non-starter but he'd given her other things to think about.

CHAPTER
THIRTEEN

The café closed at four o'clock on Saturday afternoons and today it was Karim's turn to close up and make sure the kitchen was left clean and ready for Sunday breakfast. Jasmine took a cup of tea and a slice of spicy apple cake up to the office to do a bit of online lurking around social media sites in search of Murray Dickinson and Carl Archer – Jasmine's two Katya-assigned tasks for the next meeting. But who to do first? Jonny had already found out a bit about Carl Archer. He was a financial consultant and old family friend of the Mayberrys. He had been at university with Clarissa and now worked in the same field as Clarissa's husband, Anthony. Oh, and Clarissa had written down his phone number on a festival flyer. Why would she do that? Most people had the numbers of their friends stored on their own phones. Perhaps Clarissa had written the number down to pass on to someone else. But why the question mark? Jasmine yawned. Carl Archer sounded dull, and she couldn't think of any reason why he might want Clarissa dead. He was divorced, or divorcing, she couldn't remember which. He'd stored his stuff in the Mayberry garage while he found somewhere new to live, so there would be no reason not to visit Clarissa, who was an old university chum and a possible shoulder to cry on. Could he have visited her with a gift of mushrooms? Why would he? Nothing in Jonny's notes suggested he was into country rambles and foraging. He sounded like a typical townie businessman, probably never went far from his spreadsheets and financial graphs. Although, he'd be able to do that on his phone, possibly at the same time as gathering mushrooms. Jasmine laughed at the idea of an expensively suited financial expert, phone in one hand, the other grubbing for mushrooms on a damp and leafy forest floor, possibly listening to stock market news through earbuds. Even Ivo would fail to come up with an image like that. Was there any reason to think Carl wanted Clarissa dead? Unlikely. He'd need all the support he could get from friends while he got over his divorce. You'd hardly poison the one person who could offer you tea and sympathy. Although, from what she'd learned so far, Clarissa Mayberry didn't strike her as a sympathetic chat over a cup of tea kind of person. But she'd not met either Clarissa or Carl, so who knew?

Jasmine decided to leave Carl for now and concentrate on Murray Dickinson. She knew from what Jonny had told her that he didn't like Clarissa, or at least her opinions. And he'd asked Jonny if he'd killed Clarissa. That was odd, wasn't it? Clarissa wasn't even dead at that point. Did it mean he had a reason to feel guilty? But if he did, he'd hardly have asked Jonny a question like that, would he? He'd have crawled away and hoped no one would think any more about it. Perhaps they *should* suspect him. He'd heckled Clarissa at her talk and posted unpleasant tweets about her on Twitter. And Twitter – no, Cross – was the place to start. She checked out Murray's profile and discovered that when not posting inflammatory insults about right-wing politicians, he ran a shop that sold organic food and ethical cleaning products. He didn't give too many personal details, but it did say he lived in Berkshire so the festival would have been local. Did he also work locally? She ran a search on organic wholefood stores in the south of England. Luckily there were not too many of them; plenty of farm shops and places that delivered fruit and vegetable boxes but not many actual shops. Several were not in Berkshire at all, which left two that were fairly local. She called the first one, *Bags of Health,* but they'd never heard of Murray Dickinson. She had more luck at the next, *BBB. Odd name,* she thought, until she googled it and discovered it stood for *Bags, Beans and Boxes.* There was plenty of information on the website: a list of products; a request for volunteers; a guarantee that all the produce was organically sourced and with a low carbon footprint. All of which was fascinating but what really sparked Jasmine's interest was the photo of the couple who ran the shop, Molly and Murray Dickinson. They sounded like characters from a kids' story book. A homely, apple-cheeked couple rather than mean-spirited hecklers and disrupters of serious lectures. It also told her that the shop had only recently opened, having moved from an ad hoc collection of glass jars and sacks in the back room of a local craft shop, where it only opened two days a week, to a small shop in a side street near the Old Fire Station arts centre, only fifteen minutes' walk from where Jasmine was right now. And better still, it was open from nine to five every day. Jasmine looked at her watch. If she set off now, she could be there just before they closed.

It was a small shop, a step up from a back room in a craft shop but not very noticeable. How did they manage to sell anything? The shop was in a narrow street with restricted parking and Jasmine was glad she'd decided to walk there. It was a residential street and probably didn't attract a passing trade of window shoppers. Her dad had struck lucky with *Jasmine's,* which was right in the centre of the town, minutes away from the station and the shops, but still tucked away and quiet. Karim had been there for more than twenty years. It was probably a lot harder to find places to set up a business now.

She opened the door and went inside, where she discovered an impressive collection of rice, beans, pulses and cereals in glass jars, all arranged on untreated wooden shelves that had possibly begun life as railway sleepers or scaffold boards. At the back of the shop were metal drums of detergent, shampoo and shower gel and in the centre of the shop were tables holding baskets of handmade soap, organic cotton dusters, natural bristle brushes, hand-painted cards and bags of locally made fudge. Molly and Murray – she assumed it was them – were tidying shelves. There was no sign of any customers.

'Can I help you?' said the woman, looking up from her dusting and smiling at Jasmine. 'We're about to close.'

'I'm sorry,' said Jasmine. 'I'm not a customer, although it all looks lovely, and I shall come back and browse.' She meant it. She could spend hours there. She could even think about a partnership and offer to use some of their produce in *Jasmine's*. Probably best to hold on to that idea until she was sure Murray wasn't a poisoner. 'I was hoping to speak to Murray Dickinson.'

Murray looked up from the shelf where he was arranging jars of locally made raspberry jam. 'How can I help?' he asked.

He didn't look like a poisoner, even an inadvertent one. Nor did he look like a poster of vitriolic abuse. Not that Jasmine had any experience of what vitriolic abusers looked like. Murray seemed like the old-fashioned kind of shopkeeper she'd met in story books when she was little. Early forties, slightly receding hairline and wearing a brown apron made, she was sure, from some kind of natural undyed fabric. Quite possibly hand-sewn by Molly, who was wearing a similar one. 'I'm hoping you can give me some information about Clarissa Mayberry. I believe you were at her lecture at the Reimagine the Light Festival.'

He stared at her over the top of a pair of horn-rimmed spectacles. 'I was there, yes. What do you want to know?'

'I assume you know she died. I believe you were there when she collapsed.'

'Are you a journalist?' Murray asked, one of his jars crashing to the floor where it shattered, fragments of glass and blobs of sticky jam landing at his feet. 'Slipped out of my hand,' he said, staring at the mess. 'Clumsy.'

'Can happen to anyone,' said Molly, reaching for a dustpan and brush that had been propped up against the wall almost as if something like this was expected. It probably was. There must be multiple spillages in a shop like this, which let customers fill their own containers. Murray perched on a stool while he watched Molly clear up.

'I'm not a journalist,' said Jasmine, hoping that Murray was still listening to her. 'I'm an investigator. The Berkshire Mycology Society have asked us to trace the mushrooms that killed Clarissa.'

'Killed by mushrooms?' Molly looked up from her dustpan with a startled expression.

'Death caps,' said Jasmine. 'We need to find out where she got them. The society are planning a leaflet to warn people not to over-forage and to be particularly careful when picking mushrooms.'

'People should be allowed to gather free food,' said Murray. 'It's not right to stop them.'

'The society doesn't want to stop them altogether, just make people aware of the dangers and encourage them to nurture the countryside and not exploit it.'

Murray stood up and returned to his shelf stacking. 'So she was poisoned,' he said, looking relieved. 'I thought I'd brought on a heart attack.'

'No, she was definitely poisoned. But even if it didn't cause a heart attack, I hear you were quite forceful with your opinions.'

'No more than she deserved, but it's not her opinions I mind. She's entitled to those. What I couldn't stand was the hypocrisy.'

'I'm not sure I understand,' said Jasmine. 'I know she has strong right-wing views, but they seem consistent.'

'She has strong right-wing views when she is Clarissa Mayberry,' he said, stacking the last of his jars and wiping his hands on his apron. 'But come and look at this.'

He led Jasmine over to a computer and clicked open an author web page, one he had bookmarked. Jasmine read about a series of books that claimed to be *red hot and raunchy*. They certainly had lurid covers with scantily dressed women and bare-chested men giving each other lascivious glances. The author's name was Clarice Mayflower.

'That's what our pure-as-driven-snow advocate of family values does in her spare time,' said Murray with a snort of disgust.

Jasmine scrolled further down the page. This was Clarissa Mayberry? If it was, it was just as well she used a pen name. It definitely would not look good on her *Austerity Myth* book page. The press would have a field day. She could imagine her journalist friend Teddy Strang rubbing his hands with glee at the thought of what he could do with it if he ever knew about it. She liked Teddy but there was no way he was going to hear about this from her. The bereaved family had enough to cope with right now. But perhaps Murray had got it wrong. 'You're saying Clarissa Mayberry is Clarice Mayflower? I suppose it's a similar name, but that could just be a coincidence.'

'It could,' said Murray. 'But it isn't.' He opened another website. This one was called *Wicked Secrets*. There was a short piece headed *Things you might want to know about our so-called moral leaders*. There was a short review of Clarissa Mayberry's book, *The Austerity Myth: poverty is all in the mind*. This was followed by a biography of Clarissa, which mentioned her degree from LSE and her work on government think tanks. The piece ended by saying that Clarissa also wrote novels using the pen name Clarice Mayflower.

So Murray had got it right? How had he discovered it? And what did he plan to do with the knowledge? Hopefully nothing, as Clarissa was now dead. Did the fact that Clarissa had led a double life have anything to do with her death? Jasmine wasn't sure what to think. She took a quick shot of the screen on her phone. The others would be interested in what she'd discovered. Even if it wasn't relevant, it would show Clarissa Mayberry in a very different light.

She thanked Murray for his time, wished them luck in the new shop and walked home.

CHAPTER
FOURTEEN

T*he residents of Little Frampton generally keep themselves to themselves,* Jonny thought as he drove into the village past houses more or less hidden from view by tall hedges, and insulated from the outside world by long drives. He doubted it was the kind of village where neighbours popped in and out of each other's houses, borrowing cups of sugar and offering to babysit. He didn't imagine there were that many babies or small children. This was a village for those who had made it several rungs up the ladder from starter home buyers. He didn't know how long the Mayberrys had lived there but it probably wasn't since the twins had been tiny. There was no sign of a village school, no bus stops and none of the things that made living in a village with a young family possible, like a village shop or a doctor's surgery. All the same, Jonny took care not to drive over the speed limit. Not only because he didn't want to knock any children that were there off their bikes, but because he didn't want to start off by upsetting Alan Biggs and appear in one of his speeding videos.

As he hoped, Alan was in his usual spot a mile from the centre of the village. A carefully chosen lay-by shortly after a bend in the road and on a straight downhill stretch where it was all too easy to relax one's foot on the accelerator. There had been extensive correspondence in the local press about the need for a speed limit along this mile-long run into the village. Some residents had lobbied for a 30mph enforcement sign, but the authorities whose job it was to place speed limits had, on several occasions, declined to do so. It was not a built-up area and there had been no accidents; it was a safe part of the road, used only by residents and deliveries to the village. It was not on a route to anywhere and there were no schoolchildren, elderly people, animals or any other vulnerable demographic using the road. Therefore, they argued, there was no need to bring the limit down below the national one until the built-up part of the village, where there could be an issue with cars turning out of drives but where there was already a limit in place. Biggs and his friends disagreed. It might not be a built-up area in the true sense but there were some houses along there with driveways onto the road. Just because people could afford to live well apart from each other didn't mean they had to put up with cars speeding dangerously past their entrances. And while there had been no accidents, there had been a number of near misses. Eventually, after a great deal of lobbying, the authorities agreed to a 40mph limit and put up a sign near the junction with the main road. A sign that was steadfastly ignored by almost every driver who passed it. Biggs and his committee complained that the limit was not being enforced and lobbied for a speed camera. In order to keep him quiet, at least for a while, the local authority had asked him to compile statistics and submit a full report to the council. Speed cameras were expensive to install and run. They needed to know that it would be financially viable. Since then, Biggs, who was retired, sat at the side of the road most days checking the speed of every car that passed him.

Jonny pulled the car off the road at the end of the lay-by. He climbed out and strolled back to where Alan Biggs was sitting in a camping chair, clipboard in hand, and a flask at his side next to a Tupperware box that most likely contained or had recently contained sandwiches. 'Good morning,' said Jonny with a friendly wave. 'How's it going?'

Alan Biggs shrugged. 'Bit quiet today,' he said.

Jonny held out his hand. 'I'm Jonny Cardew,' he said, hoping for a spark of recognition. He was not disappointed.

Biggs looked up at him and frowned. 'Related to Councillor Cardew?' he asked.

'Belinda's my wife.'

'Then you're too late. Voted off, wasn't she?'

'She was, but she's interested in what's going on locally. She still has some influence and knows who to talk to in the council offices.' Jonny hoped that was still true. Belinda seemed to have lost interest in council matters since losing her seat, but Biggs didn't need to know that. 'She's definitely keen on road safety,' he added, not too sure that was true either. But she'd been annoyed with him when he was sent a speeding ticket a year or so ago and that was evidence of her concern, wasn't it?

He'd done some online research on ways to check traffic speed and had expected Biggs to have some kind of speed gun of the type traffic police used. Anyone could buy one on Amazon, but all Alan had was a clipboard and a phone. 'Still collecting traffic stats?' Jonny asked, although what else he'd be doing sitting at the side of the road Jonny couldn't imagine.

'Yes, we're trying to get our campaign moving again. The election slowed everything down, but we've been hard at work over the summer.'

'I suppose you've got a different set of councillors to convince now.'

'Politics doesn't really come into it. We hoped it might, but it doesn't. Speed's all that matters round here. The car is king. Everyone's in a hurry these days.'

Everyone except the retired. People like Alan Biggs, who had the leisure to sit and watch traffic. 'What exactly do you do?' Jonny asked. 'I was expecting you to have more equipment than this.'

Biggs put the clipboard down on the ground at his feet. He glanced along the road to make sure nothing was approaching then held up his phone so that Jonny could see the screen. 'I've got an app. Clever little bit of kit. All I do is set two points fifty or so yards apart. I click this button here.' He pointed to a red circle on the screen. 'It takes a short video from where the car passes the first point and works out how long it took to get to the second. The app tells me the speed and logs the make and registration number of the car. When I get home, I download it to my desktop, transfer it all to a spreadsheet and save it in my records.'

'Does the app record the names of the car owners?'

'No. I could find out easily enough for a small fee but really that's a job for the police. All I do is pass on the numbers and hope that someone acts on them.'

'By sending out a letter with a demand for a fine.'

'Not sure how often they get around to it, but like I said, I'm keeping records. Enough cars breaking the limit and the council should act on it and put in a camera. It'll be a nice little earner for them and make the village safer at the same time. A win-win situation.'

But unpopular with those who liked fast cars and were regularly late for work. Not that Jonny condoned driving too fast. 'I'll mention it to Belinda. Maybe she can have a word with the right people.'

'Every little helps, I suppose,' said Biggs, not looking too impressed. He'd been nagging away for months. Why would a retired councillor make any difference?

'But while I'm here,' said Jonny, 'there's something else.'

A car drove past and Biggs put his app into action. 'Oh, yeah?' he said, once the flurry of activity had ended.

'I don't know if you are aware that I work as an investigator.'

Biggs shook his head. He was a long way from both the Long Walk and the river, and he didn't look like a circus fan, so there was no reason he should ever have heard of the Breakfast Club Detectives, and unless they were investigating speeding drivers, he was unlikely to be interested.

'I've been asked to trace a car that was believed to be in the village last Thursday.'

'Oh, yes?' said Biggs, looking more interested. 'What time?'

'It would have driven into the village at around midday. I'm hoping you'll have a record of it.'

'A busy time of day. Not as busy as early morning but quite a few cars would have passed me. What make was it?'

Jonny swore inwardly at Magda's inability to distinguish one car from another. 'I'm afraid our witness didn't know. She said it was big and black, the kind that airport drivers use. A saloon, not a people carrier or hatchback.'

'Probably a Merc or a Hyundai. Standard executive cars. There won't have been that many at that time of day.'

'Could you check and send me details of any that match that description?'

Biggs reached down for the clipboard. 'Could do, I suppose.' He passed it to Jonny and rummaged in his pocket to find a pen. 'Will you sign my petition?'

Did this count as bribery? But Jonny had had worse. At least he wasn't being asked for money. He took the clipboard and scanned the list of names. Surprisingly, Tristan Mayberry had signed it, as had Magda Nowak. But not Clarissa, Anthony or Amelia. Jonny scribbled his own name. There was no reason not to. It was a small price to pay for information when he was more used to forking out twenty quid notes. And slowing down traffic was good. He could well be helping to condemn unknown numbers of people to speeding fines or, as he had once been, sent on a speed awareness course. But it was all in a good cause.

He tore a page out of his notebook, wrote down his email and handed it to Biggs, who stuffed it into his pocket. 'Might as well knock off now,' he said, looking at his watch. 'The wife will have my dinner on the table. Stickler for mealtimes, she is. But I can eat while

I download this morning's videos.' He shoved the clipboard into a backpack along with the flask and sandwich box. Then, having folded up the chair, he set off along the road into the village. 'I'll check last Thursday's notes,' he called over his shoulder to Jonny, who was wondering if he should have offered him a lift. 'I'll get them to you as soon as.'

'Thanks,' Jonny called to his rapidly disappearing back. 'I'm very grateful for your help.'

Arriving home, Jonny decided he couldn't do much more about who was driving the black car until he heard back from Alan Biggs. It occurred to him that Anthony Mayberry drove a black Audi. Could that have been the car Magda saw? But she would have recognised it, wouldn't she? Although she'd also said that she rarely saw Anthony, so it was possible that she didn't know what car he drove. Jonny himself usually kept away from the house when their own cleaner, Mrs Gage, was at work. Perhaps Anthony Mayberry felt the same way Jonny did, that cleaners preferred not to have men under their feet while working. And that reminded Jonny that the next task on Katya's list was to find out more about Magda herself.

Once home, he turned on his computer and opened the notes Jasmine had made after her meeting with Magda. There was nothing about why Magda had stopped working for the Mayberrys. She'd told Jasmine that she didn't like the family, so perhaps the feeling was mutual. Had one of the Mayberry family done something to upset Magda? She'd told Jasmine she wouldn't be working there again and had given the impression that she'd asked for a different placement. But perhaps Clarissa had complained about Magda, attempted to get her struck off the Windsor Mops books, maybe. And Magda had decided to take revenge. Poisoning was a bit extreme, but it wasn't generally known that death caps could kill. At least that was something the fungus society leaflet might help with. But perhaps Magda had known what death caps looked like and meant only to make Clarissa ill. She might have had an opportunity to pick the mushrooms – out for a walk during a coffee break, perhaps – and leave them in the Mayberry kitchen. There would have been a risk of poisoning the whole family, but since she hated all of them that could have been what she hoped would happen. Upset stomachs all round to get her own back for the way they'd treated her? Mrs Gage might know what had happened for her to be moved and she was due for a visit on Monday morning. Jonny could leave later than usual for his breakfast at *Jasmine's* and see if he could extract some gossip from her.

It was Jonny's turn to cook that evening. Since his retirement and Belinda's ousting from the council, they shared the cooking. Belinda cooked on Monday, Wednesday and Friday and Jonny did Tuesday, Thursday and Saturday. On Sunday they went to the Feathers in Frampton-on-the-Hill for a carvery lunch and didn't feel the need for anything more than a bowl of soup in the evening. Tonight Jonny planned to cook lamb chops, recently delivered from an organic butcher, peas from the garden, of which there was a plentiful supply in the freezer, and duchess potatoes using a recipe Karim had given him. He had just started peeling the potatoes when he heard a ping from his laptop, which he had left open in the living room, within earshot of the kitchen. He'd left it there because he hoped Alan Biggs would contact him as promised by the end of the day. Jonny dried his hands and went to see who the email was from. He wasn't disappointed; it was from Alan. An attached list of car makes and numbers and a short sentence saying he hoped it would help. He'd also attached stills from all the car videos he'd recorded that day and another link that would enable Belinda, and everyone else they knew, to sign his online petition about speeding traffic in the village. Alan was beginning to remind Jonny of a terrier who wouldn't let go of a rat it had caught.

Jonny opened the attachment and then the Zip file containing the photos. Thursday had been a busy day. Jonny ignored more than fifteen delivery vans. Did no one in the village do their own shopping? He also ignored cars that weren't black, apart from Tristan's green Polo and the white Evoque, which he knew Amelia had borrowed, both of which, Jonny noted, had been driving over the limit. He wondered how Anthony would respond to the inevitable speeding fines that would soon land on his doormat.

That left three black cars that might fit Magda's description. One, driven right on the limit, was too early. The others were at approximately the right time, but then Jonny remembered that Magda had seen the car as she was leaving. He checked Jasmine's notes and discovered that Magda drove a silver-grey Clio. Alan and his camping chair were always in the same spot, about three-quarters of a mile from the drive to Lime Tree Cottage. Magda would have driven past him a couple of minutes after she left and the car she saw would have been there a couple of minutes before that. He looked at the time stamps on the two photos of the black cars. One had driven into the village at around the time Amelia had left it. Too soon for Magda to have seen it. He clicked on the photo of the other one and wrote down the registration number. Then he looked at the view of the car itself. Alan sat on the left-hand verge as one approached the village. This gave a good view of both driver and passenger seats of cars driving into, rather than away from, the village, so unless there was someone lying down on the back seat, there was only one person in the car. He was unable to tell much more than that. The photo was blurred, but he thought from the size of the driver that it was male, a man with shortish hair and dark glasses. Not much to go on.

He opened Alan's list, on which he'd noted down the registration numbers he'd extracted from his slowed down videos and where he'd also made a note of the speed the cars were driving at the moment they'd passed him. The black Merc that Jonny had identified as the one Magda must have seen hadn't been speeding, and Jonny was relieved that Alan had chosen to send a list of all the cars, not only the ones he was about to report to the traffic police. Jonny tapped the number into a box on a website he'd used before, paid a small sum of money and was supplied with details of the registered owner. *Interesting,* he thought, assuming it was the owner who was driving and not someone he'd lent the car to. Jonny should have recognised the car, although he would only have seen it briefly. He took a screen shot of the details and printed them ready to take with him to the meeting the next day, thinking that it wasn't going to progress their case very far. But that's how it was being a detective. Half the stuff one discovered would turn out to be irrelevant. It didn't detract from the excitement of finding something that was useful, though. And hopefully Jonny would do that quite soon.

CHAPTER
FIFTEEN

Ivo lay in his bunk and watched some leaves floating down from the sycamore tree that grew on the other side of the fence separating *Shady Willows* from the road. It would soon be time for him get out the leaf blower and make sure the paths were clear of leaves, which could make them slippery. It was Sunday morning and he'd have liked a lie-in. Unfortunately, Harold, being a dog, didn't know it was Sunday morning. Or perhaps he did, but it didn't make any difference. He still wanted his early morning walk. And then Ivo realised it was not only Harold who needed his attention. There was a detective meeting the next day and he still hadn't sorted his notes about Tristan Mayberry. If that was all, he could probably wing it. He remembered what the two girls had told him, and it was plenty to support his theory that Tristan was now near the top of the list of suspects. He hadn't decided if this was a case of accidentally poisoning his mother or whether he could have done it deliberately. But by Katya's criteria, he had the means and the opportunity, and Ivo thought he probably also had a motive, although he hadn't uncovered what that was yet. But the lack of notes concerning Tristan was not all. Ivo still had nothing to report about Amelia

Mayberry. He lay in bed, thinking about what he needed to do. Walk Harold first, he decided, or he would get no peace. Then a strong cup of coffee and a session on Google.

Walking Harold was always a good time to think things through, and this morning was no different. As he walked, he tried to remember what he did know about Amelia, and so far that was little except what Jasmine had written in her notes after talking to Magda. All he knew so far was that she spent most of her time at home listening to music in her bedroom. But she was eighteen. She must have some kind of social life and go out occasionally or she'd die of boredom, wouldn't she? Were she and her father supporting each other through what must be a very difficult time for both of them? For a moment, Ivo tried to think himself into the head of a bereaved father. Anthony Mayberry had told Jonny that Amelia had taken her mother's death badly and any father would be worried about what was best for his daughter. Jonny had found Anthony Mayberry cold-hearted and commented that he appeared to have very little time for his family. He'd packed his son off to college to get some A levels, but he would have done that long before Clarissa's death and Ivo had no idea whether sending him to a crammer was supporting his son or just getting him out of the way.

Returning from their walk, Ivo opened up Google on his phone and did some research. The college Tristan attended claimed to cram students through as many exams as fast as they could. Their current intake had signed up within days of the results coming out in mid-August and courses had begun almost immediately. They had to, Ivo supposed, if they were going to cover a two-year syllabus by the next exam session the following June. Why hadn't Anthony done the same with his daughter? Ivo knew the twins had both attended St Cuthbert's school, so he logged into their web page and clicked on a news tab. The latest entry was headlined *Better results than ever this year*. Ivo read it and found some photos of happy students jumping up and down, clutching printouts of their results. There was no complete list of results. The school wouldn't want to publicise a student like Tristan, who had failed everything. There were, however, a few cameos of students who had done particularly well, one of whom was Amelia Mayberry, who had scored top grades in four subjects and was headed to Cambridge University to study plant sciences. Ivo navigated to a site that told him the subjects needed at A level for the course. One of them was biology. Another search told him that A level biology included the study of the natural environment – so mushrooms? Had he uncovered another suspect?

A level exams ended in June, so did that mean Amelia had been sitting around for more than two months doing nothing? Or was her current lack of inertia the result of losing her mother? But no, that couldn't be right. Magda's last visit to the house had been before Clarissa's death and she'd suggested that Amelia had been idling her time away in her bedroom since the end of the exam season. What did post A level students from posh schools usually do with the long summer that followed their exams? Why hadn't Amelia headed for a boozy few weeks surfing in Cornwall or sunning herself on a beach in the Balearics?

Ivo returned to the St Cuthbert's website and harvested the names of Amelia's contemporaries who had also done well in their exams. He pasted them all into a Google search and came up with a goldmine of information – an offshoot of TikTok called PoshTok. There he found #stcuthshols, a series of video reels, one of which was a group of nine students descending from a ferry at Zakynthos. Ivo read the comments, things like *Here for serious sun and **** and *Good job Mummy doesn't know how to use TikTok*. One reel was of a couple of young men waving, with the comment *Miss you Melia. See you soon at Boogie's*. Melia? Short for Amelia. Did that mean she had declined to join her friends on holiday? Or had something prevented her from going? Her mother's death would have done that, but the reel was dated nearly two months ago, so unless Amelia was gifted with second sight, there was no reason she couldn't have joined them. It would hardly have been lack of money. The Mayberrys were loaded, at least when compared to

Ivo. And even if they were not actually super rich, if they could afford St Cuthbert's fees, a holiday in Greece would be a drop in the ocean financially. Had Clarissa prevented her from going? Amelia was eighteen and could do as she pleased, but unless she had a job as well as school, she wouldn't be able to pay for a holiday herself, so it was possible her mother had refused to cough up. Ivo felt he was straying into what Katya would call unfounded theory territory. Another barmy idea. He could hear her words echoing in his head. So he didn't dwell on that and instead turned his attention to Boogie's, which Ivo knew was the name of a nightclub in town.

During lockdown, Ivo had been housed in a hotel in Slough, where socialising was strongly discouraged – against the law, apparently. But leaning out of the bedroom window it had been possible to strike up a friendship with the occupier of the room next to his own and Ivo had become friendly with a lad of his own age called Scooty Brown. Before the pandemic, Scooty, like Ivo, had been living on the streets. But unlike Ivo, the streets he occupied had been in Slough, not Windsor, where it was a case of survival of the toughest. And Scooty was tough. He trained every day in his room doing press-ups and pull-ups using the door to his shower room. He also did an exercise Ivo had never dared to try, which involved hanging from the windowsill by his toes. Good for upper body strength, Scooty had told Ivo. They'd kept in touch after lockdown and met occasionally in the Eton meadows, where Ivo walked Harold and Scooty ran circuits while Ivo timed him using the stopwatch on his phone.

They'd both been lucky. Around the time Ivo was hired at *Shady Willows,* Scooty had been taken on as a bouncer at Boogie's. And that gave Ivo an idea. He pulled out his phone, scrolled through his contacts and gave Scooty a call. Ivo thought he wasn't going to answer but eventually he heard Scooty's voice grunting at him, and realised that eight on a Sunday morning might not be the best time to rouse a bouncer who had probably not been asleep for more than a couple of hours. 'Sorry,' said Ivo. 'I shouldn't have called so early.'

'Not a problem,' said Scooty. 'I wanted to go for a long run this morning anyway. I assume it's something urgent?'

'Kind of,' said Ivo. Was an imminent meeting with Katya and his lack of notes urgent?

'Saw you in the local paper,' said Scooty, sounding more awake than he had when he first answered the call. 'Detective now, are you?'

That was right. Ivo, the whole team, had been featured by the paper after solving the case of a man found dead in a carousel. 'Yeah,' he said modestly. 'I'm hoping you can help me with some detective work now.'

Scooty laughed. 'I'll get me deerstalker and magnifying glass.'

'It's not that sort of detecting,' said Ivo. 'I'm looking for a girl called Amelia Mayberry, who could be a regular at Boogie's.'

'Got a pic?'

Ivo forwarded the photo he'd found on the St Cuthbert's web site.

'Not sure,' said Scooty, having received the picture. 'I may have seen her, but all these posh girls look the same to me.'

'I know where she lives, but I need to talk to her away from home.'

'Trouble with Mummy and Daddy?'

'In a way. Her mother died recently, so she's probably not been clubbing for a while. Plus all of her friends have been on holiday.'

'That's right. They'll have been away sunning themselves in the Med. But that crowd are drifting back now. Want me to keep an eye out for her?'

'If you could let me know when she's there, I can drop in and have a word with her.'

'Any idea what it costs to get into Boogies?'

Ivo hadn't thought of that. 'How much?'

'Fifty quid on a Saturday. Less during the week.'

Ivo couldn't believe it. He and Brian had gone to nightclubs in Greece that were free. Drinks were expensive though, particularly the low alcohol ones that Ivo insisted on because he didn't want to end up like his mother. She'd died of alcohol poisoning, leaving Ivo destitute and homeless while he was still in his teens. 'Each?' he asked, trying to keep the alarm out of his voice.

'Per couple, but singles pay the full whack.'

Would Katya let him claim it as an expense?

'Tell you what,' said Scooty. 'Next time I see her I'll give you a buzz and you can come and meet her out back.'

'Will you recognise her?'

'They have to sign in. I'll keep an eye on the door list.'

Ivo wondered if she would come out to see someone she'd never met. Not if she was sensible, he thought. But she was eighteen; how sensible was she likely to be? 'Tell her she can bring a friend if she feels safer.'

'See what you mean,' said Scooty. 'There's an office you could use. There's no one there in the evenings and it's on the CCTV system. She should feel safe in there.'

'Great,' said Ivo. 'Thanks.'

'No probs, mate. Just get me a mention if you get to arrest a murderer. My boss would be that chuffed.'

Ivo laughed. 'I'll do what I can.'

He ended the call, feeling that he'd made progress. At least he had something to report to the team. He just hoped it wouldn't be too long before Amelia Mayberry fancied a night out with her mates, and also that this didn't involve exploring a new club.

CHAPTER SIXTEEN

Jonny fiddled nervously with a flyer that had been pushed through the letter box that morning. It should have gone straight into the recycling bin. He wasn't interested in having his hedge trimmed right now. And even if he was, they had a hedge trimmer who had been visiting them regularly every year once the birds had finished nesting and who kept the hedge that grew between his house and the one next door as neat as any he had seen in the area. But if he threw the leaflet out immediately, he would have no reason to sit and read it at the kitchen table. He wanted to talk to Mrs Gage, but he wanted to give the appearance of just happening to be there, sifting through the mail. Unfortunately, the post had offered very little to sift through that morning, so he had no alternative but to read every word on Jack Hedges' leaflet, several times. Was that the man's real name? Very unlikely, Jonny thought, unless it was an example of nominal determinism. Must happen sometimes, although he couldn't think of any other examples.

It was a relief when Mrs Gage bustled into the kitchen, carrying a bright yellow toolbox in one hand and an industrial, also yellow, vacuum cleaner in the other. Both were emblazoned, as was Mrs Gage's t-shirt, with the Windsor Mops logo, a picture of a woman wearing a knotted scarf on her head and brandishing an old-fashioned feather duster. Jonny had never seen Mrs Gage use a feather duster, but as he usually escaped to *Jasmine's* for a spot of washing-up when Mrs Gage was due, he couldn't swear that she never did.

She'd clipped open her toolbox and started extracting bottles of cleaning products, dusters and scouring pads before she noticed Jonny sitting at the kitchen table. He expected her to scowl at him and make some derogatory remarks about men who hang around the house when they should be at work. Jonny was not sure she had come to grips with the idea of retirement and if she had, she probably thought he should be out on a golf course somewhere. She liked to get on with her work without her workspace being cluttered with residents. Even Belinda, who was home much more now than she used to be and who was much braver than Jonny when dealing with the Mrs Gages of this world, had decided that Monday mornings were an excellent time to do a Waitrose shop followed by a visit to the library or the hairdresser.

Jonny dropped his flyer into the bin reserved for paper and smiled at Mrs Gage, still expecting a scowl in return. But she didn't scowl. Today she greeted Jonny with a smile of her own. The only time Jonny had seen this before was when he had Harold with him, but as he was on his own that morning, he was surprised by it. 'I'll be out of your way soon,' he said, 'but I just wanted a quick word before you start work.'

'That's okay,' she said, giving a bottle of ceramic hob cleaner a violent shake. 'I've always got the time for a chat.'

A lie, Jonny thought. She'd not work a moment over her allocated time so a chat with him would probably mean a short cut somewhere else. But all in a good cause if it helped him uncover a possible suspect in the who-poisoned-Clarissa-Mayberry case.

'I'll put the kettle on, shall I?' she said. She filled the kettle and switched it on, rinsed two mugs and added a teabag to each. Then she reached into a cupboard for a packet of biscuits and sat down next to Jonny. 'Not going to sack me, are you?' she asked, offering him a chocolate digestive.

He wouldn't dare. If they wanted to dispense with Mrs Gage's services he, or more likely Belinda, would call the agency and cancel her visits. 'Of course not. We couldn't manage without you,' he told her. They probably could. He was retired and Belinda had time on her hands at the moment. But they both liked having the house cleaned for them and they could afford it. They were contributing to the economy, weren't they? And if they sacked Mrs Gage they would probably be blacklisted by everyone who worked locally from plumbers to chiropodists. He might need Mr Hedges after all.

'I was hoping you might be able to tell me a bit more about one of your Windsor Mops colleagues, Magda Nowak. You remember I asked you for her phone number?'

'I remember,' said Mrs Gage. 'I hope you didn't let on that it was me gave you her number.'

'Absolutely not, but thank you. You saved us having to call round all the agencies in Windsor.'

'Not that many.'

'All the same, every second counts.'

Mrs Gage sniffed.

'Do you know Magda well? I don't suppose you get to meet the other Mops very often, do you?'

'Why wouldn't we? We don't work together but we can still be friends, can't we?'

Jonny had a vison of a gathering of Mops discussing their clients over tea and biscuits and he wondered what she said about him and Belinda.

'She did a couple of rounds with me when she first started so I could show her the ropes. Nice girl,' she added.

'It seems she didn't get on with her previous clients. I wondered if you'd heard anything about that.'

The kettle boiled and Mrs Gage made the tea, passing Jonny a mug that Belinda's cousin had given them after a visit to a National Trust property somewhere in Devon. It was decorated with a picture of a house, a kind of art deco castle designed by Edwin Lutyens. Mrs Gage was using a mug Ivo had given them as a thank you for looking after Harold when Ivo was threatened with eviction from his flat for not having read the bit in his contract about not keeping pets. Ivo had ordered it from a website, and it was decorated with a photo of Harold he'd uploaded from his phone. Mrs Gage adored Harold and Jonny guessed the mug was her favourite. If she gave him some useful information, he might get Ivo to order the same mug again as a gift. One she could take home with her.

Mrs Gage was shaking her head. 'It was an unfortunate incident, but I'm afraid things like that happen from time to time. Some clients are very difficult. Not you and Mrs C, of course. You're a pleasure to work for.'

Jonny was pleased to hear it. 'What happened?' he asked.

'The woman who owned the house, that Clarissa Mayberry – dreadful woman, by all accounts – accused her of stealing. She claimed several things had gone missing while Magda was working there and threatened to call the police.'

Would that be a motive for revenge? 'And did Mrs Mayberry call the police?'

'No, her husband intervened and said he'd got rid of them himself. Took them to a junk shop, he said. If you ask me, he was lying.'

'You think Magda was guilty?'

'No, she's as honest a girl as you'd hope to meet. I think—' said Mrs Gage, taking a lengthy gulp of her tea, 'I think it was the daughter took them. Right little layabout, Magda said.'

'But the family is well off. Why would the daughter need to sell stuff?'

'She'd fallen out with her mother. Magda heard them arguing and the mother saying she was cutting off the daughter's allowance.'

'You know the mother, Clarissa Mayberry, died a few days ago?'

'I heard. Poisoning, wasn't it?'

News obviously spread like wildfire among Windsor Mops employees. 'From death cap mushrooms,' said Jonny.

'Nasty,' said Mrs Gage. 'And it happened just a couple of days after Magda's last visit. If you ask me, she's well out of it. She's been given a new job. Cleaning at the college, I think. Not sure what Mr Mayberry will do now, but I don't see Windsor Mops sending him anyone else. They'll have him on their blacklist.'

Jonny didn't know they had a blacklist and wondered, apart from accusing cleaners of stealing, what one had to do to be added to it. But Mrs Gage had said they were a pleasure to work for, so he and Belinda were probably safe for now. He reached for his notebook, a royal blue moleskin, and wrote down everything Mrs Gage had told him. 'Thank you very much,' he said. 'That's all very helpful.'

'You don't think Mrs Mayberry was murdered, do you?' she asked, rubbing her hands and grinning at the idea. 'Are you and your detectives looking into it?'

'We're just trying to discover how the mushrooms got into the house.'

'Something fishy about all of it, if you ask me.'

'It was probably just a tragic accident.' Jonny tried to sound convincing. The last thing anyone wanted was rumour of murder passed around the affluent houses of Windsor Mops clientele. He looked at his watch. Time for washing-up duties. Jasmine would be wondering where he was. 'I'll get out of your way.' He tucked the notebook into his jacket pocket and stood up.

'Oh, before you go,' said Mrs Gage, 'I've been wanting to talk to you.'

'Oh? Nothing serious, I hope?' Had she remembered something she wanted to complain about?

'I've got this friend. Her dog's just had a litter of pups. Labradoodles, lovely temperament they have. And I know you and Mrs

Cardew were talking about getting a dog. Shall I have a word with her? See if she can reserve one for you?'

Jonny didn't recall discussing dogs while Mrs Gage was in earshot, but Belinda could have mentioned it. He would like a dog. But a Labradoodle? Small and fluffy, weren't they? Or was he thinking of some other kind of doodle? It was a long way from Harold who, since he had stayed with them, was the kind of dog Jonny would like. Harold was a rugged, down-to-earth kind of dog. Walking Harold was like going to the pub with a long-standing friend. Walking something small and fluffy wouldn't be the same at all. He didn't think they would bond. 'Thank you,' he said. 'I'll talk to Belinda and see what she thinks.'

'Well, don't take too long. They are very popular.'

Jonny assured her that he would let her know as soon as they'd discussed it.

A*RRIVING AT* J*ASMINE*'*S,* he found that all the washing-up was done and Jasmine was getting started on lunch. He must have chatted with Mrs Gage for longer than he thought. But it had been worth it to get to the bottom of why Magda had left the Mayberrys.

He bought himself a cappuccino and carried it through to the dining room, where he found a vacant seat by the window. He got out his phone and searched for images of Labradoodle puppies. They were adorable, with big, appealing eyes gazing out from behind fringes of fur. Fluffy, yes, but not all that small – two feet tall and weighing about sixty-five pounds. Jonny put the phone back in his pocket. He'd tell Belinda about the puppies when he got home. He wasn't sure how she'd feel, but he was definitely a Labradoodle convert.

But they had a case to solve. Dogs could wait. He sipped his coffee and read through the notes he'd made that morning. He remembered Katya's three conditions for murder suspects. Magda had the means; she could easily have slipped out and picked some mushrooms. She must have had plenty of opportunities, working in the house with access to the kitchen. She did have a motive, although it wasn't a strong one. She had, after all, been given another job, one that sounded a lot nicer than working for the Mayberrys. But there was enough there for the team to consider. They were not in competition with each other, but Jonny doubted if the others had found anything as concrete as this.

CHAPTER
SEVENTEEN

Katya looked out of her window, trying to decide how much layering to do. It was always difficult at this time of year. Summer was finished but autumn hadn't really got going. There'd been days recently when she set out wearing jumpers and scarves only to peel them off by midday. So was today going to be a coat day or a jumper one? Certainly not both. That was still a few weeks away and not something she anticipated with any pleasure. Some people did. 'I just love this weather,' people would say, gazing at frost-encrusted trees, crunching through fallen leaves, and stamping into frozen puddles for the pleasure of listening to the ice crack. But those were people who had warm houses to go home to and who didn't have to worry about paying the fuel bills. Not those like Katya, who lived on a pension and had stingy landlords who claimed that draught proofing and double glazing were luxuries they didn't care to shell out for. She decided on a wool shirt and lightweight jacket with a hood. Outside it was drizzling, but it was only a short walk to *Jasmine's;* she had enough to carry without the extra bother of an umbrella. Katya was not good with umbrellas. She struggled to put one up without impaling someone in the eye. Then she struggled again trying to get the wretched thing down again when it was wet without showering everyone within spitting distance. On top of that, she'd lost more than she cared to remember – on buses and trains, in shops and libraries or just forgetting where in her flat she had put them. If she took one with her today, she'd almost certainly leave it behind unless there was a downpour just as she was leaving. She didn't think they were in for a downpour today so the umbrella, even if she could find it, stayed at home.

She arrived at *Jasmine's* as the last lunch customers were departing. A carefully planned bit of timing that she'd tried before because Jasmine would have food left – the remains of the soup, a few crusty rolls, even some sandwiches if she was lucky. There was not much to be done with leftovers and Katya felt she was doing Jasmine a favour by finishing them off for her. Today there was a good bowl or two of tomato soup and some cheese-topped bread rolls. Katya sat at a table in the kitchen and ate them while watching Jasmine and Jonny do the washing-up. Jonny was going on about some dog he was thinking of getting. He showed Katya a picture on his phone. Quite an appealing little thing. Not at all like Harold, but that was not necessarily a bad thing. And then she glanced at the price. That much? For a dog? Why didn't he go to the dog rescue place? There were always dogs there that needed a good home. She wondered if Jonny knew about that but decided not to mention it.

Once they were all in the office, seated around the board, Katya tapped her pen on the table. 'Let's get going,' she said. 'I don't want to keep you too late, so just a quick catch-up and see where we're headed.' She didn't feel she was headed anywhere right now. The phone number she'd asked Lugs to check belonged to a family friend and they had no reason to believe he had anything to do with Clarissa's poisoning, or that he was even in the area at the time she'd eaten the mushrooms. And Lugs' theory suggested it was usual to look to the family first – notably spouses – when considering suspects, not family friends. She hoped the rest of the team had more to show for themselves. 'I hope you've all been busy,' she said. They all nodded, so with any luck they had done more than she had in the last day or two. 'Is it any clearer from your latest discoveries if we are looking at accident or murder? Don't all speak at once,' she said when none of them replied. 'Ivo, what do you think?'

'I'm beginning to think one of the kids killed her,' said Ivo. 'Or maybe they were in it together.'

Katya sighed. It was always Ivo who came out with outlandish ideas. Lugs might tell her to look to the family first, but the children? Ivo didn't realise how uncommon matricide was. Occasional mercy killings, she supposed. But while teenagers tended to have massive falling out episodes with their parents, it didn't usually lead to murder. But she should listen to what Ivo had to say. He could be quite perceptive. 'Do you have any evidence?'

'Something must have happened to Tristan. I don't know what it was yet. I still need to work on that, but he turned from a straight-A student into one who failed all his A levels. He's having to retake them at a private college, but according to some of his fellow students, he doesn't do any work.'

'There could be plenty of reasons for that,' said Jonny. 'Girlfriend trouble, or drugs.'

'There's more than that,' said Ivo. 'There was a course field trip, which he turned up for because it was close to their house. They were specifically warned not to pick mushrooms because they could be poisonous.'

'He had the means,' said Katya, writing it down. 'But I don't think he has much of a motive.'

'Some parents really put on the pressure at exam time,' said Jasmine. 'Perhaps his mother had been nagging him about his lack of motivation.'

'Is that a reason to kill her?' Jonny asked.

'We only know the students were warned about some mushrooms being poisonous – he might not have known they were deadly. Perhaps he just meant to make her a bit ill – shut her up for a few days.'

'That's possible,' said Katya. 'I don't think it's enough to accuse him outright, but worth looking into a bit further.'

'What about the sister?' Jasmine asked.

'Amelia? I discovered quite a lot about her as well. She's a brilliant student who was supposed to be going on a post exam holiday with her friends but pulled out at the last minute. There are video reels and comments on Instagram that hint that her parents had stopped her allowance.'

'Why would they do that?' Jasmine asked.

'I don't know yet, but hopefully I'm going to meet her soon.' He explained how Scooty was going to call him when Amelia next turned up at Boogies.

'I hope you're not planning to accuse her of killing her mother,' said Katya.

'Of course not. I'll just get her chatting and hope she drops some hints about a falling out.'

'Well, take care,' said Jasmine. 'She could have protective friends, six-footer types with medals for boxing.'

'I'm guessing this bouncer bloke, Scooty, can keep an eye on him,' said Jonny. 'But I could go as well.'

'Definitely not,' said Jasmine and Katya at the same time. 'You'd be mistaken for a meddling dad and probably get beaten up yourself.'

'No one's getting beaten up,' said Ivo. 'Scooty's a six-foot-two, super fit bouncer and we've both lived rough. We know how to look after ourselves.'

'You've done well, Ivo,' said Katya, not wanting to dampen his enthusiasm. 'Keep an eye on those two, but like Jonny says, take care.'

'Will do,' said Ivo. 'And remember Harold does a good job with violent types.'

That's true, Katya thought. To date, Harold had detained two murderers and he wasn't going to let Ivo come to any harm on his watch. Just a sight of Harold would make any attackers think twice. 'Who's next?' she asked.

'I discovered who owned the car that drove to the village the day before Clarissa died,' said Jonny. 'It was Carl Archer.'

'The old family friend,' said Katya. An interesting coincidence, since he was also the owner of the phone number that Clarissa had scribbled down on the festival flyer. Family friends tended to visit each other but, since his name kept cropping up, it could be worth looking into. 'No reason why he shouldn't visit Clarissa, I suppose. Do we know if they'd fallen out at all?' If they had, could Carl Archer be a suspect? Katya wondered what he knew about death caps. He might have slipped into the woods and gathered some before visiting Clarissa. But would he have sat there watching her eat them? He'd hardy join her and risk poisoning himself.

'We can't ask him if they had fallen out, can we?' said Jasmine with a laugh. 'It would be like accusing him of killing her.'

'Perhaps he did,' said Katya. 'I asked Lugs to trace the number we found on Clarissa's flyer. He identified the number as Carl Archer's, but I can't work out why Clarissa wrote it down. If they were friends, wouldn't she have saved his number on her own phone?'

'And why the question mark?' Ivo asked.

'Good point,' said Katya. 'And it gets even more interesting.' She paused for a moment to let that sink in. 'Lugs managed to get the call logs for Clarissa's phone. She made calls to family, the agent and the festival people – no big surprises there. There was another number that called her a day or two before she died, and Lugs found that was also registered to Carl Archer.'

'He had two phones?' Jasmine asked. 'It's not that unusual. One was probably for work.'

'Clarissa received three calls from that number she'd written down and then she blocked it. She called it once but it wasn't answered.'

'Did Clarissa call Carl Archer on his usual number?' Jasmine asked.

'A couple of times. Once later on the day we assume he visited her, and again on the morning of her lecture.'

'The number was registered to Carl Archer,' said Jonny, 'but he might have been paying for someone else. One of his kids, perhaps. Is there any way Lugs can trace where the calls were made from?'

'Not without a warrant,' said Katya. 'And it would need to be an official inquiry for that. She wrote *Find out more* under Carl's name, but she couldn't think what direction that was going to go in. It was time to move on. 'Anything on Murray Dickinson?'

'Absolutely,' said Jasmine. 'And it's fascinating.' She stood up and pinned a sheet of paper to the board. Then she looked at the others to see the impact it was having. Jonny and Ivo stared open-mouthed and Katya looked puzzled.

'That's not Clarissa, is it?' Ivo asked, as he looked at the pouting expression of a scantily dressed woman who gazed out of the picture in what could only be described as a suggestive way. She was wearing a bright green, skimpy two-piece outfit with matching high-heeled shoes. She was lounging on a chaise longue, a mane of red curls flowing over the armrest.

'No,' said Jasmine. 'It's an image from a website that sells artwork for things like adverts and book covers. It's very popular, apparently.'

'And this is relevant because?' Katya asked, a note of irritation in her voice.

Jasmine pinned up another picture. This time of a book cover with the same image and the title *Miss Ruby Tress* printed in curly, gold letters. In smaller letters, *Miss Tress series Book 1*, followed by the name of the author, Clarice Mayflower.

'I still don't see what this has to do with our enquiry,' said Katya.

Jasmine pinned up the third and final picture. It was the picture she'd taken of the website.

Ivo gasped. 'That's Clarissa, isn't it? You're telling us she wrote that book? I thought she wrote about how everyone should eat proper meals.'

'She did,' said Jasmine. 'But she wrote books like this as well. You might call it moonlighting,' she added with a giggle.

'How did you find it?' Jonny asked, looking at his phone, on which he'd opened the Amazon app. 'It's not mentioned with Clarissa's other books.'

'I'm not surprised,' muttered Katya. 'Even Amazon has standards.'

'It's only available on a rather specialist website. You have to be a signed-up member and pay a subscription.'

'So how did you find it?' Ivo asked. 'Did you sign up and pay for it?'

'No. This is all thanks to Murray Dickinson. He'd really got it in for Clarissa Mayberry and had done a lot of research. He sent me a list of websites that he'd used to collect information about her. He'd even bought the book and let me take pictures of it on my phone.'

'Did you read any of it?' Jonny asked.

'Only the first page. I couldn't face any more than that. Describing it as pornographic doesn't do it justice.'

'And this is only book one?' Katya asked.

'There are six altogether.'

Jonny looked thoughtful. 'After she was taken away in the ambulance, Murray asked me if I thought he'd killed her,' he said. 'He muttered something about having been interrupted. I think he was planning to out her in public. Do you suppose she knew what was coming?'

'And dosed herself with poisonous mushrooms rather than face being outed? Hardly.'

'No, but knowing what Murray was about to reveal might have brought on enough stress to aggravate the effect of the poison.'

'Murray told me his attack on her opinions was only the warm-up. He accepts that everyone is entitled to their own opinion. It was her hypocrisy that got to him. His heckling at the festival was well planned. He just didn't get to the final reveal before she collapsed.'

'Does that make it more likely that she was deliberately

poisoned?' Ivo asked. 'Do you think Murray hated her enough to do that?'

'Not necessarily. There'd be other people who knew about it. I still think we should look closer to home. The family must be at the top of the list,' said Katya.

'If they even knew about the books,' said Jonny. 'She might have kept it a secret from them.'

'So who is going to go and ask them?' said Ivo. '"Did you know your wife-slash-mother was writing porn?" It's not something I'd volunteer for.'

'I could ask Anthony in a tactful way,' said Jonny.

'That might be the best way to go,' said Katya. 'Just a casual question about what else Clarissa had written. Although you'd need to have your inner lie detector in place. If it was a motive for murder, he'd hardly admit he knew all about it, would he?'

'Does that let Magda off the hook?' Jasmine asked. 'If she knew about the books, she'd be more likely to use it to put pressure on Clarissa. Blackmail her for a pay rise, perhaps. But unless she is very strait-laced, I can't see her wanting to kill Clarissa because of it.'

'Maybe not,' said Katya. 'But she could still be after revenge for being accused of stealing. We shouldn't discount her just yet.' She made a list on the board, which she headed *Suspects* and added Magda's name to it. 'I'll put Murray on the list as well. The timing would have been difficult for a planned killing, but you never know.'

'He does have a motive,' said Jasmine. 'Possibly the strongest of all of them. He really hated her.'

'What about the agent?' Jonny asked. 'Do we know if she was responsible for publishing this book as well as her more serious stuff?'

'Patsy Kline? It's worth thinking about,' said Katya, adding Patsy's name to the list. 'She might be angry that Clarissa had used someone else for these books, or worried about what it would do to her reputation if it got out that she'd had anything to do with them.'

'Six possible suspects,' said Jonny, counting the names on the list. 'Seven if we include Carl Archer.'

'We don't know much about him, do we?' said Ivo. 'Except that he has two phone accounts.'

'We know he was at the house the day before she died,' said Jonny. 'Unless he'd lent his car to someone else.'

'Can you see from the speed guy's photo?'

Jonny shook his head. 'All I could see was a bloke wearing dark glasses. Not sure that's enough to identify him.'

'We're getting off track,' said Katya. 'We should be deciding what to do next. Any ideas?'

'I think we need a timeline,' said Jonny. 'Clarissa died at eight o'clock on Friday evening. We know that the first symptoms appear around six hours after the mushrooms are eaten and then there is a period of apparent recovery before liver damage takes hold around twenty-four hours later.'

Katya was scribbling some figures on a piece of paper. 'So working back from the time she died, Clarissa must have eaten the mushrooms sometime on the day before. It's probably safe to assume she didn't get up in the middle of the night for a snack of poisonous mushrooms.'

'We know what she was doing for most of the Thursday,' said Jasmine. 'Magda was there cleaning in the morning. She saw Tristan leave for college at around nine and Amelia drove off in her mother's car just before Magda finished work. Then we know Clarissa had a visitor shortly after that, possibly Carl Archer. Do we know what time he left?'

'No,' said Jonny. 'But when Alan went home at around four that afternoon he'd not videoed the black Merc going in the opposite direction. And there is no record of Amelia returning in Clarissa's car before that either.'

'Is there another route out of Little Frampton?' Ivo asked.

Jonny opened up Google Maps on the computer and pointed at the village with a pencil. 'Little Frampton has three streets that split off from the main road shortly after passing the place where Alan was sitting. They twist around but merge into one on the other side of the village. It's possible to leave that way, but at this point it's just a lane that has access to the more remote houses. Eventually it brings you back to the main road a few miles south of the turning into the village that most people use.'

'In other words,' said Ivo, 'it is a way in and out of the village but not one anyone would choose to use because it would be a lot further.'

'But,' said Jasmine, 'if Merc man had spotted Alan's camera on his way into the village, he might have wanted to avoid it on the way out again and used the longer route. So we've no idea what time he left.'

Katya picked up a pen and wiped a section of the board clean. She drew two columns for the Thursday and Friday leading up to Clarissa's death. She pointed to the Thursday column and wrote the times the twins left the house and Magda's cleaning hours. Then she added *Merc man 1pm?* She turned away from the board, pen in hand. 'Do we know Anthony Mayberry's movements on that day?'

'He was away for a few days,' said Jonny. 'We know he'd left before Magda arrived to clean, and his car didn't appear on Alan's list, so it was probably very early. I don't know what time Alan gets up, but I imagine he'd want to be in place for the morning drives to work.'

'Anthony could have gone for an early morning walk and left the mushrooms in the house before he left for work.'

Katya sighed. 'There are two things wrong with that,' she said. 'If Anthony picked the mushrooms with the intention of poisoning Clarissa, how would he know that she would be the only one to eat them?'

'Perhaps he poisoned her accidentally because he didn't know what they were,' said Ivo.

'Still doesn't work,' said Katya. 'None of the rest of the family were ill. If it was an accident, wouldn't they all have eaten some? And if it wasn't an accident, how would he make sure Clarissa ate them but no one else did?'

Jonny stared at the list on the board. 'Are we ruling out Murray and Patsy?'

'Not necessarily. Either of them could have visited the house after four that evening.'

'Sounds like it could have been quite a party,' said Jonny, laughing.

'We need to make a plan,' said Katya. 'Find out where everyone was that afternoon. Let's hope Ivo's friend gets back to him soon so he can talk to Amelia. Jonny, you could go and see Anthony again and get him to talk about where he was that Thursday evening.'

'We've got car registration numbers for Anthony, Clarissa and Tristan, as well as Carl Archer. Do we know what cars Magda and Murray drive?' Jonny asked.

'Magda has a silver-grey Clio,' said Jasmine. 'I let her use Dad's parking space when she came to see me, so I made a note of it. And there was a small white van parked outside Murray's shop. It had their logo on it, so I assume it was his. But you'd have spotted either of those on Alan's video list, wouldn't you?'

'Only from a bit before nine up to four o'clock. Magda could have returned later, I suppose. If Murray was in the area, it was before nine or after four o'clock. I noticed an ANPR camera on the main road a couple of miles before the turn off for the village. I'm wondering if Lugs could tell us which cars passed it early that evening.'

'Good idea,' said Katya. 'But he won't be allowed to give us that information unless we have evidence that a crime was committed. But...' She fiddled with her pen as she thought. 'There could be a way around that. I'll talk to him and see if I can't twist his arm.'

'We need to know when Clarissa was taken ill with the first symptoms,' said Jasmine. 'We're assuming it was Thursday evening, but what if she'd eaten the mushrooms for breakfast?'

'She'd have felt ill during the afternoon,' said Jonny. 'If Magda was telling the truth, she was fine on Thursday morning. 'It's possible the only person who was with later that day was Amelia.'

'And Carl Archer, who visited her at lunchtime,' said Katya.

'He didn't say anything about it when we met,' said Jonny. 'But he didn't mention that he'd been there at all.'

'And that makes him look guilty,' said Katya. 'But guilty of killing her or just not wanting Anthony to know he'd been there, I'm not sure.'

Jasmine was making notes on a piece of paper. 'There was someone in the house all day from when Magda arrived until Merc man left. She would have been on her own from then until the twins got home, sometime after four. We can question Amelia and Tristan about how their mother seemed that evening, but wouldn't they have told someone if she'd already been feeling ill?'

'Not if she was taken ill during the night and they were both asleep. That suggests she ate the mushrooms during the afternoon. A late lunch, perhaps,' said Jonny.

'We'd need someone to corroborate all of that. I'm not sure how reliable any of them are,' said Katya. She cleared up her notes and put them in her bag.

'I'll keep tabs on the twins,' said Ivo. 'What will the rest of you do?'

'I could try and talk to Anthony again,' said Jonny. 'Carl as well, perhaps.'

'I wonder if it's worth asking around the village,' said Jasmine.

'All good ideas,' said Katya. She looked out of the window and noticed the drizzle had stopped and the sun was shining. Just as well she hadn't bothered with an umbrella. She could walk home taking her time and mull over everything they'd talked about. Her team had worked hard. It was just a pity she couldn't see where it was taking them.

CHAPTER
EIGHTEEN

Ivo and Harold arrived back from their evening walk, a brief one on this occasion. It had rained on and off all day, the river path was slippery and for an otherwise rugged dog, Harold wasn't very keen on getting his paws wet. Once home, Ivo could do a quick check that all was well at *Shady Willows* before turning in for the night. It was after eleven and most of the cabins were in darkness; their occupants were likely to be sound asleep. The only exception was one at the far end of the site, where Ivo could see light shining through a crack in the curtains and the flicker of a TV. He could also hear the murmur of voices and a few cackles of laughter. Nothing unusual about that. The resident of this cabin was a bit shaky on his legs and was often visited by a couple of neighbours for an evening of film watching or cards. Ivo guessed from the flickering that this was film night. A comedy, he assumed, hearing the laughter. There was no need for him to interfere. A single light and silence at this time of night and he would have knocked on the door to check whether the man had fallen or was feeling unwell. Most of the residents hated the idea that anyone was checking up on them and Ivo knew when to leave well alone.

He returned to his own cabin and let himself in. He hung Harold's lead on a hook by the door and was about to put the kettle on when his phone rang. He checked the ID and Scooty's name flashed up on the screen. 'Looks like we're off out again,' he said to Harold as he answered the call.

'Amelia Mayberry's just come in,' said Scooty. 'Arrived a few minutes ago with two other girls. They've already had quite a bit to drink. They told me Amelia needed cheering up, so they were treating her to a night out.'

That was good. He hoped that after a few drinks and an evening with friends, Amelia would be feeling chatty. 'Give me fifteen minutes,' said Ivo, checking the time.

'Bring the van,' said Scooty. 'I can keep a space for you right by the back entrance. One of the managers has just left. I'll stick a cone in it for you.'

'Great,' said Ivo, putting the phone in his pocket. 'See you soon.' He dragged on a grey hoodie and loaded Harold into the back of the van, leaving a note pinned to the door with his mobile number in case of an emergency.

Scooty was waiting for them, leaning against the back door of the club, where he was chatting to another bouncer. Scooty introduced him as Big Al. A name that Ivo felt suited him well. Al matched Scooty in height and, Ivo suspected, toughness. He could imagine the two of them doing weights together. There must be a minimum height for bouncers and probably minimum levels of fitness. There were rowing and rugby clubs nearby, both of which would be full of large young men only too keen to get hammered after a match or a race. From the noise of the music, matched in volume by laughing and shouting from inside the club, they were well on their way to that state. Big Al and Scooty were in for a busy night.

'You can use the small office,' said Scooty, ushering Ivo inside. 'The girls are there already. One of them felt ill so I told them they could sit in there until she felt better. I gave her some water to drink and told them there was someone who wanted to talk to Amelia.'

Scooty led them along a dingy passage with black-painted walls and into a small room with a sofa on which sat a girl with her head bent over a bucket. The other two sat next to her, one holding her hair back, the other trying to persuade her to sip some water. Ivo could see what Scooty meant when he said the girls in the club all looked the same to him. All three had glossy, shoulder-length hair, faces caked in make-up and short, sparkly dresses. But it was easy to tell which one was Amelia. While two of the girls had deep suntans, the third was pale. It wasn't hard to guess which one had missed out on a holiday in the Mediterranean.

The pale girl looked up at Ivo from her place on the sofa. She looked nothing like her twin brother. Ivo had seen him in a photo but they could be misleading. He had seen Clarissa's photo as well and thought that Amelia was a little like her mother – the same slightly-too-large nose and piercing blue eyes. But he didn't want to make a mistake and talk to the wrong girl. 'I'm looking for Amelia Mayberry,' he said.

'I'm Amelia,' said the palest of the three girls. Ivo had been right. She looked Ivo up and down in a way that made him feel uncomfortable. He was sure, from what he'd learnt so far, that Clarissa Mayberry would have had the same effect. She stood up and draped an arm around Scooty's shoulder. 'Scooty told me a detective wanted to talk to me,' she said, in a way that suggested she was amused by the idea. 'Is that you? You don't look like a detective.'

Ivo nodded. 'We don't all have grubby raincoats and five o'clock shadow.'

She laughed. 'I was thinking more Morse,' she said. 'An opera bore with a flashy car.' She turned to the other two girls. 'Josie, if Tilly's stopped puking, she could probably do with some fresh air. Why don't you take her outside while I talk to the detective?'

Very cool, Ivo thought. She made it sound as if talking to detectives was something she did every day. Perhaps she did. He knew very little about her except that she was alarmingly clever. And confident. She didn't seem anything like the girl who, according to Magda, sulked in her bedroom all day listening to music. Perhaps she also watched old Morse episodes on Netflix. That was unusual for an eighteen-year-old, wasn't it? Even one whose options had been severely limited by an overbearing mother.

Josie nodded at Amelia, and picking up the bucket in one hand and grasping Tilly with the other, she headed for the door. Scooty followed them. 'I'll keep an eye on them,' he said. 'No one's going to want the room. Take your time and I'll sort a taxi to get the girls home when you're done.'

Ivo took Tilly's place on the sofa and Harold curled up at his feet.

'Nice dog,' said Amelia, holding out a hand for Harold to lick. 'I'd have liked a dog, but my mother was allergic. At least, she said she was. Probably just an excuse because she hated going out for walks.'

'Do you?' Ivo asked, thinking she didn't look like a typical rambler.

'What, hate going for walks?' She shrugged. 'It'd be okay with a dog, I suppose.'

'Been for a walk recently?'

'You mean have I been out in the woods picking poisonous mushrooms in order to bump off my mother?'

Nothing like getting straight to the point. It was as if she could read Ivo's mind. 'What is it you're going to Cambridge to study?' he asked. 'Plant science?'

She laughed. 'Changed my mind.'

'You're not going to Cambridge?'

'I am, but I've decided to do Law. I'm better at arguing than poisoning people with plants. Isn't it obvious?'

In a way, it was. Ivo could easily imagine her in court, tearing witnesses to shreds. It made him feel inadequate. He wished he'd brought Jonny with him, or even Katya. They'd both be better at asking the right questions than he was. He also wondered if he could trust a word she said.

'Are you really a detective?' she asked. 'I'm not familiar with the local CID. Never been involved in any criminal activity.'

He shook his head. 'Not a police one, no.'

'Ah, a private investigator. Much more interesting. More Cormoran Strike than Morse, I guess. Perhaps a dash of Sherlock Holmes or Hercule Poirot?'

She certainly knew her crime fiction. They might even share a taste for TV crime drama. 'Nothing so exciting. I'm one of a group and we've been asked to trace the source of the mushrooms that killed your mother.'

'See,' she said, her eyes shining a steely blue. 'I was right. You do think I killed her.'

'Did you pick the mushrooms? It could have been an accident. You might not have meant to kill her.'

'Sorry to disappoint you. It wasn't me and I didn't pick any mushrooms. And if I had, I promise you I would have known what I was doing. It wouldn't have been an accident. It would have been cold-blooded, premeditated murder. Quite sorry I didn't think of it actually.'

She was very scary and Ivo believed her. He couldn't say why, but he was sure she was telling the truth. 'You didn't like your mother very much, did you?'

'You're joking. Not like her very much? I hated her guts. But I'm going to uni in a few weeks. I'd hardly need to kill her when I'm about to leave home, would I?'

She had a point. Unless it was a parting gesture. But as Amelia said, why bother? He tried a different tack. 'How did your mother seem the couple of days before she died?'

'Dunno. I avoided her as much as possible when the stupid bitch stopped me from going on holiday.'

'What about your brother?'

'You think Tristan killed her?'

'He might not have meant to. But he is doing a college course that involves looking at what grows in woodland.'

'Is he? I didn't know that.'

Did this family never talk to each other? It was no surprise that Tristan had gone off the rails if his nearest and dearest didn't even ask what he was studying. 'It's part of the A level Geography syllabus.'

She looked impressed. 'You've done your background research, haven't you?'

'He might have picked some mushrooms on the field trip and taken them home.'

Amelia shook her head. 'He's a gormless prat. He probably wouldn't know a mushroom from a cauliflower.'

'He can't be all that gormless. By all accounts he was a grade A student like yourself until he got into the sixth form. What went wrong?'

Amelia shrugged. 'He got into bad company, started missing school.'

'Drugs?' Ivo asked.

'No, well, he probably dabbled a bit. We all do that. This was, you know, bad boy stuff. Nicking cars for joyriding, getting into fights, that sort of thing. He wanted to leave school and get a job at Legoland, but my parents wouldn't let him. Dad tried to bribe him to get down to some study – new laptop, better car, that sort of thing, but he wasn't interested.'

'And your mother?'

'She shouted a lot and then lost interest. Too busy with her writing, I suppose.'

That was interesting. Did Amelia know the extent of her mother's literary efforts? 'What do you know about your mother's writing?'

Amelia gave him an odd look. 'What do *you* know about it?'

'I know she wrote political stuff, economics and that. And then...' He stopped, not sure if he should say more. He didn't want to shock Amelia and if she didn't know already, discovering her mother was churning out pornography would definitely do that.

'The other stuff,' Amelia added with a giggle.

'You know about that?' Surely she hadn't bought any of it.

'Oh, yeah. I even read a few pages. It's dreadful.'

'You don't approve of raunchy literature?'

'I don't have a problem with raunchy. But this is brutal, sexist, Marquis de Sade sort of stuff. It's not even well written, for God's sake. My mother was a first-class graduate. She should have known how to string a sentence together. She had to sell it through a specialist website. Regular bookstores like Amazon wouldn't touch it.'

'What did your father and brother think of it?'

'They didn't know anything about it. God, you don't think I bought the book, do you?'

Ivo wasn't sure what he thought.

'I found it when I was on her computer,' she said. 'I was trying to hack into her bank account to pay for my holiday.'

'Since you didn't go on holiday, I'm guessing that was unsuccessful.' Just as well. If she'd succeeded and her mother discovered, she'd probably have had her arrested and that wouldn't have done her Cambridge prospects any good at all.

'Yeah, worse luck. I knew her log in details but she'd installed some double layer security app and it texted her a warning so she banned me from going away with the others. She even stopped Dad from paying for it.'

Ivo wasn't surprised. Even someone as unlikeable as Clarissa Mayberry was entitled to keep their bank account secure.

'She softened a bit when my exam results came. Probably because that secured my place at Cambridge and she knew she'd be shot of me in a few weeks. She even let me borrow her car a couple of times. Didn't let up with Tristan though. He was packed off to that crammer with dire threats about what would happen if he didn't pass some exams. Not sure what she would have done with him. Being cast out of the family home could be just what he wanted.

She'd probably have made him stay and dig the garden over or clear out the drains.'

Ivo was not surprised that Tristan seemed to have dropped out of everything. He was beginning to feel quite sorry for him.

'I did spot one thing when I was trawling though mother's financial stuff,' said Amelia.

'Oh, yeah?' Ivo was beginning to think Amelia was every bit as obnoxious as her mother.

'She had another account at a bank I'd never heard of. She can't have used it often, or perhaps she hadn't had it for long, because she'd taped her user details to the underside of her desk. You don't do that once you've memorised them, do you?'

'You didn't try to steal from it for your holiday?'

'No. She'd not used it much – there'd been no withdrawals from it. She would have noticed.'

'Like she wouldn't have noticed money missing from her other account?'

'She might have eventually, but it's the one she used for her political and business stuff. Loads of transactions in and out.'

'So this other account, you say she hadn't withdrawn anything, but who was paying into it?'

'Mostly a company called Rabid Dog Inc.'

'Sounds unpleasant,' said Ivo, with a glance down at Harold.

'I poked around a bit and discovered it's the business name of the people who publish her books – the nasty ones. They're sold with a lot of other stuff, not just books, on a site you can only use if you pay a subscription to join. I didn't bother because I can imagine what's there.'

'You didn't want to find out?'

She looked at him quizzically. 'I know I'm no saint, but frankly I was shocked by what my mother had been doing. To be honest, if you find out someone killed her, I'd say they'd done everyone a favour and leave it there.'

'You don't think your father would want to know why she died?'

'Dad's okay. I'd worry about what the truth might do to him.'

'You'd rather your father was left in the dark than see justice done?'

'Yeah, I would, but if you really want to know more about the way my mother's mind worked, you should talk to her agent.'

'Patsy Kline? You know her?'

'She came to the house a couple of times recently and I overheard them having some blazing rows.'

'Did you hear what they were about?'

'No, but I'm guessing Patsy had her doubts about continuing to represent my mother.'

Ivo wondered what Katya knew about that. He wouldn't ask more about it now. That was Katya's territory and he didn't want to encroach. He'd let her know what Amelia had told him and leave it there. It was time he and Harold went home.

The door opened and the other two girls came in. Tilly looked a lot less green than she had earlier. 'She's feeling better,' said Josie. 'We're thinking of heading home. Scooty's going to call a taxi.'

'Do you live in town?' Ivo asked, wondering if he should offer them a lift.

'Out towards the Walthams,' said Josie.

That was way off his route home, and the other side of town from Little Frampton, where the Mayberry family lived. 'I can give you a lift home if you like,' said Ivo to Amelia. 'It's just a few miles upriver from where I live.'

Amelia smiled at him. 'It's okay, thanks. We're all staying at Tilly's. I used Mother's car and parked it in their drive.'

Josie slipped an arm around her shoulder. 'Poor Melia,' she said. 'First bit of freedom she'd had since... oops.'

'S'okay,' said Amelia. 'You're allowed to mention the D word. And Dad's got his best buddy staying, so he won't be lonely.'

'Where's Tris this evening?'

'Dunno,' said Amelia. 'He went off in his own car. He's probably breaking into an off licence or tearing up the M4 in a stolen beamer.'

'I thought you couldn't break into those,' said Tilly, wide eyed.

Amelia shrugged. 'My bro is useless at most things, but he knows his way around posh cars.' She turned to Ivo. 'So, Mr Detective, have I been any help?'

Ivo wasn't sure how to take that. He had mixed feelings about Amelia, mostly repellent ones, but not without a glimmer of admiration. 'Thanks for talking to me,' he said. He delved into his pocket and found a card with his phone number. 'Give me a call if you think of anything else.'

Amelia looked at the card. 'Handyman?'

'That's right. Detecting is a sideline.'

'And you also fix things?'

'Yes, sometimes. Small things, mostly,' he added, assuming any repairs to the Mayberry household would be carried out by expensive tradespeople who drove electric vans with upmarket writing on the side.

Amelia put the card in the top pocket of her jacket. 'Then I'll be sure to let you know if I have anything small that needs fixing.'

IVO AND HAROLD stood on the pavement at the back of Boogies and watched the three girls climb into a taxi. He loaded Harold into the van and set off back to *Shady Willows*. It had been an interesting experience. Harold's first visit to a local nightclub hadn't impressed him very much. He was more of a café culture type. There weren't too many food opportunities in a place like Boogies. And it was way too noisy. Even in the office there was the constant thump of loud music from the other side of the wall. Harold wasn't used to loud music. Nor, when he gave it some thought, was Ivo. But he had learnt a lot more about the Mayberry family. Dysfunctional was how Ivo would describe it. At first, he'd been sure the killing was accidental. It hadn't seemed likely to be murder, certainly not a premeditated one. Now Ivo was not so sure. The problem was that everyone who had any connection to the family disliked Clarissa and had a motive.

CHAPTER NINETEEN

There were times, Katya reluctantly admitted, when being retired put her at a disadvantage, the main one of which was not having access to police records. The poisonous mushroom case was beginning to get her down. It was all very well for these fungus society people to want to know what had happened to Clarissa, with the obviously magnanimous wish to stop it happening again. For a reasonable financial outlay, they could point out the dangers; not only the risk of eating poisonous fungi but the risk of over-foraging and depleting nature. They had made it sound so easy; discover what had happened and they'd produce a leaflet or put up signs or whatever it was they were planning. She should be grateful, Katya supposed, to be the recipient of their generosity, but the job was turning out to be way more difficult than she'd ever thought it would. Yes, knowing where the death caps had come from would help. They could add it to their map of where to watch out for free food that would likely kill you. But while a short investigation of the woods around Little Frampton would answer that question, it wouldn't solve the actual problem of who had given Clarissa the mushrooms, assuming she hadn't picked them herself, which looked unlikely. Nor did it tell them why she had been given them. The more Katya thought about it, the more she suspected it was a gift with sinister intentions. She might not be working for the police any more but she did still have connections. She had a plan, but she would need help from Lugs. There were some things she knew he wouldn't be able to do for her and she'd never ask him to do anything that would risk his career. But there were a few grey areas that, with a little bit of softening on her part, he might just be persuaded to do. There was one thing that might help with the softening. She'd call in at *Jasmine's* on her way to the police station.

~

'NOT HAVING BREAKFAST THIS MORNING?' Jasmine asked Katya, who was standing at the counter instead of sitting at her usual table.

Katya shook her head. 'I'm off to see Lugs. I'll take a bag of your best buns and two coffees.'

Jasmine picked up the tongs. 'Which ones do you fancy?'

Like Katya, Lugs had a sweet tooth. She pointed to a chocolate croissant and a raspberry Danish. 'Two of each,' she said. 'And two cappuccinos with a generous sprinkling of chocolate.'

Jasmine handed her the bag and two cardboard mugs with snap-on lids.

Katya placed them carefully into her bag alongside a list of names and car registration numbers. 'Ivo not in yet?'

'No,' said Jasmine. 'He was out late talking to Amelia Mayberry. He called me this morning to say he'd be in later to type up his notes.'

Ah yes, Ivo's planned visit to Boogies. She didn't see him fitting in there somehow, but with a friend who was a bouncer she supposed he'd be all right. Ivo's ability to find ways of talking to people was becoming quite impressive. 'How did he get on?'

'He said he'd learnt some interesting stuff about both Amelia and her brother. He'll email round the notes he made. He's probably worked out a new theory.'

'The trouble is,' said Katya, paying for her purchases, 'we can put together scenarios for any of these people in the way of opportunities and motives, but there's very little actual evidence.'

Jasmine nodded. 'It's really difficult to know if it was an accident or murder, or somewhere in between.'

'Clarissa died a day or so after she ate the mushrooms,' said Katya. 'There's no actual crime scene.'

'I hadn't thought of that,' said Jasmine. 'Did you ever work on cases like that? No crime scene, I mean.'

'I can't remember an actual case, but they must have happened.'

'You'd rely on witnesses, I suppose.'

'Katya nodded. That's right. We do need witnesses. A sighting of someone gathering mushrooms or someone encouraging Clarissa to eat them.'

'Would that make it more likely that it was a planned murder?'

'Probably, or someone who wanted her to feel ill for a day or two but had no intention of actually killing her. It's a puzzle because whoever did it must have stayed around long enough to make sure Clarissa and no one else ate the mushrooms and then cleared off so they'd not be suspected.'

'Do you think Lugs will be able to help?'

'Hope so. And I'd better get going before this coffee gets cold.'

IT WAS a short walk to the police station and Katya asked if the inspector was in his office. 'Up to his eyes in paperwork,' she was told.

So he would either be annoyed at being interrupted or pleased that he could take a break for some proper coffee and Karim's buns. She headed up the stairs and tapped on the door, opening it before Lugs had a chance to tell her to push off.

'Not too busy for coffee, I hope?' she asked, eyeing the pile of paperwork on his desk.

'It's like the flipping Forth Bridge,' said Lugs, removing his glasses and rubbing his eyes. 'I get to the bottom of one heap only to find another one building up right next to it. But I've always got time for you, Katya. Particularly when you're carrying a bag that just might contain pastries.'

'And coffee,' said Katya, sitting down. She handed him a coffee and pushed the bag of buns in his direction. 'I thought the paperwork was all online these days.'

'Most of it is. But we still get a lot of paper to deal with and it all needs to be logged online. I quite miss the days when I was out and about for much of the time.' He picked up the mug of cappuccino and prised off the lid. 'So what can I do for you? Still working on the death cap poisoning?'

'I am, and going nowhere fast.' She rummaged in her bag and found the piece of paper on which she'd written a list of cars. 'I'm hoping you can check if any of these were picked up by the ANPR camera on the road away from Little Frampton between late on Wednesday afternoon and early on Friday morning.'

Lugs took the list from her. 'You know I can't do that unless a crime's been committed.'

'I do know that, and you don't need to give me any details. But we know a man called Alan Biggs will be sending you details of people he saw speeding through the village. You'd have a reason for checking them out on the ANPR and you might just take a peek to see if they were there at other times. We know the owners of the cars already, so I'm only asking you to confirm they were there. You'd not be giving me any of their personal details. We've already questioned the relevant drivers and none of them admits to being there at those times. So if they were on camera we'd know they were lying and you might begin to suspect a crime had been committed.' Phew. It had taken a long time to work that out and memorise it. She just hoped it was persuasive enough. And it was almost true. They had questioned the people on the list, just not about the time they were driving on that stretch of the road.'

Lugs laughed, drained his coffee and finished his second pastry. 'Very devious of you and a very back-to-front way of going about it.'

'So will you do it?'

'I don't see that it can do any harm. Like you said, I won't be passing on any personal details. I'll get on to traffic and ask them to check.'

'Thanks, Lugs. You're a star.'

CHAPTER
TWENTY

Belinda Cardew was eating a piece of toast while reading emails on her laptop. Something Jonny disapproved of. When he and Belinda had breakfast together, it was usually a meal they took their time over and chatted to each other. Besides, toast crumbs were hell to get out of laptop keyboards without a very thin brush, and right now Jonny couldn't see one of those anywhere near Belinda. And then there was the issue of keys sticky from marmalade. The marmalade they were both eating this morning was a gift from Mrs Gage, who had made a huge batch back in January and was still doling it out to people she cleaned for when she was in a generous mood. She collected jars from the recycling bins of her clients and this particular batch was in a pickled gherkin jar, somewhat larger than a usual jam jar so both Jonny and Belinda were inclined to be lavish with it. Apart from which, it was delicious and there was probably plenty more where it had come from, so there was no need to hold back. But Jonny shuddered when he thought about Belinda's sticky fingers possibly jamming her keys. He dipped a tissue into a glass of water, and having squeezed it until it was merely damp and not wringing wet, he passed it to Belinda, who wiped her fingers and returned to her typing.

There was a ping from an incoming email and Belinda stopped typing and clicked it open. 'This is interesting,' she said, turning the laptop so Jonny could see it.

He put on his glasses and leant over to read it. 'Patsy Kline?' he said, wondering why the name sounded familiar.

'I'm trying to get some public speaking engagements. I've plenty of experience after all the speeches I made for the council. I thought I'd work up a repertoire. The breakfast clubs could be one topic.'

'Good idea. Is this Patsy Kline offering you an engagement?'

'No, she's an agent. Someone at the festival recommended her after our breakfast club presentation and I emailed her to find out what she could offer to someone like me.'

Of course, that's how he knew the name. Patsy Kline had been Clarissa Mayberry's agent. A horrifying but fleeting thought passed through his mind about Clarissa's steamy novel. But he doubted Patsy Kline dealt with that kind of stuff. He'd no idea what kind of an agent did. More likely Clarissa dealt with the publisher direct. Or perhaps it was a site where anyone could upload whatever they wanted to. He pushed the thought away and paid attention to what Belinda was telling him.

'She'd be interested in representing me,' she said, reading Jonny the salient parts of the email. 'She sent a link so that I can look at the kind of speakers she works with. I think I'd fit in quite well. They're not all rabid right-wingers like Clarissa. In fact, very few of them are. There are several people who spoke at the festival.'

Jonny read through the list and recognised some of the names. It looked like Belinda would be in good company. There were one or two retired politicians and Jonny always felt politicians sounded more sensible once they'd retired. There were people who'd travelled a lot and a couple of conservationists. No detectives, he noted. Not that he'd want to talk in public about that. Or anything else. He'd shied away from any kind of public speaking since his son, Marcus, had begun working for him and was happy to take over anything that meant addressing rooms full of people. Marcus had obviously inherited his mother's talents in that area rather than Jonny's more introverted way of doing business.

Belinda closed the website and returned to the email. 'She's going to be in the area and has asked me to join her for lunch later today.'

'That's short notice, isn't it?' But if she was in the area already it would make sense. No need for Belinda to travel into London when she could have a nice, relaxed lunch fifteen minutes from home.

'Short notice is quite flattering,' said Belinda. 'It means she's in a hurry to offer her services before anyone else snaps me up.'

'I suppose so.' She could have a point. He just hoped Belinda wouldn't rush into anything. There was probably plenty of competition and she should shop around before committing herself. 'Where does she want to meet you?'

'She wants me to recommend somewhere. I was thinking of *Jasmine's*. She's coming by train and it's only a short walk from the station.'

'Good idea. It's also where the breakfast club got started. She'll be able to look at the plaque on the wall and the photos of you opening it.'

'I'd forgotten Jasmine had put those up.'

They were good photos that Karim had taken – Belinda in her council days looking stunning a fuchsia pink suit, unveiling the plaque that announced the new breakfast club. 'I'm going there this morning. I'll make sure she reserves a table for you.'

'Why don't you join us?'

'I'd like that. As long as she doesn't try to sign me up for any public speaking events.'

'If she does, you'll just have to recommend Marcus instead. I won't let her browbeat you into anything.'

Belinda had paperwork to finish and would probably want to change out of her slouching-around breakfast gear into something more glamorous. Jonny decided to walk into town and spend some time in the detective office, finding out all he could about Patsy Kline and whether she was a reliable person to do business with. He'd be inclined not to trust someone who represented the likes of Clarissa Mayberry, but he shouldn't judge Patsy Kline on the strength of one unpleasant client. And meeting her might give him an insight into her dealings with Clarissa. Wasn't she on Katya's list of suspects?

Arriving at *Jasmine's,* he arranged for a reserved table in a quiet corner and made his way up to the office, where he logged into the computer and searched for Patsy Kline. He didn't learn a lot, but his searches confirmed that she was a well-respected literary and public speaking agent. The two were often linked. The authors she represented were mostly social and political commentators, and more often than not, the authors were also speakers. She didn't work for fiction authors of any kind, so it was quite possible she knew nothing of Clarissa's sideline in pornography. Her photograph suggested she was highly respectable – a thin, not to say gaunt, woman with severely bobbed hair, wearing a black business suit and large Iris Apfel-style spectacles. It was hard to imagine her in off-duty mode. Jonny checked some social media sites but didn't find anything about her personal life. Either she was wedded to her work, or she kept her home life strictly offline. He wasn't going to find anything more about her so he logged off, called Katya and explained that Patsy was having a lunch meeting with Belinda, but that he'd be there as well and could she suggest how he might find out more about Patsy's dealings with Clarissa Mayberry. 'Just sit and listen,' was Katya's advice. 'Remember what she says, but don't lead her.' He could manage that. As long as she didn't mention mushrooms.

BELINDA MET Patsy at the station and sent Jonny a text to say they were on their way. She'd managed to persuade Patsy that a taxi to *Jasmine's* would not be necessary as it was only a hundred yards or so from the station. Jonny watched as they arrived, wondering how

Patsy had managed the walk down the stone stairs and cobbled lanes at the back of the station on perilously high heels. Perhaps it would be sensible to get her a taxi back. It would be a lot further by road but would avoid the steep steps and uphill cobbled lane.

They sat down at the table Jasmine had reserved for them. Patsy draped her hooded raincoat over the back of her chair and studied the menu. She didn't look like an eater of breakfasts, but Jonny supposed she didn't need to be. As long as the speakers she represented gave value for money and were popular with the punters, what they were speaking about wouldn't be of too much interest to her. Nevertheless, he introduced Jasmine as the co-founder of the breakfast club and together they showed her the menu, explained how the club worked and what membership involved.

'But it is your wife who is the speaker?' Patsy confirmed, smiling at Belinda, who had changed into a sky-blue trouser suit. Flat shoes, Jonny noticed.

'That's right,' he said. 'Belinda is a far better speaker than I am, and I doubt Jasmine has the time. But Belinda will be running her own club soon, so she knows as much as Jasmine and I do.'

'The festival committee were certainly pleased with her presentation,' said Patsy.

Jonny passed her a lunch menu. 'It's all home cooked using fresh ingredients,' he assured her.

Patsy ordered a green salad. 'But no dressing,' she insisted. 'And a bottle of sparking mineral water.'

Jonny wondered if she would be offended by his roast beef sandwich and Belinda's tuna salad, but she seemed not to notice.

'I gather you were a double act at the festival,' she said. 'Do you want me to represent both of you?'

'Jonny ran a slide show,' said Belinda. 'We haven't actually discussed whether or not he would want to go on doing that.'

'Illustrated talks are always well received, but we could offer both according to the facilities at the venue. Did the equipment you used belong to you or the festival organiser?'

'The festival provided it,' said Jonny. 'They'd already hired it for the speaker who cancelled. I'm not sure Belinda would want me muscling in on her presentations.'

'We can discuss it,' said Belinda.

Patsy made some notes on an iPad. 'I'll draft some publicity and you can let me know what you decide.'

They talked about fees and travel arrangements, whether Belinda would be prepared to stay overnight. And then the conversation flagged. Jonny watched Patsy pick at some lettuce leaves and decided it might be time, in spite of Katya's warning, to introduce the topic of Clarissa Mayberry.

'Ah, yes,' she said, when Jonny told her he had been at her festival talk, was in fact there when she collapsed. 'Poor Clarissa.'

She didn't sound too bereft about the loss of Clarissa as a client. 'You'll miss her, I expect,' he said.

'Not really.' Patsy stared malevolently at a slice of tomato and prodded it with her fork. Jonny imagined she might be seeing Clarissa's face in it.

'You weren't friends?' Belinda asked.

'To tell you the truth, I was about to fire her as a client.'

'I thought she was a popular speaker,' said Jonny. 'And you see her books everywhere.'

'She had a following, certainly, but she broke her contract with me. I had no alternative but to consider terminating it.'

'Why?' asked Belinda. 'I'll have to be careful not to do the same.'

Patsy patted her arm. 'You should ask your lawyer to check the contract. But I'm sure you won't have a problem. It was the section that gave me rights to publish all Clarissa's work for a specified period after she'd submitted it to me. There were certain books that I refused to put forward to publishers. We had a row about it and Clarissa took them to another publisher using a pen name. Her contract still had six months to run.' Patsy appeared to have had enough of her salad. She put her fork to one side and took a sip of her water. 'I'm sure nothing like that will happen to you,' she said, smiling at Belinda. 'I don't believe you publish any books, do you?'

'No,' said Belinda, who looked as if she was trying to stifle a giggle, Jonny having described Clarice Mayflower's Miss Tress books in some detail to her after he researched it online.

'Dreadful stuff,' said Patsy, dabbing at her mouth with a napkin. 'Badly written tosh. I couldn't possibly have my name connected with that kind of thing.'

'And yet you were with Clarissa at the festival on the day she died.'

'We agreed to meet there. I wanted to settle things amicably. Clarissa was threatening to sue me. Not that she had a leg to stand on. My lawyer knows how to draw up a watertight agreement. She suggested shortening the contract, cancelling upcoming engagements and paying me compensation for missed engagements.'

'But then she died. How does that leave you now?'

'There's a death clause, which claims a sum on her estate should she die before the term of the contract is complete. She hadn't formally withdrawn from it, and I hadn't given her official notice, so the contract still stands.'

'Is it a large claim?' Belinda asked the question Jonny didn't like to.

'It covers loss of my commission, cancellation fees and a percentage to compensate me for the loss of future work.'

It could be a tidy amount. Jonny wondered what Patsy's average earnings were per client and decided this death payment would probably be a somewhat larger sum. Most people probably didn't expect to die mid-contract and so were happy to sign away whatever Patsy asked for. If Belinda went ahead and signed up with Patsy – something he was about to advise her strongly against – he would take a good look at that part of the agreement. Was it enough, he wondered, to give Patsy a motive for murder? It could be, depending on the current size of her client list and the amount of work she was getting for them. But did the timing work? She'd need to have fed

Clarissa the mushrooms the day before the festival talk, so she would have to have visited Clarissa early on the Thursday morning. Magda had not mentioned seeing her, so it would have been very early. 'When was the last time you saw Clarissa before that?' he asked.

'Several weeks ago,' she said, rather to Jonny's disappointment. She could, of course, be lying. Or she might have arranged to have a basket of mushrooms delivered to Clarissa, by an employee perhaps, or more likely someone who hated Clarissa as much as she did. But an accessory of any kind was dangerous. As soon as it was known that Clarissa had died, they would have spoken up and given the game away. There was no guarantee that Clarissa would be the one to eat the mushrooms, of course, unless whoever delivered them stood over her and watched, and that would have been risky. But if Patsy was lying and had visited the house, her car would have shown up in Alan's video. It may have done, but Jonny didn't know what kind of car Patsy drove.

Belinda was looking at her watch. She had an appointment that afternoon and Jonny, too, had things to do. He settled the bill and offered to walk Patsy to her car.

'Patsy came by train,' said Belinda. 'I told you that, didn't I?'

Yes, of course she had. He'd not forgotten, but he needed a reason to talk to Patsy about cars and her possible ownership of one. 'I'll walk with you to the station,' he said.

'That's very kind,' said Patsy. 'I wonder if I could ask you to carry my briefcase for me. These cobbled streets make it hard for me to walk in heels.'

'Of course,' said Jonny, failing to point out it was only a few yards of road that were cobbled. But then there were the steps. He'd probably need to carry her briefcase up them as well. 'I imagine you usually drive to appointments.'

Patsy agreed that she did.

'What kind of car do you have?' he asked, hoping that she'd accept this as a typically blokey way of keeping up the conversation, rather than a means to identify her as a possible murder suspect.

'It's an Audi Q5. Luckily, it's exempt from ULEZ charges.'

Jonny watched as she went through the barrier to catch her train and then decided to sit in one of the station's many coffee bars and write a few notes. The matter of the contract and its death clause was very interesting, and if her car had been seen in Little Frampton early on Thursday morning, Patsy Kline would definitely be a suspect.

CHAPTER
TWENTY-ONE

Ivo woke up to the sound of rain beating against his windows. Autumn was on the way, but he was ready for it. The last two weeks had been unseasonably warm and dry, and he'd been able to tidy up the site, check the drains and make sure all was ready for a change in the weather. Plus a visit to a nightclub, which was a new experience for him. An exhausting one. He couldn't see the point of drinking too much in a dark room with too many people, too much loud music and nowhere to sit down. Was he beginning to sound like a grumpy old man? At twenty-two? Well, he didn't care. He knew who his friends were, and parties had never been his thing. Harold hated the rain, so he wouldn't take him out until later when hopefully the rain had stopped, and they could go for a nice long walk. It was also payday, so he would do a supermarket shop and then tidy the flower beds outside his cabin.

While it was still raining, he made himself a cup of tea and opened his email. There was nothing from Katya, who was trying to track down anyone who'd driven into Little Frampton the day before Clarissa Mayberry had died. The last thing she said was that she was going to talk to Lugs about cars that had been picked up on the ANPR near to the Mayberry home. If it was just finding out which cars had been spotted, Ivo didn't see how it would help them very much. He didn't think Lugs would tell them who owned the cars. But Katya had her methods and Ivo would be the last person to argue with them. Ivo had methods as well, and his own meeting with Amelia Mayberry had been interesting. She'd not been at all what he'd expected and was clearly a very different character from her brother. Ivo had been shocked by some of the things she'd admitted. At the same time, he couldn't help admiring her spirit. He noted down everything she had said and emailed it to Katya. If anyone had set out to kill Clarissa Mayberry, her daughter must be high on the list of suspects. According to Katya's three conditions, Amelia had a motive – her mother putting a stop to her holiday opportunity – she was in the house with her mother most of the time, and the means. Amelia was highly intelligent, could have researched poisonous mushrooms, and even lived close to where they were likely to grow. As far as Amelia was concerned, it would be much easier to take a stroll in the woods and pick some mushrooms than to go online and buy regular poison in a bottle. He wasn't sure if it was even possible to buy poison online but would be surprised if it wasn't. And Amelia was probably capable of finding her way around the dark web, which could supply pretty much anything an evil killer might want. But why bother, when poison was growing free just beyond her garden fence? Ivo typed all of this and sent the email off to Katya. He doubted that Katya would agree with him. She rarely did. She'd tell him it was all too far-fetched. But on this occasion, just maybe, he hoped she'd see things differently.

Having sent his email, Ivo looked out of the window. The rain had stopped, and weak sun was starting to break through the clouds. 'Time for a walk,' he said to Harold, who was snoring loudly in his basket. Ivo prodded him awake and reached for his lead. He'd pulled on his wellies and they were about to leave the cabin when his phone rang with a number he didn't recognise. He picked it up and answered it. The caller identified himself as Thomas Johnson and he said that his neighbour had found one of Ivo's leaflets on a bus when returning from her book club at the library. Thomas Johnson had rain seeping in through a badly fitting door frame and the neighbour had suggested giving Ivo a call. It was an old cottage, he explained, he lived on his own and he'd had a bad back recently and hadn't been able to fix things the way he used to. Ivo thought Mr Johnson sounded like an elderly gentleman and this was something that needed seeing to right away. He wrote down the address, which sounded familiar, tapped it into his maps app and told Mr Johnson that he could be there within the hour. Harold looked at him sadly when he picked up the keys to the van and Ivo promised they'd go for a walk as soon as the door was fixed. He loaded his toolbox and Harold, with a towel because the ground would still be wet from the rain when they went for their walk, into the van. Then he returned to the cabin and flicked through some notes he'd made at the last detective meeting. Little Frampton. He knew the address had sounded familiar. It meant Thomas Johnson lived in the same village as the Mayberrys. That was great. Fix a door and do a bit of detective work at the same time. Katya would be proud of him. With any luck, Thomas would be a chatty type. He lived on his own, so he'd probably be full of gossip about the village and its residents, whose every movement he watched from his window. And when he'd finished the job, Ivo could take Harold for a walk in the woods and do a bit of mushroom hunting of his own. He wasn't sure how finding the mushrooms would help the case, but it wouldn't do any harm and would give him an idea about how many people were out there foraging and how far it was from Limetree Cottage where the Mayberrys lived.

As he drove into the village, Ivo got the impression that it was a rather upmarket place, with big houses separated from each other by high walls and long drives. He noted the drive to Limetree Cottage as he passed. But as he drove through the main part of the village and into the lanes on the far side, the houses were more modest. Thomas Jones lived in a house at the end of a row of three cottages. These were what Ivo had always imagined cottages to be, two-up-two-down houses with tiny, flower-filled gardens and no garages. Limetree Cottage was poorly named, he thought. It had at least five bedrooms, a sweeping drive and double garage. It should have been called Limetree House. Although in a village like this, with so many well-off commuters, and quite a lot of lime trees, it was possible that there was an even bigger place already called Limetree House.

Ivo pulled up in front of Thomas Johnson's house and lifted out his tools. Dogs were not always welcome in people's houses, and it was a cool day, so he left the van windows open and Harold sitting on the front seat, watching Ivo soulfully as he knocked on Thomas's door. It was opened by an elderly man who walked with a stick. He glanced down the path at Ivo's van, where Harold was gazing out from the passenger seat window. 'You can bring him in,' he said. 'I like having a dog about the place. I've always had one of my own, but when the last fella passed away, well, it didn't seem fair to get another. Not at my age.'

That was sad. Ivo was never lonely when he had Harold for company, and he was still young enough to get out and about. There was no sign of a car outside and he didn't imagine there was a great social life in the village. Thomas Johnson probably didn't get out much and must be lonely. Ivo had passed a church but there was no school or a village shop. He wondered if there was still a pub.

Thomas showed him the warped door. There was nothing much wrong with it. Or nothing a sheet of sandpaper and a plane couldn't fix. Ivo sanded it down and fitted a new draught-excluding side panel that meant it closed snugly and would help to keep the house warm. 'That should be fine now,' he said. 'But call me if you have any trouble with it. Is there anything else I can do while I'm here?'

'You could stop and have a cup of tea. Gets a bit lonely when my neighbour's away.'

Ivo could understand that. It was why so many people liked *Shady Willows*. There was always someone to talk to. And of course, many of them, like Thomas, had been dog owners who now enjoyed

Harold's company. 'Love to,' he said, sitting down on a threadbare sofa and telling Harold to sit on the floor next to him. 'Will your neighbour be away for long?'

'Just to the end of the week. Gone to visit her sister in Stroud. But she left me some lovely fruit bread. Can I toast you a slice?'

That suited Ivo very well. He would enjoy a slice of fruit bread and a gossip. And Harold might be able to pick up a few crumbs.

Thomas made the tea and toasted a couple of slices of the bread, which he spread generously with butter. He put a blue and white striped plate down in front of Ivo as he sat himself down in front of an electric imitation log fire. Harold looked up hopefully and Ivo broke off a crust and fed it to him. 'Have you lived in the village for long?' he asked.

Thomas chuckled. 'Born and bred here. Mind you, it's changed a fair bit. The school and shop closed and most of the houses were bought up by commuters. All done up and extended, extra bathrooms and the like. Used to be a community, now people don't talk to each other no more. Even the church has to share a vicar with two other villages. We only get services every third week. The church hall was turned into another posh house. Our little row of cottages is all that's left of the old village. I reckon once we're gone, they'll knock the three of them together and sell them as one big house. We've already had offers. I turned them down flat.'

'What do your neighbours think? Would they sell up?'

'Not if they can help it. These cottages used to be homes for farm labourers, then the council bought them, and we were all given the option to buy from them at a knock-down price. Back in the eighties, that was. Good for us as was living here, but not so good for the young ones growing up in the village. They've all moved into town now.'

'Do you know many of the other people in the village?'

'Them in the posh houses? Yeah, I did odd bits of gardening for some of them before my back problem.' He rubbed his back and shuffled uneasily in his chair.

'Did you work for the people at Limetree Cottage?' It would be interesting to get a villager's perspective on the Mayberrys.

'Raked up leaves there once, but only when they first moved in. But it ain't a cottage no more. They built on a bloody great extension, didn't they? And then they got in some contract garden people. Had it *landscaped,* would you believe? What's wrong with good old-fashioned gardening? I can remember when a proper old village family lived there. Grew vegetables, they did, and kept chickens.' He sipped his tea noisily. 'Used to have a few hens myself, but they got eaten by a fox one night. Didn't bother with them after that. Mrs Thomas two doors down gets me eggs from the farm shop over at Wittingham now.'

'Have you met the Mayberrys?'

'Who?'

'The family that live in Limetree Cottage.'

'Oh, them. I've seen the kids hanging round the village. Spoiled brats, I reckon. Quite a few of those in these parts. Always smoking and having noisy parties.'

'There were parties at Limetree Cottage?' Would Clarissa really have put up with teenage raves?

'I don't think so, now I come to think of it. Plenty of other families with teenagers, though. But I can't really complain. They're mostly away at boarding schools so parties are just weekends and holidays.'

'Did you ever meet Mrs Mayberry?'

'The lady what died? Yes, she came round here once, collecting for some charity. Didn't give her anything. Charity begins at home, that's what I think. Not some earthquake-ridden hellhole on the other side of the world.'

So Clarissa had been a supporter of a charity. That surprised Ivo. From what he'd learnt about Clarissa Mayberry, she'd been more of a pull yourself up by your bootstraps type. She'd have people out of their houses clearing up molten lava with a dustpan and brush. But perhaps giving to foreign disasters was different. She probably thought it could stop them from coming over here. And supporting charity would look good on her publicity leaflets. As long as it didn't suggest handouts to shirkers.

'Stupid woman,' Thomas continued. 'Poisoned herself with mushrooms. That's what happens when you let townies in. Us country folk would know the difference between a field mushroom and a death cap just by looking at it. Those town types just want something for nothing. Foraging, they call it. Theft's a better name. It's not like they can't afford to buy food. They don't even need to go to the shops. There's a van delivers boxes of veg once a week.'

'Do you get veg delivered?'

'No, not me. Have you seen how much those people charge? No, my neighbour drives me to Tesco on a Thursday afternoon. I can get all I need there. Seen the van, though. It's got some stupid name.' The old man scratched his head and thought for a moment. 'Got it,' he said suddenly. '*Threebies*. It's painted on the side of the van. Winnie next door had to explain it for me. It stands for *Beans, Bags and Boxes*. I suppose they couldn't get all of that on the side of a van. It's a shop in Windsor, apparently, where you go to fill up your own containers with food. Sounds a bit of a palaver to me. Costs an arm and a leg as well. Daft, isn't it? Pay twice as much for your food and don't even get it properly packaged.' He laughed and poured Ivo a second cup of tea.

Ivo drained his cup and packed up his tools.

'You off now?' Thomas asked.

'I'll be back as soon as you have more work for me,' Ivo promised. 'I thought I'd take Harold for a bit of a walk while I'm out this way. We usually walk along the river, but it would be nice to see the woods. Can you recommend somewhere?'

'I'll tell you where I used to take Nipper – that's my last dog. You can leave your van here. Walk back down to the village and take the footpath that runs between Limetree Cottage and Limetree House. That will take you onto a nice path into the woods.' He stood up and showed Ivo to the door. 'Don't be picking the mushrooms, though,' he added with a cackle.

Ivo put Harold on the lead and walked back to the village. Thomas obviously had him down as one of the townies. Probably rightly. Ivo doubted he'd know the difference between a mushroom and a death cap.

Once they reached the path into the woods, he let Harold off the lead and pulled out his phone, tapping into the notes Jasmine had sent him about her visit to Murray Dickinson's shop. Feeling pleased with himself, he closed the notes and put the phone back in his pocket. His memory had not let him down. Murray Dickinson, assuming he drove the van himself, delivered boxes to the village. It wouldn't be too hard to find out if he delivered on Thursdays. And if he did, he'd just shot to the top of the list of suspects.

CHAPTER
TWENTY-TWO

Jasmine was surprised to see Magda as she was about to close the café. 'You're just in time. What can I get you?' They still had some of her dad's blackcurrant pastries and she remembered how much Magda had enjoyed them when she was there before. 'One of those?' she asked, pointing to the plate on the counter.

'Thank you, and a black coffee.'

'Choose a table,' said Jasmine, indicating the empty room. 'I'll bring it over.'

'I'm sorry. I didn't know if you'd still be open. I need to tell you something.'

'It's fine,' said Jasmine, turning the sign on the door to *Closed*. 'It's time to close and there's no one else in here. I usually sit down with a cup of tea before I start clearing up.' She made herself a cup of mint tea and carried it to the table Magda had chosen on a tray with Magda's coffee and the pastry on a plate. She sat down next to her and pushed the sugar in her direction. 'What is it you want to tell me?'

Magda tipped in two sachets of sugar and stirred the cup

thoughtfully. 'It's just, well, I remembered something. It may be nothing, but you asked me about people coming and going from the house where I worked for Mrs Mayberry.'

'You saw someone visit the house?' That could be interesting, but why hadn't she mentioned it last time they spoke? She'd been very specific about everything else. She'd hardly be likely to have forgotten a visitor. Unless it was just someone dropping off a parcel or stuffing a flyer through the letterbox. Jasmine herself would probably not have thought twice about one of those. Not if she was trying to account for everyone who'd visited the café on a particular day.

Magda shook her head. 'Not at the house. It was on the path that goes to the woods.'

'The one between Limetree Cottage and the big house next door?'

'Limetree House, that's right. People get them muddled and Mrs Mayberry got annoyed when things were delivered to the wrong address. With two similar names like those, it happened a lot.'

'Is that what you wanted to tell me about? Something delivered to the wrong house?'

'No. Not exactly.' She picked up a napkin and took a pen out of her bag. 'I don't know if you have been there, but the two houses are like this.' She drew two squares and pointed at one of them. 'This one is Limetree Cottage. The driveway turns into it from the edge of the path like this.' She drew a line that curved from between the two squares. 'For Limetree House, the turning is further down the road, but people get confused. When you see the sign for the cottage it looks as if it's a turning off another driveway, but it's actually the footpath into the woods, which goes straight between the two houses.' She drew another line for the path to show how it forked away from the driveway to Limetree Cottage. 'The first time I went there I made a mistake and missed the driveway. I drove up the path, but it narrows where it passes the end of the Mayberrys' property. There is a back gate to the garden at that point.'

All very interesting, Jasmine thought. But apart from telling her

Limetree Cottage had a back gate, she couldn't see that it was useful information. 'And you saw someone there? I suppose that's not unusual if it's a public footpath.'

'It's not unusual. I have often seen people going for walks there. Sometimes they have dogs. But this was different. It was the last day I worked at the house. I was about to turn in off the road to but there was an Amazon van in the drive, and I didn't have room to turn in and park like I usually did. I had to wait in the road for the man to deliver the package and leave. And from where I had stopped, I had a good view of the path. I was worried that I would be late for work. I could have left the car there and walked up the driveway, but it was raining so I stayed where I was. Mrs Bossy Mayberry would just have to wait for a bit. She'd probably complain about me to my employer, but I was getting fed up with her moaning about me. My manager was quite sympathetic and was arranging somewhere else for me to work, so I'd be moved soon anyway. I didn't care what she thought of me any more.'

'Okay,' said Jasmine. Where was this going? An Amazon delivery was hardly unusual, and surely even a difficult employer like Clarissa Mayberry would understand a few minutes' delay caused by a delivery van blocking the drive.

'While I was waiting, I saw someone, a woman I think, walking down the path towards the road. I didn't take much notice of her. It's a public path to the woods so not that unusual, but it was a wet day and people don't usually go for a walk in the rain unless they have to walk a dog. But this person didn't have a dog – she was on her own. There's a gate into the Mayberrys' garden and she opened it and went in, slamming it shut behind her.

'Did you see her come out again?'

'No. The Amazon van left so I was able to drive in. But there was no one like that in the house, so she must have left again almost at once.'

'And you didn't recognise her?'

'I couldn't see that well. It was a wet morning and my windows had steamed up. Anyway, she was wearing a long coat with a hood.'

'Could it have been Mrs Mayberry or Amelia?'

'I don't think so. This woman was tall and Amelia is average height like her mother.'

'You're sure it was a woman? It couldn't have been Tristan?'

She shook her head. 'He was still in his room asleep when I arrived at the house. I heard him moving around a bit later when I went to clean the bathrooms.'

He could have gone out and then slipped in again through the gate before Magda was in the house, she supposed. But going for an early morning walk in the rain didn't fit the image she had of Tristan. It didn't fit the description Ivo had given her, that had suggested he was a lazy layabout. 'Did you notice anything about her build or the way she walked?'

Magda shook her head. 'I could tell she was in a hurry. And even with a raincoat on she looked quite slim. Oh, I do remember she was wearing wellingtons, but most people do when they walk in the woods on a wet day.'

That was quite helpful. It probably meant that the walk had been planned. Jasmine was trying to remember what the weather had been like that day. Jonny had told her that the weather had been good for most of the festival, unseasonably hot in fact. But it had rained one night and on into the next morning. Something was ticking over in her brain. Something she had read recently about mushrooms. That in autumn they can spring up overnight after a heavy shower. So if one was planning to go mushroom foraging, last Thursday morning – a wet night after a dry spell – would have been an ideal time. 'Was she carrying anything?'

'I think she had a camera.'

'She was taking photographs?'

'No, just carrying it from a strap over her shoulder.'

'In a shoulder bag?'

'I don't know. It just looked like a small black box on a strap.'

That was unusual. Didn't most people take photos on their phones these days? Would they take them at all in the rain?

Magda finished her coffee and scraped up the remaining crumbs of her pastry. She stood up to leave. 'I hope I haven't wasted your time. It's probably nothing.'

'Not at all. I think it could be very useful.'

'I didn't like Mrs Mayberry, but I'm sorry she died the way she did. Do you think the person I saw might have had something to do with her death? Do you think they killed her?'

Jasmine thought it was possible, but wasn't prepared to tell anyone other than the rest of the team. At this stage, it was an uncorroborated piece of information. 'I don't think we should jump to conclusions. No one has suggested that it was anything more than an accident. We just want to know how Mrs Mayberry came to eat the mushrooms, to try to avoid it happening to someone else.' And yet the more they found out about Clarissa Mayberry, the more people they discovered who might actually want her dead. But now was not the time to share that with Magda. The last thing they wanted was to encourage gossip among the Windsor Mops. And if Jonny's Mrs Gage was anything to go by, gossip was the lifeblood of the Mops. 'Are you still working for Windsor Mops?' she asked.

'Yes, but now they have sent me to a different place to clean. They are good employers and keep their promises to the staff.'

'Do you like the new place better?'

'Much better. It's a family with a nice modern house and well-behaved children. I'm there three days a week. The children are at school and the parents both work, so I have the house to myself. I can clean properly when a house is empty. The other two days I go to an old lady who lives in one of the Guards View flats. They are for retired people. The lady I clean for doesn't go out, but she is very nice and we have time for a chat.'

. . .

Jasmine saw Magda out and returned to her kitchen cleaning from what she felt had been a very productive discussion. She was fairly sure they could now pinpoint the time the mushrooms arrived in Clarissa's kitchen. She wished the Amazon driver had delayed things for a little longer, when Magda might also have seen where the woman went when she came out of the garden. If, as she suspected, the small box contained death cap mushrooms, what had the woman done with them? She doubted that however hungry Clarissa may have been, she wouldn't just gobble down a box of mushrooms someone had left in the kitchen in a box. They must have been added to something that was already prepared and that Clarissa planned to eat. A garnish, perhaps. Raw mushrooms were tasty sprinkled on a salad or stirred into a bowl of soup. And if that was the case, this must have been done by someone who knew what Clarissa's eating plans were for that day. That pointed the finger firmly at one of the family, didn't it?

Was what Magda had told her evidence of foul play? If they had found real evidence, they would have to hand it over to the police. Was seeing someone acting suspiciously enough to report to the police? A woman walking in the woods in the rain, using the back gate into the Mayberry garden carrying a small box. Jasmine wasn't sure. She'd write it all down and share it with the team.

CHAPTER
TWENTY-THREE

A waiter, clad in black trousers, white shirt and a William Morris patterned waistcoat, covered the neck of the champagne bottle with a white damask table napkin and gently eased out the cork. 'Congratulations, madam, sir,' he said, pouring them each a glass and handing them menus printed on gold-edged card. 'Are you ready to order?'

'Give us a moment, would you?' said Jonny, reaching for the dish of upmarket nibbles that was sitting in front of them.

The waiter nodded and left them.

'Don't eat all the cashews,' said Belinda, helping herself to an olive. 'Or you won't have any room left for the meal and that would be a great pity at a place like this.'

Jonny leant back in his chair and grinned at Belinda. 'Is it really forty years?'

'Hard to believe, I know.'

Things were very different forty years ago. Jonny working for his father, the boom and bust of the nineties yet to take off, Maggie Thatcher still in power and Belinda pregnant. They'd gone for a low-key wedding. 'My mother said we wouldn't last five years.'

'You've stayed with me just to prove your mother wrong?'

Jonny winked at her. 'There were other attractions.'

'Thank God for that.' Belinda spread out her fingers and studied the rings she was wearing. Wedding and engagement rings and now a new one, an eternity ring, a gift from Jonny that morning. 'You're an old romantic, aren't you?'

'Best forty years of my life. I felt I should mark the occasion. It was either the ring or a puppy. Either way, the financial outlay was about the same, but puppies last fifteen or sixteen years and eternity rings last for... well, eternity. And rings are low maintenance and have fewer running expenses.'

'You've just given me an idea for your next Christmas present. I should have worked that out sooner with the massive hints you and Mrs Gage have been dropping recently.' She picked up the menu and read it. 'But more immediately, what are we going to eat?'

Jonny took a sip of champagne and studied his menu. 'Normally I would have gone for the garlic mushrooms in creamy white wine sauce as a starter, but I'm a bit off them right now.'

Belinda laughed. 'I'm afraid Clarissa Mayberry's demise won't have done a lot for the mushroom market. Any progress on whether it was an accident or not?'

'No real evidence that it wasn't an accident, but we're discovering several people who might have wanted her dead.'

'Intriguing. It's usually family members who come under suspicion first, isn't it?'

'They're not in the clear. Not the son and daughter, anyway.'

'What about the husband?'

'He was away for a few days when it happened, so we don't see how it could have been him.'

'Does his alibi check out?'

'That would be something for Katya to ask Lugs to do, but we don't have enough evidence against him yet.'

'Any other family?'

'None that we've come across, so no obvious suspects. There's a close family friend, but we've not found any suggestion that he wanted to do away with Clarissa. We know she didn't get on with Patsy Kline either, and Murray Dickinson's not exactly in the clear. But never mind them. We're here to celebrate forty years of a marriage that I've loved every minute of. What do you think of this place?' The Morris had been recommended by a colleague after it opened over a year ago. Jonny had been too busy to trying to be a detective to come here sooner but a fortieth anniversary was quite a landmark.

'It's very nice,' said Belinda, looking around at the flowery wallpaper, matching chair covers and curtains. 'They might have overdone the William Morris theme a bit, though.'

She was probably right. Every surface was covered with lilies, birds, peacock feathers and swirling designs in muted greens and reds. What he did like, though, was the layout of the dining room, which was roomy and had comfortable chairs. Tables were artfully arranged in a series of alcoves. He returned to the menu and decided on salmon with dill and crème fraîche followed by spatchcocked poussin with fermented chilli bean butter. Belinda had yet to make a decision, so Jonny left her to re-read the menu and passed the time by peering over the top of an art deco screen, decorated with a design of ferns and poppy seedheads, at his fellow diners. A couple in an alcove on the far side of the room had finished their meal and were standing up ready to leave. He watched as they headed towards the entrance, where one of the waiting staff had waylaid them. 'Belinda,' he hissed. 'You see that couple over there by the service desk?'

Belinda lowered her menu and stared across the room. 'The well-dressed middle-aged couple? What about them?'

'The man is Anthony Mayberry. I don't know who the woman is. She looks a bit familiar, but I can't quite place her.'

'I don't think I know her. Could you have seen her at the festival? We didn't go to a lot of the same events so it's possible you saw her there and I didn't.'

'Maybe, but she wasn't one of the speakers. I would have remembered her if she was.' He was sure he had seen her recently, but thinking back over the last week or two he couldn't think where that might have been. Can you take a photo on your phone without them noticing? You've got a better view than I have.'

Belinda put her menu down, angled her phone towards a tall, cut-glass vase containing a single white lily that was perched on the side of the reception desk, and took a picture. Then she moved slightly to her right and took another one, this time framing the couple at the service desk. She was just in time. The man signed something and the two of them left.

She passed the phone to Jonny. 'Excellent,' he said. 'A nice clear shot of both of them.'

He handed the phone back to Belinda, who put it away in her bag. 'No more phones tonight. We're here to celebrate,' she said. 'Not spy on people. But...'

'Noticed something?' She was a far better people-watcher than he was.

'No coats,' she said. 'And it's quite chilly this evening.'

'Perhaps they parked close by.' But Belinda was right; the woman was wearing a flimsy dress – pretty, but not designed to keep her warm.

'And,' Belinda continued, 'it didn't look as if they were paying for their meal. No bank cards or phone apps. Just a signature on a slip of paper.'

'So?'

'I think they must be staying in the hotel, not just dropping in for a meal.'

That was a good point. Jonny had forgotten that this was also a hotel. It was better known as a restaurant, but there were maybe eight bedrooms. Perhaps he should have booked one of them for Belinda and himself. Would that have made it more of a celebration? 'Would you have liked to stay here? I'm sure they can find us a room if we ask nicely.'

Belinda shook her head. 'That's not what I was getting at. Going out for a meal was a lovely idea and quite enough of a celebration. We can save overnight jaunts for our fiftieth. Anyway, I haven't brought my toothbrush.' She picked up the last olive, popped it into her mouth and chewed thoughtfully. 'Doesn't it strike you as odd that less than two weeks since his wife died, Anthony Mayberry is having a flirty meal and an overnight stay in a posh hotel with another woman? A very pretty one.'

'It could be a business meeting.' Financial advice people were probably regular winers and diners of clients.

'To be continued in the bedroom?'

'They might have a room each. They might be planning to finish their meeting over breakfast.'

'No, you only have to notice the body language to tell they are not business colleagues.'

Jonny wasn't good at body language. He'd have to take Belinda's word for that, but there was something else. 'They're only a few miles from where Anthony lives, so why stay in a hotel at all?'

'A house with a couple of teenagers isn't exactly conducive to a steamy romantic night with a lady friend. Particularly one who wasn't their mother.'

'I suppose there's no reason why a widower shouldn't find himself a new lady friend.'

'None at all, but after less than two weeks? If you ask me, this has been going on for a while.'

'Body language again?'

'Yes, it's obvious this isn't a first date.'

How did she know that? If he was going to be the kind of detective that spied on people having steamy affairs, he'd need to learn more about couples and their body language. There was probably a book about it, and hundreds of websites.

'If those two had been seeing each other for a while,' said Belinda, 'they'd have had a motive for getting rid of Clarissa, wouldn't they?'

'But when I met Anthony, he seemed so bereft. He was grief-stricken without Clarissa.'

'That could have been guilt. Or a smokescreen,' she said, 'to make sure he was the last person anyone suspected.'

Jonny scooped up the last of the nuts as the waiter arrived to take their order. He'd changed his mind and ordered mackerel paté as a starter. He stuck with the poussin as a main course. Belinda was still undecided until the waiter recommended scallops with a chorizo and hazelnut sauce followed by lamb shanks in red wine. Their short stint of veganism at the festival now a mere memory, Jonny was enjoying tucking into meat once more. Belinda obviously felt the same.

The waiter tapped their order into an iPad and handed Jonny the wine list. Cabernet Sauvignon or Merlot? he wondered. The waiter stood to one side while he made up his mind.

'The couple who just left,' said Belinda. 'They were sitting over there by the aspidistra. Are they regulars here?'

'The lady stays here about once a month,' said the waiter. 'Has been for a while now. I think I've seen the man a few times. Are they friends of yours? Should I send a message to their room for you?'

'No. They're not exactly friends. We just thought we'd seen them before somewhere. No need to bother them.'

Jonny was trying not to laugh as he handed his menu back to the waiter. 'You were right,' he said. 'They are staying here, and in *their* room. A good bit of detective work. Katya would be proud of you.'

'Not really,' she said, modestly. 'It just confirmed what I'd already worked out.' She took a sip of her wine and nodded approvingly. 'A good choice. Perhaps we should have invited them to come and share it with us. We could have asked Anthony to introduce his friend.'

'Send a message to their room? Hell, no. I can't imagine what we might have interrupted. And if either of them does turn out to be a suspect, we wouldn't want to let on that we know.'

'So what happens next?'

'Airdrop that photo to my phone and I'll find out who the woman is.'

'How?'

He wasn't sure, but he'd start by going through his notes and see if anything there jogged his memory. He must have come across her while working on the case because here she was with Anthony Mayberry. It would be too much of a coincidence if he'd met her any other way. He'd check with Katya or one of the other detectives, who might have come across her in their own searches. If that failed, he could contact someone on the festival committee and see if they recognised her.

Their food arrived and Jonny remembered how hungry he was. 'Let's forget all that and enjoy our meal.'

'Fine with me. Do you remember the first meal we had together?'

He did. It was beans on toast in a scruffy bedsit Belinda was living in while interning for the local MP's surgery. They'd met when Belinda pushed a leaflet through his parents' letter box while out canvassing. Jonny had just been going out but kept her talking. He had absolutely no interest in the man she was canvassing for but had decided Belinda was the woman he was going to marry. A week later they'd gone to see *A Fish Called Wanda* and Belinda had invited him back to her place for something to eat. It was also that evening that Jonny had told her about his secret ambition to be a detective rather than spend his life in cardboard packaging. 'So what are you waiting for?' she had said. 'Go for it. Send off for an application form.' A month later Jonny's father died of a heart attack and the decision was taken out of his hands. He'd spent the next thirty-nine years in cardboard. Then he retired and within days a body was discovered in the Long Walk and everything changed.

CHAPTER
TWENTY-FOUR

Jonny was the first to arrive for the next detective meeting. Not a surprise, really. Jasmine had to clean the café kitchen, Ivo rarely finished his handyman rounds before mid-afternoon, and Katya... Jonny had no idea what might be keeping Katya. She was usually there first, having given herself time for a bite to eat in the café before the meeting started. She was probably having a quick catch-up with Lugs and would arrive puffing up the stairs with a fistful of notes. Hopefully today she might have news of cars that had driven through the village on the crucial Thursday when Clarissa was poisoned.

While he waited, Jonny downloaded the photo Belinda had taken the other night of Anthony Mayberry and his friend, so that he could ask if any of the others recognised the woman. He cleaned and primed the coffee machine, set out four mugs and emptied a packet of bourbon biscuits onto a plate. After that, he sat looking out of the window and wondering what else he could usefully do while waiting.

He decided he would follow up other incidents of mushroom

poisoning. It would be useful to the fungus people when making their map of death cap sightings. There had been reports of a case in Australia quite recently, when several people had died after eating the mushrooms fed to them during a family meal – probably not very useful for a local map. Interesting though, because poisoning by mushrooms rarely made it into the press. He didn't remember ever hearing about cases in the UK, although he remembered Jasmine had found statistics about it. He typed *death cap poisoning* into Google and most of the links took him to the case in Australia. Then a headline caught his eye from the website of a local paper: *Teens cautioned after mushroom party.* He clicked on the news page that carried the story and found it had happened quite recently, and not far from where he was right now. A group of students from a local school – no mention of which school – had been celebrating the end of their exams with a party at the home of one of the boys, whose parents were away on holiday. Police had been called to the house at midnight after neighbours complained about the noise. The young people involved had carried cushions and rugs out into the garden and were cooking over a camping stove while playing music from a phone through speakers. From the account of the first response officer on the scene, they appeared extremely good-natured and friendly, greeting the police constable with invitations to join them. Apparently, according to the constable's notebook, one of them had told him *the stars were twinkling silver and gold lights in the sky and the moon was a glowing magenta disco ball.* At this point the constable began to think this wasn't the usual type of teenage party. He examined the kitchen for alcohol and found only a few empty beer cans and a half-finished bottle of red wine. 'Nice Mr Policeman,' one of the girls had said, taking him by the hand. 'Come back to the garden and have some food. We're cooking omelettes. They make you feel wonderful.'

They returned to the garden, the constable calling for backup on the way, and examined the contents of the frying pan. 'Where did the mushrooms come from?' he asked. They pointed to the boy whose parents owned the house. 'Picked them,' he said, waving a lazy arm towards a field visible beyond the garden fence. 'My mum makes tea with them when she's feeling stressed.'

The youngsters were taken into custody which, according to the arresting officer, they agreed to placidly, finding the whole experience *a bit of a laugh*. The under-eighteens among them were given strong coffee and their parents sent for to take them home. The two boys who were over eighteen were detained for further questioning and later released after a police caution. The tea-making mother was also questioned on her return from holiday, but no further action was taken.

Jonny read through the piece again. No names were given – rightly, he thought. No real harm had been done. If they hadn't been playing loud music, it was likely no one would ever have known about it. All the same, he did wonder if this might have had anything to do with the Mayberry twins. Both had recently finished exams and the description of the house, the young people involved, and the fact that no charges were made, suggested money and influence. Privileged students could get away with far more than their less fortunate peers. Two incidents in the area, both involving mushrooms, seemed an unlikely coincidence. He made some notes and put them to one side. It was a timely discovery for their meeting, at which Katya would no doubt ask for updates on their suspects.

KATYA PUFFED up the stairs to the office feeling pleased with herself. She was late, but not by much. Jonny would have made coffee and Jasmine would have a selection of leftovers after closing the café for the day.

She was, as expected, the last to arrive. Jonny poured her a cup of coffee and put the plate of biscuits down where she could reach them easily. Jasmine pushed a plate of sandwiches in her direction. *Sandwiches and biscuits*. That was more than she'd ever got while she was working. Police budgets tended to cover only plain biscuits – custard creams if one was really lucky. This lot knew how to spoil her. She wondered if that meant they'd all uncovered useful evidence and wanted to celebrate. Or if they had nothing to show for the last couple of days and were trying to soften her up before delivering the bad news that they were making no progress at all. Hopefully it was the first of those, since Ivo was looking excited and was clutching a fistful of notes he had just printed. She wondered what ludicrous theory he had put together this time. Harold settled himself under the table, knowing that Katya's arrival meant the start of the meeting, and no one would take much notice of him for the next hour or so other than passing him the occasional biscuit.

'Mm,' she said, taking a bite of her sandwich. 'This is delicious. Tomatoes don't usually taste this good.'

'They're from Ivo's friend's greenhouse,' said Jasmine. 'They brought them in for me to taste.'

'Are you going in for market gardening, Ivo?'

He shook his head. 'Brian only has a small greenhouse. He just likes to grow things as a way of relaxing. He had a bit of a glut this year.'

'Well, tell him from me he's doing a great job. But right now we'd better get on with the meeting. Are we any closer to identifying suspects? I've got some info from Lugs, but it's highly confidential. Only to be shared if there's a real possibility of one of these people being involved. So let's hear what you've got first. Who'd like to start?'

'I will,' said Jonny, opening up the file of notes he'd made. 'I've been quite busy. First, Belinda is going on the public speaking circuit.'

'Fascinating,' said Katya. 'Does it have anything to do with our case?'

'In a way. She's looking around for an agent and Patsy Kline's name came up.'

'Clarissa's agent?' said Jasmine.

'That's right. Neither of us liked her very much, so we probably won't use her, but we did have lunch with her to talk about the possibility. Naturally, since I was with Clarissa when she was taken ill, we talked about her and it turns out there was some bad feeling between them.'

'What kind of bad feeling?' Ivo asked.

'Patsy was about to terminate her contract because she said Clarissa had broken its terms by publishing with someone Patsy didn't approve of. In fact, it wasn't just the publisher. She disapproved of Clarissa's whole sideline in pornography. She thought it would stain her wholesome image.'

'She had a point,' said Katya. 'But was it legal to terminate the contract?'

'I think Patsy would know, and if she didn't, she'd have a team of legal people.'

Katya took a thoughtful sip of her coffee. 'I don't suppose Clarissa was short of legal people either. The whole thing could have turned into a nasty, long and expensive court case.'

'Which Patsy would want to avoid,' said Jasmine.

'But would breaking a contract be a motive for killing her?' said Ivo.

'No,' said Jonny. 'I don't think so.'

'So why mention it?' Katya asked.

'Because,' said Jonny, knowing he'd kept the best bit back so far, 'Patsy's contracts have a death clause.'

'A what?' asked Ivo, looking puzzled.

'If the client dies before the end of the contract, Patsy is entitled to a percentage of the estate in lieu of what she would have been able to claim from the fees they were paid.'

Jasmine stared at him in surprise. 'People actually sign on those terms?' she asked.

'I suppose most people like to think they'll survive to the end of their contract.'

'And if they're dead, they won't care much one way or another,' Ivo added.

'Is it usual for agents to have a clause like that?' Jasmine asked.

'No idea,' said Jonny. 'But it's something I will be looking into before Belinda signs anything.'

'So,' said Katya, tapping her pen on the table. 'We don't know how much Clarissa was bringing in or how long her contract had to run, but her book was doing surprisingly well and she did a lot of speaking engagements. It could have been a substantial amount.'

'That would give Patsy a motive for killing Clarissa, wouldn't it?' said Ivo.

'Possibly. It's certainly worth noting,' said Katya, adding it to the Patsy column on the board. 'We should try to find out if Patsy's business is doing well or if she was badly in need of money.'

'It's hard to find out things like that,' said Jonny. 'She'd keep quiet about it and it's possible no one would know she was in trouble until she declared herself bankrupt.'

'We'll keep it in mind,' said Katya. 'If more evidence appears, there might be a way we can get a look at their records. Lugs would know about that. But thank you, Jonny. You've given us plenty there to chew over. Who's next?'

'I haven't finished,' said Jonny.

'There's more about Patsy?'

'No, this is something quite different.'

'Okay,' said Katya. 'Fire away.'

'It was our fortieth wedding anniversary yesterday.'

'Congratulations,' said Katya, sighing. How likely was it that Jonny's long marriage had anything to do with this case? Was he just expecting them to be impressed by his enduring relationship? Something to celebrate these days, she supposed. But not likely to solve the case for them.

Jonny noticed her expression. 'Before you accuse me of going off track,' he said, 'we went out for a meal at the Morris. It's on the river just beyond Staines.'

'Yes,' said Katya. 'I know where it is. Is this relevant?'

'Very posh,' said Jasmine. 'Was the food good?'

'It was excellent,' said Jonny. 'We might go back there for our forty-first.'

'Did you have mushrooms?' Ivo asked.

Jonny laughed and shook his head. 'They do a lovely mushroom in white wine and garlic starter, but I didn't really feel like trying them. It's too soon after...'

'Don't blame you,' said Jasmine. 'I'm having to force myself to serve them in the café at the moment.'

'Okay,' said Katya impatiently. 'Everyone's gone off mushrooms. Does your meal out affect our case?'

'It does,' said Jonny, who, in Katya's opinion, was testing her patience by spinning it out for as long as possible. 'We saw something very interesting.'

'And relevant, I hope. What was it?'

'It's *who* we saw there,' said Jonny, drawing out the suspense but not going any further.

Katya gave him a *get on with it* look. 'I'm guessing it wasn't the terrible twins.'

'Not far off,' said Jonny. 'We saw Anthony Mayberry.'

'You can't blame him for not wanting to eat at home right now,' said Ivo.

'He was with a woman.'

'Maybe a client? Financial advice over dinner?' Katya suggested. 'I'm sure it happens.' She could only assume that, never having had enough money to need advice. Odd that. Shouldn't those with very little money be more in need of it?

Jonny turned to the computer and opened the photo Belinda had taken. He turned the screen so that Katya could see it more easily. 'That doesn't look like a business meeting, does it?'

'Can I see?' said Jasmine, leaning across to look over Katya's shoulder. 'Definitely not. Very lovey-dovey.'

'And they were not just eating there,' said Jonny.

'How do you know?' asked Ivo.

'They didn't pay the bill for the meal, just signed for it. And they didn't have coats, so we thought they must have had a room in the hotel.'

'Did they see you?'

'No, we were tucked away in an alcove, and anyway, they were far too wrapped up in each other. We did ask the waiter if they were regulars.'

'And are they?'

'He told us he saw the woman about once a month and Anthony had sometimes been with her. He assumed we knew them and asked if we would like to send a message to their room.'

'He definitely said *their* room?' Jasmine asked. 'Are you sure?'

'Quite sure. And Belinda can back me up.'

'I'll make note of it,' said Katya, 'but we shouldn't jump to conclusions. Do you think it gives Anthony a motive?'

'Bound to,' said Ivo. 'They could have planned it together.'

'I'm sure I've seen this woman before, and quite recently. Do any of you recognise her?'

None of them did.

'There's something else,' said Jonny. 'And it could knock that theory on the head.'

'You mean you have another suspect?' said Katya. 'You have been busy.'

'Not so much another suspect – at least, not yet. But this made me think.' He handed out copies he'd made from the news page that had reported the magic mushroom party. 'It doesn't mention the twins – no names at all – but it seems like too much of a coincidence. Two mushroom-related events within a few weeks of each other.'

They were quiet while they all read it.

'Different kinds of mushrooms,' said Ivo. 'I don't see how they can be connected.'

'Well,' said Jonny. 'This is just an idea. But suppose one or both of the twins were at that party. It sounds like the kind of crowd they'd mix with. They were both angry with their mother. What if they decided to get their own back by sending Clarissa on a magic mushroom trip?'

'But Clarissa was poisoned by death caps, not magic mushrooms,' Ivo pointed out.

'They could have made a mistake. The two aren't so different to look at and both grow in the fields around here.'

'A hell of a mistake, though,' said Katya. 'Does either of them have an air of guilt about them? Ivo, you've met them both.'

'I've not met Tristan, only his friends, but they said he was behaving normally.'

'That's suspicious for a start,' said Jasmine. 'Who behaves normally when their mother has just died? What about the sister?'

'Amelia's a cool type,' said Ivo. 'I wouldn't put it past her to cover up something of that sort. She's got a lot to lose. She wouldn't want anything to stop her going to Cambridge and then having a dazzling career.'

'All the same,' said Jasmine. 'I can't see them making a mistake like that and not showing some sign that it had gone horribly wrong. And anyway, Magda saw something that will kill that idea.' She told them about Magda's sighting of the woman in the lane that led to the woods.

'Let me get this clear,' said Katya. 'A woman went through the garden gate with something in a box.'

'Having been in the woods, where we know the death caps grow,' said Ivo. 'Must be a suspect.'

'Did Magda see her come out again?'

'No,' said Jasmine. 'The Amazon van drove away so she was able to get her car into the drive before the woman came out.'

'Did she see her again once she was in the house?'

'No. Clarissa was in her office working and the twins were still in bed. There was no one else in the house.'

'And no sign of the box of mushrooms in the kitchen?'

Jasmine checked the notes she'd made after her first talk with Magda. The kitchen had been tidy and free of clutter. But, and no one had spotted this until now, there was a flask on one of the worktops. That had to have been Clarissa's. Soup for her lunch, perhaps. Tristan had crawled out of bed later that morning and headed for college, and Amelia only came out of her room after Clarissa told her she could borrow her car. 'We need to know what happened to the flask,' said Jasmine.

'I expect someone emptied it and cleared it away. Possibly Clarissa herself after she'd finished its contents,' said Katya. 'We need to find out who the woman in the lane was. Did Magda give you any kind of description?'

'Only that she was tall and wearing a raincoat with a hood. And she was slim.'

'Hmm,' said Katya. 'A slim, tallish woman wearing a hooded raincoat. There must be hundreds of them.'

Jonny looked up from his notes. 'Patsy Kline has a hooded Burberry. And she's slim and quite tall.'

'And she had a grudge against Clarissa.' Katya drew a circle around Patsy's name on the board.

'Whoever it was obviously knew their way around the house and garden,' said Ivo. 'And that Clarissa worked in her office and the twins got up late. She could leave her box of whatever it was without being seen.'

'Or,' said Jasmine, 'it was someone who was often at the house, so even if she'd been seen, they wouldn't have been surprised.'

'We know that Anthony has a woman friend. Could it have been her?' said Katya.

'She has to be a suspect,' said Jasmine. 'We just need to know who she was.'

'What about Murray?' said Ivo suddenly.

'What on earth makes you think Murray was in the woods in the pouring rain? And he's not a woman.'

'It might have been his wife,' Ivo suggested.

'Molly's quite short and dumpy,' said Jasmine.

'We know Murray delivers veg boxes in the village,' said Ivo. 'And he hated Clarissa.'

'Everyone hated Clarissa,' said Katya. 'It's not helping. The woman Magda saw was carrying something the size of a camera box, not a full-sized vegetable carton. And how would Murray know his way in and out of the house?'

'I don't know,' said Ivo. 'But it would account for why Magda didn't see a car near the lane. She might have seen Murray's van and ignored it.'

'He wasn't on Alan's list of cars driving into the village that day,' said Jonny. 'But he could have been there before Alan set up for his speed watching. Any luck with Lugs and the ANPR?'

'He wasn't on that either.'

'But he would have been, wouldn't he?' said Jasmine. 'If he delivers in the village on Thursdays?'

'He might have had deliveries in other villages and used the back route in,' said Ivo.

'Was there anyone you recognised on the ANPR?' Jonny asked.

'Lugs checked for the day before Clarissa died. He looked at early morning before Jonny's friend was doing his speed checks, and evenings after five when he would have finished. He was able to tell me, off the record of course, that Anthony Mayberry passed it at seven forty-five on the Thursday morning.'

'We know that he left home before Magda arrived,' said Jasmine.

'He wasn't seen returning later in the day, was he?' Jonny asked.

'No. I thought that was a bit odd,' said Katya. 'But now we know that he wasn't at home on the Thursday night. He'd have been called by the hospital when Clarissa collapsed and probably went straight there. He might not have returned home until the early hours of Saturday morning. Jonny, did you check the owners of cars on Alan's list who were not speeding?'

'Only the ones that fitted Magda's description – the black expensive ones.'

'But there were others?'

'A couple.' Jonny opened the list Alan had sent him.

'So your friend sat there all day and there were only two cars that didn't break the speed limit?'

Jonny nodded. 'Looks like he's got a point about speeding. There was a white Seat Ibiza and a Land Rover. The Land Rover was leaving the village at around eleven. The Seat came in from the main road at eight forty-five.'

'Can you find out who owns them?'

Jonny logged into the site he had subscribed to and tapped in the numbers. 'The Land Rover belongs to a Mrs Joan Farmer. She lives at an address just outside the village. It's a cattery.'

'So unless Clarissa was a closet cat murderer, she's probably not relevant. And Magda would have noticed a Land Rover parked anywhere near the lane.'

'She could have walked there from the cattery,' Jasmine pointed out.

'We'll check her out, but I don't see her as a suspect.'

'She might just have dropped off some mushrooms for Clarissa because she's a good neighbour,' said Ivo. 'Perhaps she was out for a walk and thought she'd give them to Clarissa because she was passing her house.'

'Like I said, we'll check her out.' Katya made a note on the board. 'What about the Seat?'

'Belongs to Paul Simpson, living at an address in Southampton.'

'I wonder what he was doing in the village that early in the morning?'

'Hmm,' said Katya. 'Perhaps Magda was wrong and we're looking for a slim man. In a hooded raincoat it might be hard to tell the difference. I wonder where it was parked. Magda didn't mention a white Seat, did she?'

'No,' said Jasmine. 'But it could have been left further up the road. Give me the address, Jonny, and I'll check him out.'

Jonny scribbled the address on a piece of paper and handed it to her.

Jasmine took it from him. 'I'll check the cattery lady as well.'

'I could do that,' said Ivo. 'I said I'd call back and see Thomas Johnson. He enjoys a chat. There might be some gossip about her.'

CHAPTER
TWENTY-FIVE

Jasmine found the address Jonny had given her for Paul Simpson, the owner of the white Seat, on Google street view. She sat and stared at the image for a few minutes, thinking that seeing where Paul Simpson lived wasn't much use. It didn't give her any clue about what he might have been doing in Little Frampton early in the morning of the day Clarissa had eaten death cap mushrooms. She needed to know a lot more about him. Without much optimism, she typed the name into Google and added Southampton after it. And she was in luck. Up popped an article from a Southampton newspaper about an independent bookshop in the city, recently opened by a Paul Simpson. Nothing to indicate that this was the same man, but she typed the name of the shop into Google and came up with its Facebook page. Clicking on the gallery she found plenty of photos, one of which was very interesting. The bookshop was in what appeared to be a quiet street, mainly residential but with a small parade of shops: an artisan baker, a flower shop and Simpson's Books. Between the shops and the road was a lay-by where cars could park at right angles to the street – handy for some quick shopping. And, it seemed, for the shopkeepers. One of the cars was a white Seat and after zooming in, Jasmine could see that it had the same registration as the one that was spotted driving into Little Frampton on the fateful day.

Delving a little deeper, Jasmine discovered that Paul Simpson ran the shop with Leonora Simpson, an artist whom Jasmine assumed was his wife. It was only when she dug deeper still that she discovered they were brother and sister. The actual Mrs Simpson was a pharmacist working in the city. The Bookshop, although new, was popular among locals, many of whom had left comments about how lovely it was to have a small bookshop run by helpful, friendly people. Jasmine found articles in the local paper about the opening of the shop only a few months earlier. Paul had been working as a teacher until he won twenty-five thousand pounds on the lottery. The paper published a piece about how he had become burnt out and suffered from anxiety attacks caused by teaching and all its attendant paperwork and inspections, commenting that this small windfall had saved his life.

Nice as it was, Jasmine didn't think that twenty-five thousand pounds was enough to set up a bookshop and wondered if he'd had to take out a loan, in which case she suspected his anxiety problems could well be made a lot worse by increasing interest rates and the cost-of-living crisis, which probably meant far fewer people bought books. But she found a photo of him and his wife tagged at a family barbeque at the end of the summer, in which he looked happy and relaxed and not in the least anxious. So perhaps the sister had also invested in the bookshop.

A little searching told her that Leonora Simpson was recently divorced, so she may have had money to invest as part of a divorce settlement. She'd been married to a financial manager, so Jasmine imagined it would have been a generous settlement. She must also have reverted to the name she used before her marriage. It would be a weird coincidence if she'd married a man who was also called Simpson. Leonora was currently living with her two children in a flat over the shop. Jasmine clicked further into the barbeque photos and found that Lenora and her children had also been there. Leonora was a slender woman who favoured bohemian-style flowered skirts and fringed waistcoats. She looked a little familiar, although Jasmine was unable to place her. Photos could be misleading anyway, so she was probably mistaken. The children, Jasmine thought, looked sporty, both wearing shorts and with the kind of suntan that resulted from a life outdoors. She zoomed in closer and was able to identify a logo on one of the t-shirts, a small sailing boat and the letters SLSC, which she copied into Google and discovered was the badge of the Solent and Lymington Sailing Club. That made sense, since they lived in Southampton.

They looked like a pleasant, happy family running a small but thriving business. Not unlike her own, perhaps. She could find nothing at all that linked Paul Simpson or anyone else in the family to any of the Mayberrys or to Little Frampton. The only thing she could think of was that they dealt in second-hand books and the sighting of Paul's Seat in the village might mean that he was going to a house sale in search of stock for his shop. A long drive, but it wasn't impossible that someone in Little Frampton had a valuable collection of first editions.

Jasmine made some notes, copied in the photos she'd found and emailed it all to Katya, hoping she might be able to make a connection to their case.

As she was shutting down the computer and preparing to lock up the office for the day, Ivo and Harold appeared. Ivo looked smarter than usual in chinos and a navy blue open-necked shirt. 'Off out somewhere?' Jasmine asked.

'Harold and I were meeting Brian at the Jolly Ploughman for a barbeque, the last of the year, but his flight from the States had to turn back because of a bomb scare so he's not going to make it.'

'Oh my God, is he okay?'

'Yeah, it was some nutter calling in a hoax. But they've missed their flight slot so they've a layover in Seattle.'

It amazed Jasmine how quickly Ivo had adopted airline language, his only jetting experience having been a three-hour flight to Santorini a couple of months ago. 'Bad luck,' she said. 'But you and Harold could still go.' The Jolly Ploughman had a reputation for casual pick-ups. 'You might meet someone nice.'

Ivo shook his head. 'I can't speak for Harold, but that's not my scene. I thought I'd go and see Thomas Johnson.'

'Who?'

'The old boy in Little Frampton. I fixed his door and he talked to me about what the village was like in the old days and how stupid Clarissa must have been to eat poisoned mushrooms.'

'That'll be nice,' she said, thinking Thomas Johnson was a poor substitute for jet-setting Brian.

'He misses his dog,' said Ivo. 'I thought I'd take him to the pub for a beer and see if he spotted the white Seat. Do you want to come?'

Why not? She'd nothing else planned for the evening and she'd not seen Little Frampton yet.

IVO TURNED the van into the road to the village, taking care not to break the speed limit. A petition had been launched by Alan Biggs pleading for a twenty-mile-an-hour limit. *A vain hope*, Jasmine thought. They had enough trouble persuading people to drive at thirty. Alan Biggs aside, this was a village of self-entitled commuters with gas-guzzling four-by-fours. He'd probably start a revolution at any suggestion they should drive even more slowly. She looked around at the affluent houses they were passing. 'Which is Limetree Cottage?' she asked.

'It's the first house on the right after this bend,' said Ivo, slowing down even more so that she could take a good look, and getting hooted at from an impatient Subaru Outback driver who was far too close to the back of Ivo's van. Ivo pulled over onto the verge and let the car past. The driver made a rude gesture as he pulled out to overtake. Jasmine returned it with a giggle. 'So that's the lane to the woods?' she asked.

'That's right. Magda would have parked her car right there, I think, while she waited for the Amazon driver to move.' He pointed to a small lay-by on the opposite side of the road.

'Let's take a look,' said Jasmine, unbuckling her seat belt and climbing out onto the grass verge.

Ivo let Harold out of the back of the van and locked the doors. The sun was setting, but there was still a good half hour or so of daylight left. They walked up the lane, past the gate into the Mayberry's garden. Jasmine opened it and peered in. A short walk across a tidy lawn, there was a door into the back of the house. Was the kitchen at the back of the house? She tried to remember what Jonny had told her about the layout. If it was a door to the kitchen, it would be the job of a few seconds to leave a box of mushrooms and be back in the lane again before anyone in the house noticed. She closed the gate and looked back down towards the road, where the lay-by was clearly visible. Magda would have had a good view of the woman. Even in the rain she was unlikely to have been mistaken about whoever it was going through the gate.

A little further on they came to a kissing gate and a path into the woods. To Harold's obvious disappointment, they decided to head back to the van. Jasmine was wearing ballet pumps and didn't want to get them muddy, and the woods looked gloomy and damp. There would be little chance of seeing any mushrooms, not that they wanted to. Jasmine wasn't too sure she'd ever eat mushrooms again. Even ones that came from a supermarket. So there wasn't much point in spending any more time there. Ivo didn't want to keep Thomas Johnson waiting. He would be looking forward to their visit, to seeing Harold and a trip to the pub.

Ivo had called ahead, and Thomas was standing at his door waiting for them. He probably didn't get out much, Jasmine thought. And he'd dressed up for the occasion in a navy-blue suit: a jacket with wide lapels and trousers with turnups, teamed with a white shirt and boots that had been polished until he could see his face in them. He waved cheerily at Ivo and bent down to stroke Harold. 'I do miss me old dog,' he said, rubbing his back as he straightened up. 'Reckon we should walk to the pub. That car park gets chocka of an evening.'

He wasn't wrong. The village shop might have closed down and the school had merged with one several villages away, but the pub was still going strong. It sat proudly on the edge of a village green, with a view of the church and the ruthlessly gentrified house that had once been the village school. It had even resisted the urge to become a gastro pub and still served proper bar meals: pie and chips; scampi and chips; sausages and chips; and chicken curry with rice.

Ivo fished out his wallet. 'What'll it be, Thomas?' he asked.

'Pint of Best and a packet of crisps. And none of those fancy ones.'

'Ready salted?'

'Suppose they'll do. Whatever happened to those little blue packets of salt you used to get?'

Ivo and Jasmine looked at him blankly.

'That's what we got when I was little. Smith's crisps with salt in a blue twist of waxy paper.'

Jasmine didn't like the idea of clearing up after all the scraps of blue paper that would be dropped if she sold them in the café, but they'd probably still be around somewhere. Sold in some hipster place for three times the price. 'Won't you have a proper meal?' Jasmine asked. 'I'm going for a pie and chips.'

'Sausage and chips for me,' said Ivo. Harold pricked up his ears at the mention of sausages.

'Well,' said Thomas. 'If you insist. I'll have the chicken curry. Remind me of my army days.'

'You were in India?' Ivo asked.

'God help us, what do they teach the young today? We pulled out of India in 1947. I'd have been all of eight years old. No, I did a stint in Germany. They know how to cook a decent curry, them Germans.'

Jasmine reached for her bag and checked that she'd remembered her wallet. 'We'll go halves,' she said to Ivo. 'Set up a tab and we can tap in our cards when we've eaten.'

. . .

'This is nice,' said Thomas as Ivo arrived back at their table with a tray of drinks. He swallowed half of his pint, put the glass down on the table and settled back in his seat. 'But I don't imagine you two are here just to keep an old codger company.'

'You're great company,' said Jasmine, patting his hand. 'But while we are here, we just wondered if you had seen a white Seat in the village the Thursday before last.'

'The day we had that early morning downpour?'

'That's right. But you probably stayed in that morning.'

'Nah, not me. I've never minded a drop of rain. And I did see a white car. Don't know what kind it was, though.'

Ivo scrolled through his phone and found a picture of a white Seat Ibiza. He handed it to Thomas.

'Is that the car?' Thomas asked.

'Not the actual one, no, but it would have been just like it.'

'Could be the one. Seen it a couple of times, come to think of it.'

'Calling at one of the houses or just driving through?'

Thomas took a thoughtful sip of his beer. 'Let me see now.' He scratched his head and looked out of the window. 'I remember. It was parked on the village green a couple of times. Right across there.' He pointed to a row of houses on the other side of the green.

'We think it might have belonged to someone buying up second-hand books.'

'Doubt it,' said Thomas. 'Not much call for books these days. It's all computer gadgets.'

'Books haven't totally gone out,' said Ivo. 'The man who owns the car runs a bookshop.'

'No, no, you're wrong,' said Thomas.

'He really does,' said Jasmine. 'We found it on Facebook.'

'There might be a bookshop on this Facebook, but it was a lady driving the car.'

'Are you sure?' said Ivo.

''Course I'm sure. You think I don't know the difference?'

'Could you describe her?'

'Nice looking woman, fortyish, I'd say. Kind of old fashioned.'

'Old fashioned?'

'Yeah, long skirts and that.'

'Raincoat?'

'Reckon she was wearing a raincoat the last time I saw her. Tipping it down, it was.'

'Was she on her own?'

'Yes, she was. Parked the car and walked down the road a bit. Probably visiting one of the houses down by the lane to the woods. Don't know why she didn't drive up to the house. I suppose there were too many cars there already. Even the kids have their own cars these days.'

Ivo and Jasmine stared at each other.

'Could it have been the sister, Leonora?' Ivo asked. 'She might have been here buying books. You know, house clearance stuff. Thomas, did you see her when she came back for the car?'

'Nah, only went for a short walk but the car had gone by the time I got back.'

'It could have been Leonora,' said Jasmine, fishing out her phone and searching for the photo she'd found on Facebook. 'Is this her?' she asked, handing Thomas her phone.

Thomas took it. 'You two got your whole lives on these gadgets?' he asked.

'Just about,' said Ivo. 'You should get one. You could do all sorts, listen to music, watch movies, keep in touch with your friends…'

'Might just do that,' he said.

'So is this the woman you saw?' Jasmine asked, trying not to sound impatient.

'Dunno,' he said. 'Can't be sure. But she had a skirt like that one, all flowers and stuff.'

'You could see that under the raincoat?'

'She didn't have the raincoat the other time I saw her.'

'Did she go the same way that time as well?'

'No. She sat there for a bit and then Mr Mayberry came along, and they drove off together. Odd, that was. He'd parked his own car up round the back of the church.'

'Mr Mayberry?' said Jasmine in surprise.

'Yeah, didn't I say? It was probably his house she went to the second time I saw her.'

'What do you make of all that?' Ivo asked as they drove home, having seen Thomas back to his cottage.

'Perhaps the Mayberrys were clearing out old books. Didn't Jonny say the garage was full of boxes?'

'I thought he said those belonged to his friend, Carl Archer. He's storing his stuff in their garage while he looks for a house for himself.'

'Why would Anthony Mayberry meet her on the village green and not at the house?'

'No idea,' said Jasmine. 'Perhaps it was to give her a list of the books he wanted to sell and didn't want her calling at the house.'

'Why not?'

'No idea.'

'So she drives back to Southampton with this list, checks with her brother about which books they want to buy and then drives all the way back again?'

'I guess,' said Jasmine.

'Doesn't make sense, does it? You want to sell some books, you'd make a list and email it, not drag someone all that way just to give them a paper list.'

Ivo was right. It didn't make much sense. But there was a whole lot about this case that didn't make any sense at all. She sighed loudly.

Ivo glanced at her. 'Well, at least Thomas had a nice evening out.'

'Yeah,' said Jasmine. 'He's quite a character. We should do it again sometime.'

'I like the pub as well. We should bring Katya here. She's always complaining about the pubs in town being too smart. She likes her pub meals to be old style, doesn't she?'

'We'll make a night of it,' said Jasmine. 'Once we've got this death cap stuff out of the way.'

CHAPTER
TWENTY-SIX

Jonny was helping Jasmine with the lunchtime washing-up while she told him about the evening she and Ivo had spent with Thomas Johnson.

'You say this man had seen the white Seat in the village?' Jonny asked, trying to get his head around it. 'The one that belongs to, what's his name, Simpson?'

'That's right. The bookshop owner from Southampton, but it wasn't him. It was a woman driving. Ivo and I thought it might have been Simpson's sister, Leonora. And perhaps she was in the village checking out first editions or something.'

Leonora? Something nagged at Jonny's brain. The name Leonora was familiar and he couldn't work out why. He mentally trawled though all his friends and colleagues going back for years but couldn't remember a single Leonora among them. So why had the name struck a chord?

'Jonny?'

'Yes, sorry, buying first editions. Possible, I suppose. But did you say the sister was called Leonora?'

'Yes, and Thomas told us she was meeting Anthony Mayberry. Not at his house, but in the village.'

'Really? Do you think she was Magda's mysterious person in the rain?'

'I don't know. And why would they be sneaking around like that? Meeting in the village? Unless...'

'Hang on a minute,' said Jonny. 'Did you say you'd found a picture of Leonora?'

'Yes, it was on Facebook, a family barbeque.' Jasmine grabbed her phone and found the page she had bookmarked. 'That's her.' She enlarged the photo and handed the phone to Jonny.

'That's it,' said Jonny, fumbling for his own phone and finding the photo Belinda had taken at the Morris. 'Look. Same woman, isn't it?'

'You're right,' said Jasmine, holding the two phones side by side. 'You know what that means, don't you?'

'Um,' said Jonny, trying to work it out. 'Anthony and Leonora were having an affair?'

'If they were, they'd have a motive for killing Clarissa, wouldn't they? And they met in the village after Anthony was supposed to have left for work.'

'We don't know that it was Leonora in the car. Perhaps this Simpson guy has an assistant who used it.'

'I suppose we can't prove it. But you've identified the woman who was with Anthony that evening as Leonora. And that a white Seat Ibiza belonging to her brother drove through the ANPR that week and was seen in the village around the time he was allegedly leaving for work. I know Katya is always saying we shouldn't make assumptions, but two white Seats in the village would be a bit of a coincidence, wouldn't it? And if it was them... well, they'd have to be suspects.'

'It's a bit far-fetched,' said Jonny. 'I can't see why they'd want to kill Clarissa. Why couldn't Anthony just leave her?'

'Money? The children? Who knows?'

DEATH AT THE FESTIVAL

'So you think Leonora parked in the village, walked to the woods in the pouring rain, and picked some poisonous mushrooms, which she left in the kitchen, presumably without being seen. A bit risky, wasn't it? What if one of the twins had eaten them?'

'I don't know,' said Jasmine. 'But we should tell Katya and see what she thinks.'

'I suppose it's something she could discuss with Lugs. He might think it was grounds for further enquiry.'

Jonny had just put the phone back in his pocket and plunged his hands back into the soapy water when he felt the buzz of an incoming call. He dried his hands and fished the phone out of his pocket. Anthony's name flashed up on the screen. 'Talk of the devil,' he said. 'How's that for a coincidence?'

'Put it on speaker,' said Jasmine.

Jonny clicked the speaker icon and put the phone down on the draining board. 'Mr Mayberry, what can I do for you?' Jonny hoped he didn't sound as if he was about to accuse Anthony of murder, which would probably have made him end the call abruptly.

'I need to see you,' said Anthony. Jonny and Jasmine looked at each other in surprise. 'I've been going through Clarissa's desk and there's something that doesn't make sense.'

'What kind of thing?'

'It's difficult to explain on the phone. Could you call in and I can show you what I found?'

Jonny looked at his watch. 'I can be there in around half an hour,' he said, ending the call. 'That was odd. It seems I am about to discover things about Clarissa that Anthony didn't know before.'

'He's probably found her porno manuscripts,' said Jasmine.

'You think he didn't know she was writing that stuff?'

'Would Belinda tell you if she was writing a steamy novel?'

'No idea. I can't imagine her ever doing anything like that, but we don't have any secrets from each other.'

'So you know all her passwords and stuff like bank details?'

'Well, no, but I know how to find them. We wrote everything like that down in a notebook to keep with our wills in case one of us dies suddenly.'

'What about all the stuff Belinda did for the council? Wasn't any of that confidential?'

'Probably. I never asked. I don't think it was all that interesting.' He dried the last glass and placed it on a shelf above the sink. 'Are you suggesting that we keep things from each other?'

'No, not at all. Anyone can tell you and Belinda totally trust each other. What I'm saying is that if a couple wanted to keep things secret, it wouldn't be all that difficult to do. Anyone with a computer can hide stuff. Password documents or bury them among a lot of boring stuff where no one would think to look for them. You can even encrypt a document and save it online.'

'You think Clarissa kept her writing secret?'

'Wouldn't you?'

He laughed. 'Probably. Although if I had that kind of imagination, who knows what I'd do with it.'

'And it looks as if Anthony had secrets of his own, doesn't it?'

'The mysterious Leonora? Let me see that photo again.'

Jasmine found it on her phone – a smiling woman with two sporty-looking kids. She handed it to Jonny.

'When I saw her with Anthony at the Morris, I thought I knew her from somewhere. But I must have been wrong. Belinda thought I might have seen her at the festival but I'm sure I didn't.' He was about to pass the phone back when his finger slipped, and he found he'd scrolled to the next picture. 'What's that one?' he asked.

Jasmine looked at it. 'That's a close-up of the t-shirts the kids were wearing. It's a sailing club logo.'

Suddenly it all clicked into place. 'That's it,' he said. 'Sailing.'

'What do you mean?'

'They used to sail together, the Mayberrys and the Archers.'

'Okay, but lots of people go sailing in that part of the country. It's by the sea.'

'The Solent is actually a river that runs into the English Channel round the Isle of Wight. A very popular area for small boat sailing.'

'That's what I said, isn't it? Anthony Mayberry could easily have met this Leonora while he was sailing, but it doesn't explain why you thought you'd met her before.'

'That's just it. Carl Archer's wife was called Leonora. I remember now from the notes I made when I first researched Carl. There was a photo of them after some sailing race they were in.'

'You think she's the same Leonora?'

'It's a fairly unusual name. This woman is about the right age and so are the children.'

'You may be right,' said Jasmine. 'But it doesn't explain why she and Anthony are having clandestine meetings in Little Frampton.'

'And in a hotel near Staines.'

'Did you find out why the Archers divorced? Perhaps it was because Leonora and Anthony were already having an affair.'

'So why didn't the Mayberrys get divorced as well?'

'No idea. Perhaps I'll ask Anthony when I see him.'

'Are you going to see him now?'

'I said I'd be there in half an hour.'

'I'm coming with you. He might not react well if you accuse him of feeding his wife with death caps. You might need protecting.'

'I wasn't planning on accusing him of anything. I'll see what he wants to show me and drop Leonora into the conversation if it seems relevant. But if you want to come as my knight in shining armour, you are more than welcome.'

THERE WAS ONLY one car on the drive when they arrived at Limetree Cottage. Neither Tristan's battered Polo nor Clarissa's white Evoque, now Amelia's, were there. Jonny hoped that meant that Anthony was on his own in the house. He must have heard Jonny's car on the drive, because he was standing at the door by the time they had climbed out. He led them upstairs into a room Jonny assumed had been Clarissa's study. Anthony must have been clearing it out. Cardboard boxes lined the floor and were filling up with books and papers. On the desk was a computer running a screensaver of sailing boats, and in front of that was an indexed hardcover spiral notebook. Jonny guessed that it contained all Clarissa's passwords.

Jonny introduced Jasmine and Anthony nodded at her. 'Are you on your own today?' Jonny asked.

'Tristan's working late at college, trying to catch up with some revision. I've given Amelia her mother's car and she's gone to visit friends.'

'And your friend, Carl, is he still here?'

Anthony frowned. 'No, he was only here for the day when you met him.'

Odd, Jonny thought. Hadn't he been there to help with funeral arrangements? But he supposed they could have sorted all of that in one day.

'He was more Clarissa's friend than mine,' Anthony continued.

'I thought you were sailing buddies,' said Jonny. 'Family get-togethers, wasn't it?'

'That was before Carl and Leonora were divorced.'

Jonny gave Jasmine a warning look. They'd go into the matter of Anthony and Leonora later. 'What was it you wanted to show me?'

'I've been sorting out Clarissa's finances.' He sat down at the desk and flicked the computer mouse. The screen came to life showing a spreadsheet. 'I've been closing her accounts and transferring the money into a holding account until we've sorted probate. It all seemed in order until I came to this one.' He shuffled the mouse over the final entry. 'This was the account Clarissa used for her, er, her fictional writing.'

'Her *Miss Tress* stories?' Jasmine asked.

Anthony looked surprised. 'You know about those?'

'Just one of several things we discovered about your wife,' said Jonny.

'Well, I didn't approve. Can't imagine what she was thinking of.

Any hint of it in the press and her reputation would have been destroyed. We quarrelled about it, and she obviously decided to keep any money she made from it in a separate account. Maybe she wasn't declaring it for tax, who knows.'

'Did she make very much from the books?'

'Surprisingly, yes. If you look at her spreadsheet, they were bringing in five figure sums over the last three years.'

'I don't know the terms of her will,' said Jonny. 'But did she mention that particular pot of money?'

'Her will simply left everything in trust for the twins. There is a certain amount set aside to cover their college expenses. The rest will be theirs when they reach their twenty-first birthday.'

'She left nothing to you?'

'We owned the house jointly and it's mine for my lifetime, after which it will pass to the twins. It's what we agreed, when we were still on speaking terms. I have plenty of money of my own. We ran our finances quite separately.'

That surprised Jonny. He'd assumed they were a happily married couple. Then he remembered Anthony had been spotted with Leonora in the village and he'd seen them himself at the Morris, so perhaps not. 'The money in this account will be transferred into a trust for the twins?'

'It should have been, but the account is now empty.'

She'd spent it? No reason why she shouldn't. It was her money, however much one might disapprove of the way she'd earned it. 'It was hers to spend,' Jonny pointed out.

'You don't understand,' said Anthony. 'I'm afraid I was not as prompt as I might have been. It was a few days before I had copies of the death certificate, which the banks need in order to close accounts. By the time I'd got around to closing this one, it had been emptied. The day Clarissa died the balance showed around fifty thousand pounds. Two days later, it was empty.'

'A delayed transfer, perhaps?'

He shook his head. 'I have all Clarissa's bank details and passwords here.' He picked up the notebook and waved it at them. 'I was able to log in and check the transaction. Money had been going in regularly from the publisher and Clarissa had barely touched it. The only transaction was made, apparently by Clarissa, two days after her death. Unfortunately, when I contacted the bank, they started accusing me of stealing the money, assuming I was the only one able to access her accounts. They threatened me with the possibility of prosecution. Luckily, I have a very good legal accountant and he was able to persuade them that I'd had nothing to do with it.'

'Can they trace where it went?'

'Seems not.'

Probably to some anonymous offshore account. Jonny had heard of things like that. 'Could one of the twins have done it?'

'I doubt if it was Tristan. He can barely keep track of his own phone, never mind hack into his mother's account. Amelia probably has the necessary skill, but she can't have needed it urgently and the money would have come to her anyway in time.'

'So do you have any idea who might have done it?'

'Clarissa had secrets. I think she was seeing someone.'

'Someone she shared her bank details with?'

'I don't know,' said Anthony, sinking into the chair and putting his head in his hands. 'I'd been suspicious for a while.'

'Of?'

'Carl Archer. I didn't know for sure, though.'

'But I thought you were all friends? What made you change your mind?'

'I became suspicious a couple of months ago. Not sure why, but he was different somehow. And then his wife, ex-wife now, got in touch.'

'Leonora?'

'Yes.' Anthony looked surprised. 'You knew her name?'

'We did some background checks on everyone on a list of people Clarissa had seen recently,' said Jasmine.

'But surely Leonora wasn't on that list?'

'No, but it looks as if she should have been,' said Jonny.

'What do you mean?' Anthony asked, looking flustered.

'It seems to us that Clarissa wasn't the only one with secrets,' said Jasmine.

'I don't understand.'

'No?' said Jonny. 'You want me to spell it out?'

Anthony nodded dumbly.

'You were seen together,' said Jasmine. 'In the village, and Leonora was seen walking down the path to the woods the day before Clarissa died.'

Anthony stood up and started pacing round the room. 'I'd better explain,' he said as he stopped pacing and perched on the edge of Clarissa's desk.

'I think you'd better,' said Jonny.

'Come with me,' he said, leading them into another room. Anthony's own study, Jonny guessed. He scanned some shelves and eventually reached down a leather-bound album. After flicking through some of the pages, he extracted a photograph and handed it to Jonny, who passed it to Jasmine. 'That was the day I met Leonora for the first time, a few years after we left university. It was taken in the bar of a sailing club we used. Carl and Clarissa had belonged to their university team, and I also sailed a little as a student. It was Carl who introduced me to Clarissa. They were student friends then, no more than that. I don't know how long Carl had known Leonora, but she'd been away on some student exchange. The day this photo was taken was the first time he brought her with him. She was an experienced sailor. She and her brother grew up near Lymington and had been sailing since their father bought them a dinghy of their own when they were kids. Leonora was way more experienced than any of us. She'd crewed for some of the big yachts that took part in the round the island races. She was also on one of the first all-women crews in the Americas Cup.'

'Were you all married then?'

'Clarissa and I were married. Carl and Leonora were engaged. I was going to be the best man at their wedding, but...'

'But?'

Anthony closed the album and put it back on the shelf. 'I'm not proud of what happened next. We decided to have a dinghy race. It was Carl's idea, and because I was the least experienced sailor, he suggested that Leonora and I should team up in one boat while he and Clarissa took the other. It was just a one day sail, starting at Hamble, out into the Solent, round some of the buoys and back again. Well, as I said, Leonora was the more experienced sailor, so we arrived back well before the other two and we had time to get to know each other while we waited. We met a few times after that, and Leonora hinted that she'd fallen for me and was having second thoughts about marrying Carl. Well, what could I say? Carl was my closest friend. I told her that for me it had only been a bit of fun and that I was married to Clarissa, and we shouldn't meet again. And she and Carl did break up for a while. I don't know how much Carl knew, but our friendship cooled off for a while.'

'But,' said Jasmine, looking puzzled, 'they did get married and you and Carl finished up as business partners.'

'Carl and I met again at a conference a year or two back. We were in similar lines of work, so we teamed up again. Carl was pretty cut up about the prospect of divorce, for which he blamed Leonora one hundred percent, and being the good pal that I was, I believed him. He still saw their children, although he complained that this was very much on Leonora's terms. And of course, he poured all this out to Clarissa, who was sympathetic. More than sympathetic, as things turned out.'

'When did you realise it was more than that?'

'When Leonora contacted me and asked if we could meet. We met at a hotel for a drink and she told me the whole story. Towards the end of their marriage, they'd had blazing rows and Carl had accused her of being rubbish in bed. In the heat of the moment, she let slip that it hadn't been like that when she was with me. She said she'd tried to forget me and tried to put our affair behind her. But then she discovered that Carl and I had teamed up and that he was spending a lot of time with Clarissa. She said she was still fond of me, and she didn't want to see me get hurt. She suspected that Carl was out for revenge of some kind, probably set on breaking up our marriage.'

'You think she was genuine about her concern for you?' Jasmine asked. 'Not just trying to get you back for herself?'

'I did think so at first. She seemed like a sweet woman trapped in an unhappy marriage, and I know Carl can be ruthless, so I believed her. But then she started to become very possessive – obsessive, even.'

'Did you think about ending it?' Jasmine asked.

'I did, but she could be very persuasive. She was the one who told me Carl and Clarissa were meeting in secret. I still found it hard to believe that Clarissa would be fooled by Carl, but I planned to prove it one way or another.'

How? Jonny wondered. 'You had her followed, spied on her?'

'No, not exactly. I installed one of those tracker apps on her phone. But then I felt bad about it. In fact, I only used it a couple of times.'

'Any particular reasons why you used it when you did?'

'There were a few occasions when Carl was out of the office but hadn't told me where he was going. I thought he could be meeting Clarissa somewhere and if I knew where she was, I could confront them. But she must have found the tracker and disabled it. Or perhaps she'd turned the phone off. And like I said, I felt bad about spying on her.'

'Did you ask her about it?'

He shrugged. 'I could hardly do that without her getting suspicious, could I?'

'Where's the phone now?' Jasmine asked.

'I reset it and gave it to Tristan.'

And destroyed some evidence in the process. Just as well Lugs had got hold of her call log when he did. He looked helplessly at Jasmine, who was searching her bag for something. She found what she was looking for and handed Anthony a piece of paper. 'Do you know whose number this is?'

'It's Leonora's.'

'But Carl Archer is the account holder.'

Anthony shrugged. 'I guess Leonora was still on his account.' He handed the paper back to Jasmine.

'She called Clarissa using this number a few days before she died.'

'No idea why she'd do that.'

He looked uneasy, Jonny thought. 'Clarissa blocked the number.'

'Look,' said Anthony, 'I don't know anything about these calls. I'm more concerned right now about tracing that money.'

'I'm not sure we're able to do much about that,' said Jonny.

'You could report it to the police,' said Jasmine. 'Or ask the bank to trace it.'

'I don't think I could do that. They already suspected I was the one who transferred the money. I was lucky they didn't take that any further. But it's not really the money I'm worried about so much as who took it.'

'You're wondering if whoever hacked into Clarissa's bank account might also have been the one who gave her the mushrooms?'

'It had crossed my mind, yes.'

'Did Clarissa keep a diary?' Jasmine asked. 'Perhaps there could be a clue in that.'

'She had an online one. We could go back to her study and take a look at what's on her computer.'

Jonny couldn't see how that would help. But he'd go along with it. Would Anthony really be talking to him like this if he had been the one to give her the mushrooms? He was looking less like a suspect every minute. But if not Anthony, was he protecting someone? Leonora, or one of his children?

Anthony opened up Clarissa's calendar, which had the names of some people she was meeting and dates of speaking engagements. Nothing that shed any light on who might have had access to her bank account. Ivo had discovered that Amelia had tried to hack into Clarissa's current account without success, so she was probably now the prime suspect. But as Anthony said, the money would soon be hers anyway. And they could hardly start suggesting to Anthony that his daughter had poisoned her mother. Not until they had more definite evidence.

Jasmine, who had been looking at some files on the desk, picked up a picnic flask that was next to the computer. 'What's this?' she asked.

'Clarissa liked to work undisturbed,' said Anthony. 'She'd probably filled it with coffee.'

'Or soup?' Jonny asked, remembering the notes Jasmine had made. Something Magda had said about a flask in the kitchen.

'Possibly. Either way, I expect it could do with washing.' Anthony held out his hand but Jasmine hung on to the flask. 'We should get it examined,' she said. 'I'd better pass it on to Lugs.'

Jonny could tell what she was thinking. This could be the flask that Clarissa had filled with soup and left in the kitchen until she was ready to start work. Long enough for someone to sneak in and add some mushrooms. And someone, possibly Leonora, had been seen entering the garden through the back gate the morning Clarissa had eaten the death caps. If their suspicions were correct, the same person had been making phone calls to Clarissa, who had blocked their number. And now they knew the number was one used by Leonora.

The flask might still have dregs of the soup and fingerprints that they should try to preserve. He looked around and spotted a wastepaper basket, empty apart from a clean bin liner. He pulled it out and handed it to Jasmine, hoping she'd realise what it was for. She winked at Jonny and started wrapping it around the flask. It was a bit small, but she was able to cover enough of the flask to protect any fingerprints.

The door opened and Jonny looked up, expecting to see one of the twins. But it wasn't either of them. It was a woman, one Jonny recognised from photos and an evening at the Morris.

'Leonora?' said Anthony, paling visibly. 'What are you doing here?'

She crossed the room and draped her arms around him. 'Pleased to see me?' she asked.

From the expression on Anthony's face, Jonny guessed he wasn't. Particularly after what he'd told him only a few minutes ago about Leonora's obsession with him.

'Who are they?' she asked, noticing Jonny and Jasmine for the first time.

'Friends,' said Anthony. 'They're just helping me sort some of Clarissa's paperwork.'

Jasmine was still clutching the flask, its distinctive pattern showing through the bag. Leonora gasped and stared at it, frowning. 'I'll take that,' she said, reaching for the bag Jasmine was carrying. 'I'll bin it for you.'

Jasmine clung to it. 'It's evidence,' she said, 'that someone poisoned Clarissa.'

'No one poisoned her,' said Leonora. 'She was just too stupid to know what she was eating. Give it to me. Now.'

'No,' said Jasmine, holding on to it more tightly and edging behind Jonny and out of Leonora's reach.

Leonora glared at her, and still with one arm firmly around Anthony, reached into her pocket and pulled out a knife. Sabatier. Jonny recognised it as one from the knife block in the kitchen. He guessed that she came in through the garden gate again, and that Anthony had failed to lock the kitchen door. Leonora gripped Anthony more tightly and held the point of the knife against his throat.

'Empty your pockets,' she told Jonny and Jasmine. 'Car keys and phones on the floor.'

They did as they were told and Anthony groaned as Leonora pushed the knife a little harder into his neck, drawing a drop of blood. She grabbed his phone from where he'd left it on the desk and flung it onto the floor with the others. Then, still clinging on to Anthony, she stamped on each phone in turn, smashing the screens.

'Please, Leonora,' said Anthony. 'You don't want to do this. You said you loved me.'

'Shut up,' she said. 'Let me think.'

'Anthony's right,' said Jonny. 'You don't want to kill him. You'd never get away with it.'

'You're wrong,' she said. 'I can be away from here in seconds. Clarissa was always boasting about how secure her study was. She had special locks fitted so the family couldn't spy on what she was doing in here. I can lock you two in and by the time you've escaped, Anthony and I will be out at sea in my boat.'

'It'll never work,' whined Anthony. 'I'm not going anywhere with you.'

'Then I'll just have to kill you and let these two take the blame. Their fingerprints will be all over the place.' She scowled at Jasmine. 'She can also take the blame for killing Clarissa, since she's hanging on to the flask that had the poisoned soup in it.'

Jonny was trying to work out how they could overpower her. It was three against one, after all. But one false move and Anthony would be a dead man, and any struggle with Leonora would leave his own fingerprints all over the knife. He glanced at Jasmine, who looked as helpless as he felt.

CHAPTER
TWENTY-SEVEN

Ivo was packing up his tools after replacing some broken tiles in the gents' toilet at *Jasmine's* when his phone buzzed in his pocket. He expected it to be Jasmine or Jonny calling. Karim had told him they had gone off somewhere as soon as they'd finished the lunchtime washing-up. 'Jonny had a call,' Karim said. 'Someone wanted to talk to him, and Jasmine went with him. I think they were going to Little Frampton.' Ivo knew Jonny wanted to talk to Anthony, and very likely he would have taken Jasmine with him. They were probably calling in to update him. He fished the phone out of his pocket. The number didn't belong to either Jasmine or Jonny. It was one he didn't recognise. He clicked to answer it. 'Is that Ivo, the detective handyman?'

Ivo confirmed that it was.

'It's Amelia Mayberry.' The voice sounded relieved, although also breathless. 'We need your help.'

There was something nervous about her voice. He didn't think she was calling about a handyman job. 'We?'

'Me and Tristan.'

That was interesting, given that Amelia had little time for her brother. 'What sort of help?'

'When can we see you? Now?'

'Where are you?' Obviously not at home, or she could have talked to Jonny or Jasmine.

'We're in my car.'

That didn't tell him much. 'In your car at home, in a car park, where?'

'We're in the riverside car park. Where are you?'

'I'm at *Jasmine's*. I've just finished a job here.'

'Can you meet us there?'

'Sure,' said Ivo. 'If you come now.'

The car park was about ten minutes' walk away. Amelia had sounded genuinely worried, scared even, not the like confident girl he'd met at Boogies. He decided to call Katya for help. He explained as much as he could from Amelia's breathless call. 'It must be something serious,' he said. 'She was so cool and on top of everything when we met.'

'I'm already on my way,' said Katya. 'I was dropping in to use the office computer, so I'll see you in a few minutes.'

Ivo hadn't realised how gentle and motherly Katya could be. She was often tetchy and impatient, but she took one look at the twins when they arrived and bustled them up to the office. 'My poor dears,' she said. 'You both look terrified. Come and sit down. Ivo can pour you some tea while you tell us what's happened.'

'I found this in Mum's car,' said Amelia. She pulled an envelope out of her bag and pushed it across the table to Katya. Amelia's name was printed on the envelope in a shaky hand and with a pencil. 'Read it,' said Amelia.

The envelope was unsealed, and Katya carefully eased out the page of writing that was inside it. She read:

Dearest Amelia

I know we don't always see eye to eye but that's mothers and daughters for you.

If you find this letter you will know it's too late for me. Don't let anyone tell you it was an accident.

Yesterday, while you were out, Carl came to see me. He told me I was in danger from Leonora. I believed him because I think she might have been stalking me. Well, maybe not stalking, but someone called me two or three times and threatened me. I didn't recognise the number, so I blocked it and thought no more of it. Until Carl's warning I just assumed it was some nutter who didn't like my views – there are a lot of those. But Carl confirmed that it was Leonora's number. So if anything does happen to me, well... take care.

Your loving mother

'This was in her car?' Katya asked.

'In her make-up bag in the glove compartment. Dad gave me her car, but I hadn't used it much because, well, you know...'

'I understand,' said Katya.

'I used to pinch Mum's make-up quite often. She bought all this really expensive stuff. She knew I would be the only one to look in her make-up bag.'

'Dad and I would probably just have chucked it all away,' said Tristan, speaking for the first time.

'Anyway, Tristan's car wouldn't start when he'd finished at college, so I said I'd drive over and pick him up. We were held up by roadworks where they're laying all that fibre stuff for the internet and while we were sitting in the traffic jam, I thought I'd do my make-up. Tristan had made me leave in a rush, so I didn't have time before I left home. I knew mum kept a make-up bag in the car so she could tidy up before a speaking gig.'

'And that's the first you knew of her letter to you?'

'I thought we should take the letter to the police,' said Tristan.

'Once the traffic started moving again, we weren't far from the police station. And I wasn't in any hurry to get home.'

'It had already been decided it was an accident,' said Amelia. 'The police would have just said we were wasting their time.'

'You could be right,' said Katya. 'But I can have a word with a friend of mine who is a police inspector. He usually listens to me.'

'It's too late, isn't it?' said Tristan. 'Mum's already dead.'

'But Leonora could still be dangerous,' said Amelia. 'I thought of calling Carl about it but he's not answering his phone.'

'Tell us about Leonora,' said Katya. 'Why do you think she would threaten your mother?'

'Revenge. She wanted Dad. They'd been having an affair, but I think Dad had ended it. She probably thought that was Mum's fault.'

She had a point. It could be a motive for getting Clarissa out of the way.

'How do you know they were having an affair?' Tristan asked.

Amelia sighed. 'If you didn't spend all your time plugged into headphones, you might notice things now and then.'

'How can we help?' Ivo asked, feeling they were losing track of why Amelia and her brother were there.

'I think Dad's in danger.'

'What makes you think that he is?'

'Tell them, Tris.'

'Carl came round. Everyone was out except me. He was acting very angry and wanted to know where Dad was and if I'd seen Leonora.'

'What did you say?'

'That I hadn't seen either of them and didn't know where Dad was.'

'And when was this?'

'Yesterday. I didn't know about the letter then, so I didn't think I needed to do anything.'

'We should call Jonny or Jasmine,' said Katya.

'Karim said they were going to Little Frampton, so I think they might be at Limetree Cottage now,' said Ivo. 'We should warn them about the letter and check that Anthony is okay.' He tried both numbers. 'Both their phones are turned off,' he said.

'What about your father's phone?' Katya asked.

Amelia tapped in the number. 'Nothing,' she said. 'That's not like Dad. He always answers his phone if it's me calling.'

'We should get round there,' said Katya.

'I left the van at *Shady Willows*,' said Ivo.

'Then Amelia can drive us.'

'What about Harold?' Amelia's car was probably spotless and unlikely to have a dog harness.

'We don't have time to worry about that now. Can't you leave him here with Karim?'

'It's fine,' said Amelia. 'You can tie him to one of the seatbelts with his lead.'

∽

'W<small>HOSE CARS ARE THOSE</small>?' Tristan asked as they turned into the drive at Limetree Cottage and noticed the white Seat parked next to Jonny's Honda.

'The Honda is Jonny Cardew's,' said Katya, as they all climbed out of the car. 'Ivo was right. He's here with Jasmine. The other belongs to Paul Simpson, but I'm guessing it was Leonora who drove it here.'

'What shall we do?' Ivo asked.

Amelia fumbled with her keys and headed for the door. Then she thought better of it. 'We'd better not go in. We might interrupt her and Dad... well, you know, if they were having an affair...'

'Mum and Carl think she's dangerous,' said Tristan. 'And Dad's not answering his phone. He might need help.'

Katya was trying not to panic, but two of her detectives were inside this house, not answering their phones and with a woman who could well be an unbalanced murderer. Her thoughts were interrupted by the arrival of another car. A black Mercedes. Katya went over to the driver's window. 'Carl Archer, I presume?' she said as the window opened.

'Who are you?'

'DS Katya Roscoff, retired.' She offered her hand for him to shake through the window. Carl ignored it and climbed out, noticing Amelia and Tristan standing awkwardly in the drive. 'What are the twins doing? And that bloke over there with the dog?'

'The twins contacted us because they'd found a letter from Clarissa and it worried them. Ivo and I are detectives. We think two of our colleagues are inside the house. They are not answering their phones. Neither is Anthony Mayberry.'

'Quite a party,' said Carl.

'And we believe they could all be in danger from your ex-wife, who by all accounts is a little unbalanced. I understand you warned Clarissa about her.'

Carl nodded.

'What are we going to do?' Amelia asked, interrupting them and looking close to tears.

Time to take charge, Katya thought. 'I suggest Mr Archer and I go inside. I've got hostage experience and Mr Archer knows both Anthony and Leonora well. Ivo, you and Harold stay here and look after the twins. If I don't come back in five minutes to tell you everything is okay, you need to call Lugs and get him to send backup.'

~

KATYA FOLLOWED Carl into the house and found herself in a large entrance hall. 'You know the house better than I do. Where do you think they are?'

'I'll check upstairs,' said Carl, grabbing a heavy-looking marble model of the Taj Mahal from the hall table. 'You have a look round the living rooms.'

Who's in charge here? But she nodded. If they were about to discover Anthony and Leonora in flagrante somewhere, it was most likely to be upstairs and Carl was probably better able to handle the situation than she was. But if that was the case, where were Jonny and Jasmine? Jonny's car was parked in the drive, which suggested they were both still here. And if they were, then they'd more likely be downstairs. She couldn't hear voices, but did a quick check of the ground floor rooms, all of which were empty. She was about to call Ivo to tell him everything looked okay when she heard a piercing scream from upstairs followed by a woman's voice shouting obscenities. She followed the sound and arrived in a room she took to be a study, where there was a woman sitting on the floor, clutching her arm and yelling at Carl. A man she took to be Anthony Mayberry was sitting in a chair dabbing at his neck with tissues handed to him by Jasmine. Jonny was wrapping a kitchen knife in a handkerchief. Jonny was the only man Katya knew who still kept a freshly laundered linen handkerchief in his pocket. She reached into her own pocket and handed him one of her evidence bags. 'Care to tell me what's going on?' she asked.

'Call the police,' shouted the woman on the floor. 'He's broken my bloody arm.'

Katya got out her phone and made a call.

'Police are on their way,' said Ivo, answering the call immediately. 'I just called them. You were longer than five minutes. Should I call back and tell them it was a mistake?'

'No, definitely not.'

'We heard a scream. What's going on?'

'I'm not sure yet, but I need you to take care of the twins. Take them inside and make them a cup of tea or something. Tell them their father is okay but don't let them upstairs. When the police get here, send them up to the first room on the left at the top of the stairs.'

'Okay,' said Ivo. 'Do you need Harold to help?'

'No,' said Katya firmly. 'Keep him with you. He can distract the twins.' She ended the call, hoping that Ivo could handle two stroppy teenagers. Their father was still bleeding from a wound on his neck and the woman she assumed was Leonora was howling in pain from what she thought could be a dislocated shoulder. Carl stood to one side, still holding the Taj Mahal and grinning smugly.

'Police are on their way,' said Katya, putting her phone back in her pocket. 'So what happened here?'

All five people in the room started talking at the same time.

'One at a time,' she said, holding up a warning hand. 'Jonny?'

'Anthony was telling us about some anomalies he'd found when going through Clarissa's bank accounts. Someone had removed funds from one of them after she died.'

Katya couldn't see how that had led to Anthony being attacked by a woman with a knife, but supposed Jonny would get around to explaining if she gave him time. 'Go on.'

'The only person he could think might have known Clarissa's bank details was Carl. He thought he and Clarissa were having an affair.'

'Bloody cheek,' said Carl. 'It was Anthony who was having the affair. With my ex-wife of all people. I thought it was necessary to warn Clarissa about how unbalanced she was.'

'You can have your say in a minute,' said Katya. 'Hear Jonny out first.'

Carl sighed loudly and flopped into a chair.

'What about my bloody arm?' Leonora shouted.

'Shut up,' said Carl. 'It's not going to kill you.'

'There's help on the way,' said Katya. 'Jasmine, love, run down to the kitchen and see if you can find a bag of frozen peas to stop the swelling. Check that Ivo and the twins are okay while you're down there.'

'And get me a drink,' said Leonora. 'A strong one.'

'A glass of water,' said Katya as Jasmine left the room. 'Okay, Jonny, you were saying?'

'Anthony told us about his affair with Leonora.'

'I told you I'd ended it,' said Anthony.

'No,' Leonora groaned. 'You didn't mean it. We were going away together. I transferred the money from Clarissa's account so I could get cash and we wouldn't be traced through our bank cards.'

She didn't look as if she was about to make a run for it, so Katya ignored her and left her where she was on the floor.

'That's when Jasmine found the flask,' Jonny continued.

'Flask?'

'It was on Clarissa's desk. She used it for her lunchtime soup when she was working at home. We thought it could still have traces of the mushroom soup that had poisoned her. Jasmine had wrapped it up to preserve fingerprints when Leonora rushed in and attacked Anthony with a knife and demanded that Jasmine give her the flask.'

Things were starting to make sense. Katya stared down at the woman on the floor. 'It was you,' she said. 'You wanted Anthony for yourself and the only way to get him was to get rid of Clarissa.'

'I didn't think it would kill her,' said Leonora. 'The woman in Australia survived. I thought if she was ill for a bit then Anthony and I could get away.'

Looked like Carl was right. This woman was unbalanced. 'So you drove all the way up here, picked the mushrooms in the woods, sneaked in through the back gate and slipped them into the flask of soup that was in the kitchen.'

'I came to meet Tony, but he texted not to come.'

'I texted you to finish the affair,' said Anthony.

'Not really the act of a gentleman, old boy,' said Carl, smirking.

'He didn't mean it,' said Leonora. 'He loves me. He just needed a chance to get away.'

Katya was relieved when she heard a siren and saw blue lights from the police cars that crunched on the gravel drive outside. Leonora was arrested and driven to casualty under police escort. The flask and knife were sealed in evidence bags and taken away for forensic examination, and a paramedic stitched the wound in Anthony's neck – a clean wound – and he was handed a packet of paracetamol and advised to visit his GP for a course of antibiotics.

CHAPTER
TWENTY-EIGHT

It was a quiet evening in the Red Lion pub in Little Frampton. Jasmine had suggested an early meal, knowing it would be crowded later on and they'd not be able to hear themselves think, never mind have any kind of conversation. It was Ivo's idea for Thomas Johnson to join them. He had, after all, been able to help them identify not only the prime suspect, but a motive. He and Katya were discussing the menu, both approving of its down-to-earth, traditional pub grub qualities.

'Great that Lugs joined us as well,' said Jasmine.

'And he's got something important to tell us,' said Katya.

'About the case?' Jonny asked. 'Looks like he's buying us a round to thank us for what we did. Another successful case. He'll be employing us full time if we go on like this.'

Lugs paid for the drinks and carried the tray to the group at the table. 'You were right,' he said to Katya, reading the menu over her shoulder. 'This is a proper pub. I thought they'd all gone gastro in these parts.'

'Over my dead body,' said Thomas Johnson, downing half of his pint in a single gulp.

'A slightly unfortunate phrase,' said Jonny, patting him on the shoulder.

'Eh?' said Thomas.

'Congratulations,' said Lugs, raising his glass. 'Another successful case for the Breakfast Club Detectives.'

'I gather Leonora has confessed,' said Jasmine.

'Couldn't shut her up,' said Lugs. 'Boasting about it, she was. Almost like she was expecting a medal. She's been referred for psychiatric assessment.'

Jasmine reached into her bag for a leaflet, which she laid on the table in front of them. 'It's a draft from the mushroom society. Derek Weatherby sent it to me for comments.'

Jonny read it through. 'It's a bit graphic,' he said. 'I can't imagine anyone risking a walk in the woods after reading it, never mind foraging for anything.'

'But worth it if it prevents another death like Clarissa's,' said Ivo.

'There's good news for Alan Biggs as well,' said Lugs.

'He's getting his speed limit?' Jasmine asked.

'Not exactly. But the traffic people have agreed to install some of those flashing displays that tell people how fast they're driving. They are quite successful in slowing drivers down.'

'And cheaper, probably,' said Katya.

'I see Limetree Cottage is on the market,' said Thomas. 'Good job too.'

'Amelia's left for Cambridge,' said Jonny. 'The executors have agreed to release some of Clarissa's money so she can set herself up in a flat there. Anthony and Tristan have already moved out. They've gone for a father/son bonding experience in Utah.'

'To our next case,' said Katya, raising her glass. 'And thank you for the support you give us.' She clinked glasses with Lugs and took a swig of beer.

'Good luck with all your future cases,' said Lugs. 'But I'm afraid you'll have to manage without me. I'm retiring at the end of the month.'

'That was your news?' said Katya, looking at him with horror. 'You can't retire. What are you going to do with all that time?'

'You seem to manage,' he said, smiling at Katya.

'You planning to be a private detective?' asked Ivo.

'No, lad, my crime solving days are over. The wife and I are planning to buy a camper van and travel a bit. We've never seen much of the world outside Berkshire. We thought we'd drive down to Spain for some sun.'

'You're going to be a snowbird?' said Jonny.

'A what?' asked Ivo.

'It's what they call people who drive south for warmer weather,' Jonny explained.

'So will Flora Green be taking over your job?' Katya asked. 'I heard she'd passed her inspector's exams.'

'She did,' said Lugs. 'She's a bright lass and will go far. But recently promoted inspectors are encouraged to get experience in other areas. She'll be moving to Bristol at the end of the year. There'll be a new DI heading the team. Detective Inspector Charlotte Hannington will be taking over from me. She's been with North Hants but, like Flora, she's recently been promoted.'

There was a sudden silence round the table as the detectives tried to work out what this would mean for them as a team. Katya was the first to speak. 'You'll put in a good word for us?'

Lugs laughed. 'Of course. I'm sure she'll value your experience.'

Katya doubted that. She'd worked with Lugs for years, and valued him as a colleague as well as a friend. She'd already summed this Charlotte Hannington up in her mind. She'd be the cold-hearted, bossy type who had no time for interfering amateurs.

'I remember when I was in the army and we got a new CO,' said Thomas, filling a gap in the conversation. 'Not a happy experience.' He gazed glumly into his beer.

'Come on,' said Jonny. 'We'll be fine. We should be celebrating with Lugs. Retirement can bring a whole lot of unexpected new things into one's life.' He raised his glass. 'To Lugs,' he said, watching while the others did the same.

'Thanks,' said Lugs. 'I'll keep in touch.'

'Send us photos of yourself in the sun,' said Jasmine.

'And make us jealous,' muttered Katya, wondering why she'd never thought of heading off into the sunset. Was it too late? Could she buy herself a camper van and explore the world? But she looked around at the others and knew she couldn't. She raised her glass for another toast. 'To the Breakfast Club Detectives' next case.'

How will the detectives get on with the new detective inspector?

To find out read book four **Death in the Attic** launching in October 2024 **pre-order now.**

THE BREAKFAST CLUB
DETECTIVES SERIES

Death in the Long walk

Death in the River

Death on the Carousel

Visit my website www.hilarypugh.com to join my mailing list and download a free copy of the series prequel, **Crime About Town** and **On the Edge,** a short story that introduces the new detective inspector.

Acknowledgments

I would like to thank you so much for reading **Death at the Festival.** I do hope you enjoyed it.

If you have a few moments to spare a short review would be very much appreciated. Reviews really help me and will help other people who might consider reading my books.

I would also like to thank my editor, Sally Silvester-Wood at *Black Sheep Books*, my cover designer, Anthony O'Brien and all my fellow writers at *Quite Write* who have patiently listened to extracts and offered suggestions.

Discover more about Hilary Pugh and download the Breakfast Club Detectives prequel novella **Crime about Town** FREE at www.hilary-pugh.com

Also by Hilary Pugh

<u>The Ian Skair: Private Investigator series</u>

Finding Lottie – series prequel

<u>Free</u> when you join my mailing list:

https://storyoriginapp.com/giveaways/61799962-7dc3-11eb-b5c8-7b3702734d0c

The Laird of Drumlychtoun

https://books2read.com/u/bwrEky

Postcards from Jamie

https://books2read.com/u/4X28Ae

Mystery at Murriemuir

https://books2read.com/u/mgj8Bx

The Diva of Dundas Farm

https://books2read.com/u/bMYMJA

The Man in the Red Overcoat

https://books2read.com/u/4DJRge

Printed in Great Britain
by Amazon